REA

D0696428

TEXAS
STORIES

TEXAS STORIES

EDITED BY JOHN
AND KIRSTEN MILLER

CHRONICLE BOOKS
SAN FRANCISCO

Library of Congress Cataloging-in-Publication Data:
Texas stories / edited by John and Kirsten Miller.
p.   cm.
ISBN 0-8118-0845-9 (pb)
1. American literature—Texas. 2. Texas—Literary collections.
I. Miller, John, 1959-   . II. Miller, Kirsten, 1962-
PS558.T4T428 1995
810.8'032764—dc20   94-37904
                                        CIP

Book and cover design: Big Fish

Composition: Jennifer Petersen

Cover photograph: Oil Rigs by William Eggleston

Distributed in Canada by Raincoast Books,
8680 Cambie Street, Vancouver BC V6P 6M9

10 9 8 7 6 5 4 3 2 1

Chronicle Books
275 Fifth Street
San Francisco, CA 94103

TEXAS STORIES

— — — —

TEXAS STORIES

B A R R Y
G I F F O R D

— — — —

Introduction

WHEN I WAS a kid in Tampa, Florida, I once heard somebody say, "Nothin' good ever happens in Texas." I believe this was said upon hearing the news that a mad gunman named Charles Whitman had just shot and killed sixteen people and wounded a number of others from a tower on the campus of the University of Texas at Austin, before the cops put him down permanently. I know the implied admonition of that statement occurred to me when I learned that John F. Kennedy had been drilled in Dallas. Sure, terrible things happen in other places; Texas doesn't have a

---

Ultra-hip novelist and screenwriter BARRY GIFFORD compounds elements of modern and historic American culture in his novels, creating a landscape of sound bites that is unbalanced, threatening, and familiar. Many of his books are set in the Lone Star State, including Sailor's Holiday and Wild at Heart.

monopoly on violent or irrational behavior, but few areas seem to take such inordinate pride in bloody legends.

One of my favorite periods of Texas history is the time of the War Between the States, when Brownsville was seized from the Union forces by Colonel Rip Ford, a former captain of the Texas Rangers. Ford commanded a renegade army composed of young boys and men too old to have been conscripted into either the Union or Confederate forces. The self-appointed colonel organized his minions using the canard that the federals were about to flood South Texas with Negro troops. Ford falsely claimed association with the Confederate Army, which operated out of Matamoros, across the Mexican border, but they distrusted him; with good reason, as it turned out, because as the war was winding down and defeat for the Confederacy seemed certain, Ford attempted to make a deal with the U.S. government whereby Texas would rejoin the Union and his ragamuffin brigade would then join federal troops in a war on Mexico.

Fighting along the border was as ferocious and bloody as any in the rest of the country at that time. Ford's brigands managed to drive the Union boys into Mexico, where the U.S. was allied with the Juaristas in an effort to overthrow the Imperialists. Local border warlords—the Yellow Flags and the Red Flags—vied with bands of Kickapoo and Apache Indians for territory, as well as clashing with mercenary raiders such as Ford's bunch. Richard King and Mifflin Kenedy, Yankee businessmen who established the King Ranch in South Texas, had come down to profit in the steamboat trade. Rip Ford aided their betrayal of the Union by facilitating the rechartering of their boats under Mexican registry, which allowed them to transport cotton to the thousands of European ships waiting off Matamoros.

Just across the border on the Mexican side, at the end of what is now Texas Highway 4, lay the small town of Boca del Rio, or, as the Europeans named it, Bagdad. Bagdad was a wide-open place where any kind of deal went down. People from all over came to get rich quick: whores, spies, gamblers, con men, army deserters swarmed in. Wages were high and life was cheap; there was no law. Bagdad was like Tangier when it was an international port. Mosquitoes, constant sand-filled winds and murderous deviltry kept tension high. Almost immediately after the war ended, a hurricane destroyed Bagdad, cleansing it from the face of the earth.

It's this kind of past that Texans of my acquaintance seem to relish. Some of the contributors to this anthology, like Gloria Anzaldúa and Larry McMurtry (on occasion)—and some Texas writers who aren't included, such as Larry L. King and James Crumley—are also decidedly unsqueamish when it comes to Lone Star lore of blood and gore. One or two wax rhapsodic but they're Yankees or worse—Jack Kerouac was from Massachusetts and Jan Morris is British. And Don DeLillo's brilliant reinvention of the myth of Lee Harvey Oswald (who was from New Orleans, more or less) gets Texas where it hurts.

I believe it was that venerable Texan J. Frank Dobie who paraphrased a Native American Coyote myth informing us that Coyote divided animal life into three categories: animals to be eaten, animals to aid in capturing food, and animals that would eat him. Man, Coyote taught, belongs in the third category. My guess is the man to whom Coyote was referring was a Texan.

LARRY McMURTRY

- - - -

The Last Picture Show

SOMETIMES SONNY FELT like he was the only human creature in the town. It was a bad feeling, and it usually came on him in the mornings early, when the streets were completely empty, the way they were one Saturday morning in late November. The night before Sonny had played his last game of football for Thalia High School, but it wasn't that that made him feel so strange and alone. It was just the look of the town.

There was only one car parked on the courthouse square—the night watchman's old white Nash. A cold norther

---

Best-selling novelist and screenwriter LARRY McMURTRY *grew up in Wichita Falls, Texas, as the son of a cattle rancher. He has written over fifteen books and his characters have been memorialized in movies such as* Hud, Lonesome Dove, Texasville, *and perhaps his masterpiece,* The Last Picture Show.

was singing in off the plains, swirling long ribbons of dust down Main Street, the only street in Thalia with businesses on it. Sonny's pickup was a '41 Chevrolet, not at its best on cold mornings. In front of the picture show it coughed out and had to be choked for a while, but then it started again and jerked its way to the red light, blowing out spumes of white exhaust that the wind whipped away.

At the red light he started to turn south toward the all-night café, but when he looked north to see if anyone was coming he turned that way instead. No one at all was coming but he saw his young friend Billy, headed out. He had his broom and was sweeping right down the middle of the highway into the gusting wind. Billy lived at the poolhall with Sam the Lion, and sweeping was all he really knew how to do. The only trouble was that he overdid it. He swept out the poolhall in the mornings, the café in the afternoons, and the picture show at night, and always, unless someone specifically told him to stop, he just kept sweeping, down the sidewalk, on through the town, sometimes one way and sometimes another, sweeping happily on until someone noticed him and brought him back to the poolhall.

Sonny drove up beside him and honked. Billy quit sweeping at once and got in the pickup. He was a stocky boy, not very smart, but perfectly friendly; picking him up made Sonny feel less lonesome. If Billy was out the poolhall must be open, and when the poolhall was open he was never lonesome. One of the nice things about living in Thalia was that the poolhall often opened by 6:30 or 7 A.M., the reason being that Sam the Lion, who owned it, was a very bad sleeper.

Sonny drove to the hall and parked and took Billy's broom so he wouldn't go sweeping off again. The air was so dry and dusty it made the nostrils sting and the two boys hustled inside. Sam the Lion was up, all right, brushing one of the snooker tables. He was an old man, but big and heavy, with a mane of white hair; cold weather made his feet swell and he wore his old sheepskin house shoes to work in in the wintertime. He was expecting the boys and barely gave them a glance.

Once they were inside, Sonny let Billy have the broom again and Billy immediately went over to the gas stove to warm himself. While he warmed he leaned on the broom and licked a piece of green pool chalk. Sam the Lion didn't particularly care that Billy licked chalk all the time; it was cheap enough nourishment, he said. Sonny got himself a package of Cheese Crisps and made room for himself at the stove, turning Billy's cap around backward for friendship's sake. It was an old green baseball cap some lady had given Billy three or four summers before.

"Cold in here, Sam," Sonny said. "It's nearly as cold in here as it is outside."

"Not as windy, though," Sam replied. "I'm surprised you had the nerve to come in this mornin', after the beatin' you took. Anybody ever tell you boys about blockin'? Or tacklin'?"

Sonny ate his Cheese Crisps, unabashed. Crowell, the visiting team, had tromped Thalia 28 to 6. It had been a little embarrassing for Coach Popper, but that was because the Local Quarterback Club had been so sure Thalia was finally going to win a District Crown that they had literally jumped the gun and presented the coach with a new .12 gauge Marlin under-over at the homecoming game two weeks before. The coach was quite a hunter.

Two of Crowell's four touchdowns had been run over Sonny's guard position, but he felt quite calm about it all. Four years of playing for Thalia had inured him to defeat, and so far as he was concerned the Quarterback Club had been foolishly optimistic.

Besides, he could not see that he had much to gain by helping the coach get new shotguns, the coach being a man of most uncertain temper. He had already shot at Sonny once in his life, and with a new under-over he might not miss.

"Where's your buddy?" Sam asked.

"Not in yet," Sonny said. That was Duane, Sonny's best friend, who besides being an All-Conference fullback, rough-necked the midnight tower with a local drilling crew.

"Duane's gonna work himself into an early grave," Sam the Lion said. "He oughtn't to play a football game and then go out and work all night on top of it. He made half the yardage we made."

"Well, that never tired him out," Sonny said, going to get another package of Cheese Crisps.

Sam the Lion started to cough, and the coughing got away from him, as it often did. His whole body shook; he couldn't stop. Finally he had to stagger back to the washroom and take a drink of water and a swig of medicine to get it under control.

"Suckin' in too much chalk dust," he said when he came back. Billy hardly noticed, but Sonny felt a little uneasy. He didn't like to be reminded that Sam the Lion was not as young or as healthy as he once had been. Sam the Lion was the man who took care of things, particularly of boys, and Sonny did not like to think that he might die. The reason Sam was so especially good to boys was that he himself had had three sons, none of whom lived to be eighteen. The first was killed when Sam was still a rancher: he and his son were trying to drive a herd of yearlings across the Little Wichita River one day when it was up, and the boy had been knocked loose from his horse, pawed under, and drowned. A few years later, after Sam had gone into the oil business, a gas explosion knocked his second son off a derrick. He fell over fifty feet and was dead before they got him to town. Sam sold his oil holdings and put in the first Ford agency in Thalia, and his youngest son was run over by a deputy sheriff. His wife lost her mind and spent her last ten years rocking in a rocking chair. Sam drank a lot, quit going to church, and was said to be loose with women, even married women.

He began to come out of it when he bought the picture show, or so people said. He got lots of comedies and serials and Westerns and the kids came as often as they could talk their parents into letting them. Then Sam bought the poolhall and the all-night café and he perked up more and more.

No one really knew why he was called Sam the Lion. Some thought it was because he hated barbers and always went around with a shaggy head of hair. Others thought it was because he had been such a hell-raising cowboy when he was young, but Sonny found that a little hard to believe. He had seen Sam mad only once, and that was one Fourth of July when Duane stuck a Roman candle in the pocket of one of the snooker tables and set it off. When it finally quit shooting, Sam grabbed the pisspot and chased Duane out, meaning to sling it at him. He slung it, but Duane was too quick. Joe Bob Blanton, the Methodist preacher's son, happened to be standing on the sidewalk wishing he was allowed to go in and shoot pool, and he was the one that got drenched. The boys all got a big laugh but Sam the Lion was embarrassed about it and cleaned Joe Bob off as best he could.

When he was thoroughly warm Sonny got one of the brushes and began to brush the eight-ball tables. Sam went over and looked disgustedly at the two nickels Sonny had left for the Cheese Crisps.

"You'll never get nowhere, Sonny," he said. "You've already spent a dime today and you ain't even had a decent breakfast. Billy, you might get the other side of the hall swept out, son."

While the boys worked Sam stood by the stove and warmed his aching feet. He wished Sonny weren't so reckless economically, but there was nothing he could do about it. Billy was less of a problem, partly because he was so dumb. Billy's real father was an old railroad man who had worked in Thalia for a short time just before the war; his mother was a deaf and dumb girl who had no people except an aunt. The old man cornered the girl in the balcony of the picture show one night and begat Billy. The sheriff saw to it that the old man married the girl, but she died when Billy was born and he was raised by the family of Mexicans who helped the old man keep the railroad track repaired. After the war the hauling petered out and the track was taken up. The old man left and got a job bumping cars on a stockyards track in Oklahoma, leaving Billy with the Mexicans. They hung around for several more years, piling prickly pear and grubbing mesquite, but then a man from Plainview talked them into moving out there to pick cotton. They snuck off one morning and left Billy sitting on the curb in front of the picture show.

From then on, Sam the Lion took care of him. Billy learned to sweep, and he kept all three of Sam's places swept out;

in return he got his keep and also, every single night, he got to watch the picture show. He always sat in the balcony, his broom at his side; for years he saw every show that came to Thalia, and so far as anyone knew, he liked them all. He was never known to leave while the screen was lit.

"You workin' today?" Sam asked, noticing that Sonny was taking his time brushing the eight-ball table.

"The truck's being greased," Sonny said. On weekends, and sometimes week-nights, too, he drove a butane truck for Frank Fartley of Fartley Butane and Propane. He didn't make as much money as his friend Duane made roughnecking, but the work was easier.

Just as Sam the Lion was about to get back to the subject of the football game they all heard a familiar sound and paused to listen. Abilene was coming into town in his Mercury. Abilene was the driller Duane worked for. He had spent a lot of money souping up the Mercury, and in Thalia the sound of his exhausts was as unmistakable as the sound of the wind.

"Well, we barely got 'em clean in time," Sam said. Abilene not only had the best car in the country, he also shot the best stick of pool. Drilling and pool shooting were things he did so well that no one could decide which was his true vocation and which his avocation. Some mornings he went home and cleaned up before he came to the poolhall—he liked to be clean and well dressed when he gambled—but if it was too early for any of the nine-ball players to be up he would often stop and practice in his drilling clothes.

The Mercury stopped in front of the poolhall and Sam went over and got Abilene's ivory-banded cue out of the padlocked rack and laid it on the counter for him. When the door opened the wind sliced inside ahead of the man. Abilene had on sunglasses and the heavy green coveralls he wore to protect his clothes from the oil-field grease; as soon as he was in he unzipped the coveralls and hung them on a nail Sam had fixed for him. His blue wool shirt and gabardine pants were creased and trim.

"Mornin'," Sam said.

"Mornin'," Abilene replied, handing Sam his expensive-looking sunglasses. He once had a pair fall out of his pocket and break when he was bending over to pick up a piece of pool chalk; after that he always had Sam put the sunglasses in a drawer for him. Though he was the poolhall's best customer, he and Sam the Lion had almost nothing to say to one another. Abilene paid Sam two hundred and fifty dollars a year for a private key to the poolhall, so he could come in and practice any time he wanted to. Often Sonny would come in from some long butane run at two or three o'clock in the morning and see that Abilene was in the poolhall, practicing. The garage where the butane truck was kept was right across the street from the poolhall and sometimes Sonny would walk across and stand by one of the windows watching Abilene shoot. No one ever tried to go in when Abilene was in the poolhall alone.

"Let's shoot one, Sonny," Abilene said. "I feel like a little snooker before breakfast."

Sonny was taken by surprise. He knew he would not even be good competition for Abilene, but he went and got a cue any-way. It did not occur to him to turn down the invitation. Abilene shot first and ran thirty points off the break.

"Duane didn't go to sleep on you last night, did he?"

Sonny asked, feeling that he ought at least to make conversation.

"No, the breeze kept us awake," Abilene replied. That was their conversation. Sonny only got to shoot four times; for the most part he just stood back and watched Abilene move gracefully around the green table, easing his shots with the ivory-banded cue. He won the game by 175 points.

"You shoot pool about like you play football," he said, when the game was over.

Sonny ignored the insult and pitched a quarter on the felt to pay for the game. Abilene insulted everybody, young and old alike, and Sonny was not obliged to take it personally. Sam the Lion came over to rack the balls.

"I hope they hurry and get that truck greased," he said. "The way your fortune's sinking you'll be bankrupt before you get out of here."

"What'd our bet come to, Sam," Abilene asked casually. He bused the fresh rack and started shooting red balls. Sam grinned at Sonny and went over to the cash register and got five ten-dollar bills. He laid them on the side of the snooker table and when Abilene noticed them he took a money clip out of his pocket and put the fifty dollars in it.

"It's what I get for bettin' on my hometown ball club," Sam said. "I ought to have better sense."

"It wouldn't hurt if you had a better home town," Abilene said.

Sam always bet on the boys, thinking it would make them feel good, but the strategy seldom worked because they almost always lost. Most of them only trained when they felt like it, and that was not very often. The few who did train were handicapped by their intense dislike of Coach Popper. Sonny was not alone in considering the coach a horse's ass, but the school board liked the coach and never considered firing him: he was a man's man, and he worked cheap. They saw no reason to hire a better coach until a better bunch of boys came along, and there was no telling when that would be. Sam the Lion went loyally on losing money, while Abilene, who invariably bet against Thalia, cleared about a thousand dollars a season from Sam and others like him.

While Sam and Sonny were idly watching Abilene practice, Billy swept quietly down the other side of the poolhall and on out the door. The cold wind that came through the door when Billy went out woke them up. "Go get him, Sonny," Sam said. "Make him put his broom up for a while."

Billy hadn't had time to get far; he was just three doors away, in front of what once had been the Thalia Pontiac Agency. He was calmly sweeping north, into the cold wind. All his floor-sweep had already blown away, but he was quite content to sweep at the curling ribbons of sand that the wind blew past him. A time or two in his life he had swept all the way to the Thalia city limits sign before anyone had noticed him.

When Sonny stepped out of the poolhall the black pickup that the roughnecks used was stopped at the red light. The light changed and the pickup passed the courthouse and slowed a moment at the corner by the poolhall, so Duane could jump out. He was a tall boy with curly black hair. Because he was a fullback and a roughneck he held himself a little stiffly. He had on Levi's and a Levi's jacket with the collar turned up. Sonny pointed at Billy and he and Duane each grabbed one of Billy's arms and hustled him back down the sidewalk into the warming poolhall. Sam took the broom and put it up on a shelf where Billy couldn't reach it.

"Let's go eat, buddy," Duane said, knowing that Sonny had put off having breakfast until he came.

Sam the Lion looked Duane over carefully to see if he could detect any symptoms of overwork, but Duane was in his usual Saturday morning good humor, and if there were such symptoms they didn't show.

"If you boys are going to the café, take this change for me," Sam said, pitching Sonny the dark green coin sack that he used to tote change from one of his establishments to the other. Sonny caught it and the boys hurried out and jogged down the street two blocks to the café, tucking their heads down so the wind wouldn't take their breath. "Boy, I froze my ass last night," Duane grunted, as they ran.

The café was a little one-story red building, so deliciously warm inside that all the windows were steamed over. Penny, the daytime waitress, was in the kitchen frying eggs for a couple of truck drivers, so Sonny set the change sack on the cash register. There was no sign of old Marston, the cook. The boys counted their money and found they had only eighty cents between them.

"I had to shoot Abilene a game of snooker," Sonny explained. "If it hadn't been for that I'd have a quarter more."

"We got enough," Duane said. They were always short of money on Saturday morning, but they were paid Saturday afternoon, so it was no calamity. They ordered eggs and sausage and flipped to see who got what—by the end of the week they often ended up splitting meals. Sonny got the sausage and Duane the eggs.

While Penny was counting the new change into the cash register old Marston came dragging in. He looked as though he had just frozen out of a bar ditch somewhere, and Penny was on him instantly.

"Where you been, you old fart?" she yelled. "I done had to cook ten orders and you know I ain't no cook."

"I swear, Penny," Marston said. "I just forget to set my alarm clock last night."

"You're a lying old sot if I ever saw one," Penny said. "I ought to douse you under the hydrant a time or two, maybe you wouldn't stink of whiskey so much."

Marston slipped by her and had his apron on in a minute. Penny was a 185-pound redhead, not given to idle threats. She was Church of Christ and didn't mind calling a sinner a sinner. Five years before she had accidentally gotten pregnant before she was engaged; the whole town knew about it and Penny got a lot of backhanded sympathy. The ladies of the community thought it was just awful for a girl that fat to get pregnant. Once married, she discovered she didn't much like her husband, and that made her harder to get along with in general. On Wednesday nights, when the Church of Christ held its prayer meetings and shouting contests anybody who happened to be within half a mile of the church could hear what Penny thought about wickedness; it was old Marston's misfortune to hear it every morning, and at considerably closer range. He only worked to drink, and the thought of being doused under a hydrant made him so shaky he could barely turn the eggs.

Sonny and Duane winked at him to cheer him up, and gave Penny the finger when she wasn't looking. They also managed to indicate that they were broke, so Marston would put a couple of extra slices of toast on the order. The boys gave him a ride to the county-line liquor store once a week, and in return he helped out with extra food when their money was low.

"How we gonna work it tonight?" Duane asked. He and Sonny owned the Chevrolet pickup jointly, and because there were two of them and only one pickup their Saturday night dating was a little complicated.

"We might as well wait and see," Sonny replied, looking disgustedly at the grape jelly Marston had put on the plate. He hated grape jelly, and the café never seemed to have any other kind.

"If I have to make a delivery to Ranger this afternoon there won't be no problem," he added. "You can just take the pickup. If I get back in time I can meet Charlene at the picture show."

"Okay," Duane said, glad to get that off his mind. Sonny never got the pickup first on Saturday night and Duane always felt slightly guilty about it but not quite guilty enough to change anything.

The problem was that he was going with Jacy Farrow whose folks were rich enough to make them unenthusiastic about her going with a poor boy like Duane. He and Jacy couldn't use her car because her father, Gene Farrow, made a point of driving by the picture show every Saturday night to see that Jacy's car was parked out front. They were able to get around that easily enough by sneaking out the back of the show and going somewhere in the pickup, but that arrangement created something of a courting problem for Sonny, who went with a girl named Charlene Duggs. Charlene had to be home by eleven thirty, and if

Duane and Jacy kept the pickup tied up until almost eleven, it didn't allow Sonny much time in which to make out.

Sonny had assured Duane time and time again that he didn't particularly care, but Duane remained secretly uneasy. His uneasiness really stemmed from the fact that he was going with Jacy, the prettiest, most desirable girl in town, while Sonny was only going with Charlene Duggs, a mediocre date by any standard. Occasionally the two couples double-dated, but that was really harder on Sonny than no date at all. With the four of them squeezed up in the cab of the pickup it was impossible for him to ignore the fact that Jacy was several times as desirable as Charlene. Even if it was totally dark, her perfume smelled better. For days after such a date Sonny had very disloyal fantasies involving himself and Jacy, and after an hour's sloppy necking with Charlene even the fantasy that he was kissing Jacy had a dangerous power. Charlene kissed convulsively, as if she had just swallowed a golf ball and was trying to force it back up.

Of course Sonny had often considered breaking up with Charlene, but there weren't many girls in the town and the only unattached girl who was any prettier than Charlene was an unusually prudish sophomore. Charlene would let Sonny do anything he wanted to above the waist; it was only as time wore on that he had begun to realize that there really wasn't much of permanent interest to do in that zone. As the weeks went by, Sonny observed that Jacy seemed to become more and more delightful, passionate, inventive, while by contrast Charlene just seemed more of a slug.

When the boys finished eating and paid their check they had a nickel left. Duane was going home to bed, so Sonny kept

the nickel; he could buy himself a Butterfinger for lunch. Outside
the air was still cold and dusty and gray clouds were blowing
south off the High Plains.

Duane took the pickup and went to the rooming house
where the two of them had roomed since their sophomore year.
People thought it a little strange, because each had a parent alive,
but the boys liked it. Sonny's father ran the local domino parlor
and lived in a room at the little hotel, and Duane's mother didn't
really have much more room. His grandmother was still alive and
living with his mother in their two-room house; his mother took
in laundry, so the house was pretty full. The boys were actually
rather proud that they lived in a rooming house and paid their
own rent; most of the boys with real homes envied the two their
freedom. Nobody envied them Old Lady Malone, of course, but
she owned the rooming house and couldn't be helped. She was
nosy, dipped snuff, had a compulsion about turning off fires, and
was afflicted with one of the most persistent cases of diarrhea on
record. The one bathroom was so badly aired that the boys frequently performed their morning toilet in the rest room of the
Texaco filling station.

After Sonny got his delivery orders he jogged up the
street to the filling station to get the truck, an old green
International. The seat springs had about worn through the
padding, and most of the rubber was gone from the footpedals.
Still, it ran, and Sonny gunned it a few times and struck out for
Megargel, a town even smaller than Thalia. Out in the open country the norther gusted strongly across the highway, making the
truck hard to hold. Once in a while a big ragweed would shake
loose from the barbed-wire fences and skitter across the road,

only to catch again in the barbed-wire fence on the other side. The dry grass in the pastures was gray-brown, and the leafless winter mesquite gray-black. A few Hereford yearlings wandered dispiritedly into the wind, the only signs of life. There was really nothing between Thalia and Megargel but thirty miles of lonesome country. Except for a few sandscraped ranch houses there was nothing to see but a long succession of low brown ridges, with the wind singing over them. It occurred to Sonny that perhaps people called them "blue northers" because it was so hard not to get blue when one was blowing. He regretted that he had not asked Billy to ride along with him on the morning deliveries. Billy was no talker, but he was company, and with nobody at all on the road or in the cab Sonny sometimes got the funny feeling that he was driving the old truck around and around in a completely empty space.

Georgia

O'Keeffe

Texas Letters

To *Alfred Stieglitz*   [CANYON, TEXAS, 4 SEPTEMBER 1916]

YOUR LETTER THIS morning is the biggest letter I ever got— Some way or other it seems as if it is the biggest thing anyone ever said to me—and that it should come this morning when I am wondering—no I'm not exactly wondering but what I have been thinking in words—is—I'll *be damned* and I want to damn every other person in this little spot—like a nasty petty little sore of some kind—on the wonderful plains. The plains—the wonderful great big sky—makes me want to breathe so deep that I'll

---

Painter GEORGIA O'KEEFFE created the bulk of her work in the Southwest. The wife of photographer Alfred Stieglitz, O'Keeffe often fled their home in New York and took solitary journeys to Texas, and later, New Mexico. This letter reveals her immediate attraction to the the desert landscape.

break—There is so much of it—I want to get outside of it all—I would if I could—even if it killed me—

I have been here less than 12 hours—slept eight of them—have talked to possibly 10 people—mostly educators— think quick for me—of a bad word to apply to them—the little things they forced on me—they are so just like folks get the depraved notion they ought to be—that I feel its a pity to disfigure such wonderful country with people of any kind—I wonder if I am going to allow myself to be paid 1800 dollars a year to get like that—I never felt so much like kicking holes in the world in my life—still there is something great about wading into this particular kind of slime that I've never tried before— alone—wondering—if I can keep my head up above these little houses and know more of the plains and the big country than the little people.

Previous contacts make some of them not like my coming here

So—you see it was nice to get a big letter this morning— I needed it—

I walked and heard the wind—the trees are mostly locust bushes 20 feet high or less—mostly less—and a prairie wind in the locust has a sound all its own—like your pines have a sound all their own—I opened my eyes and simply saw the wallpaper It was so hideously ugly—I remembered where I was and shut my eyes right tight so I couldn't see it—with my eyes shut I remembered the wind sounding just like this before—

I didn't want to see the room—it's so ugly—it's awful and I didn't want to look out the window for fear of seeing ugly little frame houses—so I felt for my watch—looked at it—decided

I needn't open my eyes again for 15 minutes—The sound of the wind is great—but the pink roses on my rugs! And the little squares with three pink roses in each one—dark lined squares—I have half a notion to count them so you will know how many are hitting me—give me flies and mosquitoes and ticks—even fleas—every time in preference to three pink roses in a square with another rose on top of it

Then you mentioned me in purple—I'd be about as apt to be naked—don't worry—! don't you hate pink roses!

As I read the first part of your letter—saying you hadn't looked at the stuff I left for my sister to send you—I immediately thought—I'd like to run right down and telegraph you not to open them—then—that would be such a foolish thing to do

Not foolish to me—or for me—but the other queer folks who think I'm queer

There is dinner—and how I hate it—You know—I—

I waited till later to finish the above sentence thinking that maybe I must stop somewhere with the things I want to say—but I want to say it and I'll trust to luck that you'll understand

Your letter makes me feel like Lafferty's paintings—they made me want to go right to him quick—your letter makes me want to just shake all this place off—and go to you and the lake—but—there is really more exhilaration in the fight here than there could possibly be in leaving before it's begun—like I want to—

After mailing my last letter to you I wanted to grab it out of the box and tell you more—I wanted to tell you of the way the outdoors just gets me—

Some way I felt as if I hadn't told you at all—how big and fine and wonderful it all was—

It seems so funny that a week ago it was the mountains I thought the most wonderful—and today it's the plains—I guess it's the feeling of bigness in both that just carries me away—and Katherine—I wish I could tell you how beautiful she is

Living? Maybe so—When one lives one doesn't think about it, I guess—I don't know. The plains send you greetings—Big as what comes after living—if there is anything it must be big—and these plains are the biggest thing I know.

My putting you with Lafferty is really wrong—his things made me feel that *he* needed.

Your letter coming this morning made me think how great it would be to be near you and talk to you—you are more the size of the plains than most folks—and if I could go with my letter to you and the lake—I could tell you better—how fine they are—and more about all the things I've been liking so much but I seem to feel that you know without as much telling as other folks need.

To *Anita Pollitzer*   [CANYON, TEXAS, 11 SEPTEMBER 1916]

TONIGHT I WALKED into the sunset—to mail some letters—the whole sky—and there is so much of it out here—was just blazing—and grey blue clouds were rioting all through the hotness of it—and the ugly little buildings and windmills looked great against it.

But some way or other I didn't seem to like the redness much so after I mailed the letters I walked home—and kept on walking—

The Eastern sky was all grey blue—bunches of clouds—

different kinds of clouds—sticking around everywhere and the whole thing—lit up—first in one place—then in another with flashes of lightning—sometimes just sheet lightning—and sometimes sheet lightning with a sharp bright zigzag flashing across it—.

I walked out past the last house—past the last locust tree—and sat on the fence for a long time—looking—just looking at the lightning—you see there was nothing but sky and flat prairie land—land that seems more like the ocean than anything else I know—There was a wonderful moon—

Well I just sat there and had a great time all by myself—Not even many night noises—just the wind—

I wondered what you are doing—

It is absurd the way I love this country—Then when I came back—it was funny—roads just shoot across blocks any-where—all the houses looked alike—and I almost got lost—I had to laugh at myself—I couldnt tell which house was home—

I am loving the plains more than ever it seems—and the SKY—Anita you have never seen SKY—it is wonderful—

DAVEY
CROCKETT

— — — —

The Alamo

THE FORTRESS OF Alamo is at the town of Bexar, on the San Antonio river, which flows through the town. Bexar is about one hundred and forty miles from the coast, and contains upward of twelve hundred citizens, all native Mexicans, with the exception of a few American families who have settled there. Besides these there is a garrison of soldiers, and trading pedlars of every description, who resort to it from the borders of the Rio Grande, as their nearest depôt of American goods. A military outpost was es-

---

DAVEY CROCKETT was a frontiersman, hunter, and Tennessee's 'coonskin Congressman.' But it was in Texas that Crockett managed his most legendary feat, commanding American troops in the infamous battle of the Alamo. Crockett died in the battle and a folk hero was born. This excerpt is from his autobiography, The Narrative of the Life of Davey Crockett (1836).

tablished at this spot by the Spanish government in 1718. In 1731 the town was settled by emigrants sent out from the Canary Islands by the King of Spain. It became a flourishing settlement, and so continued until the revolution in 1812, since which period the Cumanche and other Indians have greatly harassed the inhabitants, producing much individual suffering, and totally destroying, for a season at least, the prospects of the town. Its site is one of the most beautiful in the western world. The air is salubrious, the water delightful, especially when mixed with a little of the ardent, and the health of the citizens is proverbial. The soil around it is highly fertile, and well calculated for cotton and grain.

The gallant young Colonel Travis, who commands the Texian forces in the fortress of Alamo, received me like a man; and though he can barely muster one hundred and fifty efficient men, should Santa Anna make an attack upon us, with the whole host of ruffians that the Mexican prisons can disgorge, he will have snakes to eat before he gets over the wall, I tell you. But one spirit appears to animate the little band of patriots—and that is liberty, or death. To worship God according to the dictates of their own conscience, and govern themselves as freemen should be governed.

All the world knows, by this time, that the town of Bexar, or, as some call it, San Antonio, was captured from the Mexicans by General Burlison, on the 10th day of December, 1835, after a severe struggle of five days and five nights, during which he sustained a loss of four men only, but the brave old Colonel Milan was among them. There were seventeen hundred men in the town, and the Texian force consisted of but two hundred and sixteen. The Mexicans had walked up the streets leading from the public square, intending to make a desperate resistance: the Texians however made an entrance, and valiantly drove them from house to house, until General Cos retreated to the castle of Alamo, without the city, and there hoisted the white flag, and sent out the terms of capitulation, which were as follows:

General Cos is to retire within six days, with his officers, arms, and private property, on parole of honour. He is not to oppose the re-establishment of the constitution of 1824.

The infantry, and the cavalry, the remnant of Morale's battalion, and the convicts, to return, taking with them ten rounds of cartridge for safety against the Indians.

All public property, money, arms, and ammunition, to be delivered to General Burlison, of the Texian army,—with some other stipulations in relation to the sick and wounded, private property, and prisoners of war. The Texians would not have acceeded to them, preferring to storm him in his stronghold, but at this critical juncture they hadn't a single round of ammunition left, having fought from the 5th to the 9th of the month. General Ugartechea had arrived but the day before with three hundred troops, and the four hundred convicts mentioned above, making a reinforcement of seven hundred men; but such rubbish was no great obstacle to the march of freedom. The Mexicans lost about three hundred men during the siege, and the Texians had only four killed and twenty wounded. The article of capitulation being signed, we marched into town, took possession of the fortress, hoisted the independent flag, and told the late proprietors to pack their moveables and clear out in the snapping of a trigger, as we did not think our pockets quite safe with so many jail birds around us. And this is the way the Alamo came into our possession; but the way we shall maintain our possession of it will be a subject for the future historian to record, or my name's not Crockett.—I wish I may be shot if I don't go ahead to the last.

I found Colonel Bowie, of Louisiana, in the fortress, a man celebrated for having been in more desperate personal conflicts than any other in the country, and whose name has been given to a knife of a peculiar construction, which is now in general use in the southwest. I was introduced to him by Colonel Travis, and he gave me a friendly welcome, and appeared to be mightily pleased that I had arrived safe. While we were conversing he had occasion to draw his famous knife to cut a strap, and I wish I may be shot if the bare sight of it wasn't enough to give a man of a squeamish stomach the cholic, specially before breakfast. He saw I was admiring it, and said he, "Colonel, you might tickle a fellow's ribs a long time with this little instrument before you'd make him laugh; and many a time have I seen a man puke at the idea of the point touching the pit of his stomach."

My companions, the Bee hunter and the conjurer, joined us, and the colonel appeared to know them both very well. He had a high opinion of the Bee hunter, for turning to me, he said, "Colonel, you could not have had a braver, better, or more pleasant fellow for a companion than honest Ned here. With fifteen hundred such men I would undertake to march to the city of Mexico, and occupy the seat of Santa Anna myself before three months should elapse."

The colonel's life has been marked by constant peril and deeds of daring. A few years ago, he went on a hunting excursion into the prairies of Texas, with nine companions. They were attacked by a roving party of Cumanches, about two hundred strong, and such was the science of the colonel in this sort of wild warfare, that after killing a considerable number of the enemy, he fairly frightened the remainder from the field of action, and they fled in utter dismay. The fight took place among the high grass in the open prairie. He ordered his men to dismount from their horses and scatter; to take deliberate aim before they fired, but as soon as they discharged their rifles to fall flat on the ground and crawl away from the spot, and reload their pieces. By this scheme they not only escaped the fire of the Indians, but by suddenly discharging their guns from another quarter, they created the impression that their party was a numerous one; and the Indians, finding that they were fighting against an invisible enemy, after losing about thirty of their men, took to flight, believing themselves lucky in having escaped with no greater loss. But one of the colonel's party was slightly wounded, and that was owing to his remaining to reload his rifle without having first shifted his position.

Santa Anna, it is said, roars like an angry lion at the disgraceful defeat that his brother-in-law, General Cos, lately met with at this place. It is rumoured that he has recruited a large force, and commenced his march to San Louis de Potosi, and he is determined to carry on a war of extermination. He is liberal in applying his epithets to our countrymen in Texas, and denounces them as a set of perfidious wretches, whom the compassion of the generous Mexicans has permitted to take refuge in their country; and who, like the serpent in the fable, no sooner warmed themselves than they stung their benefactors. This is a good joke. —By what title does Mexico lay claim to all the territory which belonged to Spain in North America? Each province or state of

New Spain contended separately or jointly, just as it happened, for their independence, as we did, and were not united under a general government representing the whole of the Spanish possessions, which was only done afterward by mutual agreement or federation. Let it be remembered that the Spanish authorities were first expelled from Texas by the American settlers, who, from the treachery of their Mexican associates, were unable to retain it; but the second time they were more successful. They certainly had as good a right to the soil thus conquered by them, as the inhabitants of other provinces who succeeded against Spain. The Mexicans talk of the ingratitude of the Americans; the truth is, that the ingratitude has been on the other side. What was the war of Texas, in 1813, when the revolutionary spark was almost extinguished in Mexico? What was the expedition of Mina, and his three hundred American Spartans, who perished heroically in the very heart of Mexico, in the vain attempt to resuscitate and keep alive the spark of independence which has at this time kindled such an ungrateful blaze? If a just estimate could be made of the lives and the treasures contributed by American enterprise in that cause, it would appear incredible. How did the Mexicans obtain their independence at last? Was it by their own virtue and courage? No, it was by the treachery of one of the king's generals, who established himself by successful treason, and they have been in constant commotion ever since, which proves they are unfit to govern themselves, much less a free and enlightened people at a distance of twelve hundred miles from them.

The Mexican government, by its colonization laws, invited and induced the Anglo-American population of Texas to colonize its wilderness, under the pledged faith of a written constitution, that they should continue to enjoy that constitutional liberty and republican government to which they had been habituated in the land of their birth, the United States of America. In this expectation they have been cruelly disappointed, as the Mexican nation has acquiesced in the late changes made in the government by Santa Anna; who, having overturned the constitution of this country, now offers the settlers the cruel alternative, either to abandon their homes, acquired by so many privations, or submit to the most intolerable of all tyranny, the combined despotism of the sword and the priesthood.

But Santa Anna charges the Americans with ingratitude! This is something like Satan reviling sin. I have gathered some particulars of the life of this moral personage from a gentleman at present in the Alamo, and who is intimately acquainted with him, which I will copy into my book exactly as he wrote it.

Santa Anna is about forty-two years of age, and was born in the city of Vera Cruz. His father was a Spaniard, of old Spain, of respectable standing, though poor; his mother was a Mexican. He received a common education, and at the age of thirteen or fourteen was taken into the military family of the then Intendant of Vera Cruz, General Davila, who took a great fancy to him, and brought him up. He remained with General Davila until about the year 1820. While with Davila he was made a major, and when installed he took the honours very cooly, and on some of his friends congratulating him, he said, "If you were to make me a god, I should desire to be something greater." This trait, developed at so early a period of his life, indicated the existence of that vaulting ambition which has ever since characterized his life.

After serving in the Spanish royal cause until 1821, he left

Vera Cruz, turned against his old master and benefactor, and placed himself at the head of some irregular troops which he raised on the sea-coast near Vera Cruz, and which are called Jarochos in their language, and which are denominated by him his Cossacks, as they are all mounted and armed with spears. With this rude cavalry he besieged Vera Cruz, drove Davila into the castle of San Juan d'Ulloa, and after having been repulsed again entered at a subsequent period, and got entire possession of the city, expelling therefrom the old Spanish troops, and reducing the power of the mother country in Mexico to the walls of the castle.

Subsequent to this, Davila is said to have obtained an interview with Santa Anna, and told him he was destined to act a prominent part in the history of his country. "And now," says he, "I will give you some advice: always go with the strongest party." He always acted up to this motto until he raised the *grito*, (or cry,) in other words, took up the cudgels for the friars and church. He then overturned the federal government, and established a central despotism, of which the priests and the military were the two privileged orders. His life has been, from the first, of the most romantic kind; constantly in revolutions, constantly victorious.

His manners are extremely affable; he is full of anecdote and humour, and makes himself exceedingly fascinating and agreeable to all who come into his company; he is about five feet ten, rather spare, has a moderately high forehead, with black hair, short black whiskers, without mustachios, and an eye large, black, and expressive of a lurking devil in his look; he is a man of genteel and dignified deportment, but of a disposition perfectly heartless. He married a Spanish lady of property, a native of Alvarado, and through that marriage obtained the first part of his estate, called Manga de Clavo, six leagues from Vera Cruz. He has three fine children, yet quite young.

The following striking anecdote of Santa Anna illustrates his peculiar quickness and management: During the revolution of 1829, while he was shut up in Oxaca, and surrounded by the government troops, and reduced to the utmost straits for the want of money and provisions, having a very small force, there had been, in consequence of the siege and firing every day through the streets, no mass for several weeks. He had no money, and hit upon the following expedient to get it: he took possession of one of the convents, got hold of the wardrobe of the friars, dressed his officers and some of his soldiers in it, and early in the morning had the bells rung for the mass. The people, delighted at having again an opportunity of adoring the Supreme Being, flocked to the church where he was; and after the house was pretty well filled, his friars showed their side-arms and bayonets from beneath the cowls, and closed the doors upon the assembled multitude. At this unexpected denouement there was a tremendous shrieking, when one of his officers ascended the pulpit and told the people that he wanted ten thousand dollars and must have it. He finally succeeded in getting about thirty-six hundred dollars, when he dismissed the congregation.

As a sample of Santa Anna's pious whims we relate the following:

In the same campaign of Oxaca, Santa Anna and his officers were there besieged by Rincon, who commanded the government troops. Santa Anna was in a convent surrounded by a small breast-work. Some of the officers one night, to amuse themselves, took the wooden saints out of the church and placed them as sentries, dressed in uniforms, on the breastwork. Rincon, alarmed on the morning at this apparent boldness, began to fire away at the wooden images, supposing them to be flesh and blood; and it was not until some of the officers who were not in the secret had implored Santa Anna to prevent this desecration that the firing ceased.

Many similar facts are related of him. He is, in fact, all things to all men; and yet, after his treachery to Davila, he has the impudence to talk about ingratitude. He never was out of Mexico. If I only live to tree him, and take him prisoner, I shall ask for no more glory in this life.

I WRITE THIS on the nineteenth of February, 1836, at San Antonio. We are all in high spirits, though we are rather short of provisions, for men who have appetites that could digest any thing but oppression; but no matter, we have a prospect of soon getting our bellies full of fighting, and that is victuals and drink to a true patriot any day. We had a little sort of convivial party last evening: just about a dozen of us set to work, most patrioti-cally, to see whether we could not get rid of that curse of the land, whisky, and we made considerable progress; but my poor friend, Thimblerig, got sewed up just about as tight as the eyelet-hole in a lady's corset, and a little tighter too, I reckon; for when he went to bed he called for a boot-jack, which was brought to him, and he bent down on his hands and knees, and very gravely pulled off his hat with it, for the darned critter was so thoroughly swiped that he didn't know his head from his heels. But this wasn't all the folly he committed: he pulled off his coat and laid it on the bed, and then hung himself over the back of a chair; and I wish I may be shot if he didn't go to sleep in that position.

Seeing the poor fellow completely used up, I carried him to bed, though he did belong to the Temperance society; and he knew nothing about what had occurred until I told him the next morning. The Bee hunter didn't join us in this blow-out. Indeed, he will seldom drink more than just enough to prevent his being called a total abstinence man. But then he is the most jovial fellow for a water drinker I ever did see.

This morning I saw a caravan of about fifty mules passing by Bexar, and bound for Santa Fé. They were loaded with different articles to such a degree that it was astonishing how they could travel at all, and they were nearly worn out by their labours. They were without bridle or halter, and yet proceeded with perfect regularity in a single line; and the owners of the caravan rode their mustangs with their enormous spurs, weighing at least a pound a piece, with rowels an inch and a half in length, and lever bits of the harshest description, able to break the jaws of their animals under a very gentle pressure. The men were dressed in the costume of Mexicans. Colonel Travis sent out a guard to see that they were not laden with munitions of war for the enemy. I went out with the party. The poor mules were bending under a burden of more than three hundred pounds, without including the panniers, which were bound so tight as almost to stop the breath of the poor animal. Each of the sorrowful line came up, spontaneously, in turn to have his girth unbound and his load removed. They seemed scarcely able to keep upon their feet, and as they successively obtained relief, one after another heaved a long and deep sigh, which it was painful to hear, because it proved that the poor brutes had been worked beyond their strength. What a world of misery man inflicts upon the rest of creation in his brief passage through life!

Finding that the caravan contained nothing intended for the enemy, we assisted the owners to replace the heavy burdens on the backs of the patient but dejected mules, and allowed them to pursue their weary and lonely way. For full two hours we could see them slowly winding along the narrow path, a faint line that ran like a thread through the extended prairie; and finally they were whittled down to the little end of nothing in the distance, and were blotted out from the horizon.

The caravan had no sooner disappeared than one of the hunters, who had been absent several days, came in. He was one of those gentlemen who don't pride themselves much upon their costume, and reminded me of a covey who came into a tavern in New York when I was last in that city. He was dressed in five jackets, all of which failed to conceal his raggedness, and as he bolted in, he exclaimed,

"Worse than I look, by ——. But no matter, I've let myself for fourteen dollars a month, and find my own prog and lodging."

"To do what?" demanded the barkeeper.

"To stand at the corner for a paper-mill sign—'cash for rags'—that's all. I'm about to enter upon the stationery business, you see." He tossed off his grog, and bustled out to begin his day's work.

But to return to the hunter. He stated that he had met some Indians on the banks of the Rio Frio, who informed him that Santa Anna, with a large force, had already crossed the Nueces, and might be expected to arrive before San Antonio in a few days. We immediately set about preparing to give him a warm reception, for we are all well aware, if our little band is

overwhelmed by numbers, there is little mercy to be expected
from the cowardly Mexicans—it is war to the knife.

I jocosely asked the ragged hunter, who was a smart, active young fellow, of the steamboat and alligator breed, whether
he was a rhinoceros or a hyena, as he was so eager for a fight
with the invaders. "Neither the one, nor t'other, Colonel," says
he, "but a whole menagerie in myself. I'm shaggy as a bear,
wolfish about the head, active as a cougar, and can grin like a
hyena, until the bark will curl off a gum log. There's a sprinkling
of all sorts in me, from the lion down to the skunk; and before
the war is over you'll pronounce me an entire zoological institute,
or I miss a figure in my calculation. I promise to swallow Santa
Anna without gagging, if you will only skewer back his ears, and
grease his head a little."

He told me that he was one in the fatal expedition fitted
out from New Orleans, in November last, to join the contemplated
attack upon Tampico by Mehia and Peraza. They were, in all,
about one hundred and thirty men, who embarked as emigrants to
Texas; and the terms agreed upon were, that it was optional
whether the party took up arms in defence of Texas, or not, on
landing. They were at full liberty to act as they pleased. But the
truth was, Tampico was their destination, and an attack on that
city the covert design, which was not made known before land
was in sight. The emigrants were landed, some fifty, who doubtless had a previous understanding, joined the standard of General
Mehia, and the following day a formidable fort surrendered without an attack.

The whole party were now tendered arms and ammunition, which even those who had been decoyed accepted; and, the

line being formed, they commenced the attack upon the city. The hunter continued: "On the 15th of November our little army, consisting of one hundred and fifty men, marched into Tampico, garrisoned by two thousand Mexicans, who were drawn up in battle array in the public square of the city. We charged them at the point of the bayonet, and although they so greatly outnumbered us, in two minutes we completely routed them; and they fled, taking refuge on the house tops, from which they poured a destructive fire upon our gallant little band. We fought them until daylight, when we found our number decreased to fifty or sixty broken down and disheartened men. Without ammunition, and deserted by the officers, twenty-eight immediately surrendered. But a few of us cut our way through, and fortunately escaped to the mouth of the river, where we got on board a vessel and sailed for Texas.

"The twenty-eight prisoners wished to be considered as prisoners of war; they made known the manner in which they had been deceived, but they were tried by a court-martial of Mexican soldiers, and condemned to be shot on the 14th day of December, 1835, which sentence was carried into execution."

After receiving this account from my new friend, the old pirate and the Indian hunter came up, and they went off to liquor together, and I went to see a wild Mexican hog, which one of the hunters had brought in. These animals have become scarce, which circumstance is not to be deplored, for their flesh is of little value; and there will still be hogs enough left in Mexico, from all I can learn, even though these should be extirpated.

February 22. The Mexicans, about sixteen hundred strong, with their President Santa Anna at their head, aided by Generals Almonte, Cos, Sesma, and Castrillon, are within two leagues of

Bexar. General Cos, it seems, has already forgot his parole of honour, and is come back to retrieve the credit he lost in this place in December last. If he is captured a second time, I don't think he can have the impudence to ask to go at large again without giving better bail than on the former occasion. Some of the scouts came in, and brought reports that Santa Anna has been endeavoring to excite the Indians to hostilities against the Texians, but so far without effect. The Cumanches, in particular, entertain such hatred for the Mexicans, and at the same time hold them in such contempt, that they would rather turn their tomahawks against them, and drive them from the land, than lend a helping hand. We are up and doing, as lively as Dutch cheese in the dog-days. The two hunters that I have already introduced to the reader left the town, this afternoon, for the purpose of reconnoitring.

February 23. Early this morning the enemy came in sight, marching in regular order, and displaying their strength to the greatest advantage, in order to strike us with terror. But that was no go; they'll find that they have to do with men who will never lay down their arms as long as they can stand on their legs. We held a short council of war, and, finding that we should be completely surrounded, and overwhelmed by numbers, if we remained in the town, we concluded to withdraw to the fortress of Alamo, and defend it to the last extremity. We accordingly filed off, in good order, having some days before placed all the surplus provisions, arms, and ammunition in the fortress. We have had a large national flag made; it is composed of thirteen stripes, red and white, alternately, on a blue ground with a large white star, of five points, in the centre, and between the points the letters TEXAS. As soon as all our little band, about one hundred and fifty in number, had entered and secured the fortress in the best possible manner, we set about raising our flag on the battlements; on which occasion there was no one more active than my young friend, the Bee hunter. He had been all along sprightly, cheerful, and spirited, but now, notwithstanding the control that he usually maintained over himself, it was with difficulty that he kept his enthusiasm within bounds. As soon as we commenced raising the flag he burst forth, in a clear, full tone of voice, that made the blood tingle in the veins of all who heard him:—

> "Up with your banner, Freedom,
> Thy champions cling to thee;
> They'll follow where'er you lead 'em,
> To death, or victory;—
> Up with your banner, Freedom.
>
> Tyrants and slaves are rushing
> To tread thee in the dust;
> Their blood will soon be gushing,
> And stain our knives with rust;—
> But not thy banner, Freedom.
>
> While stars and stripes are flying,
> Our blood we'll freely shed;
> No groan will 'scape the dying,
> Seeing thee o'er his head;—
> Up with your banner, Freedom."

This song was followed by three cheers from all within the fortress, and the drums and trumpets commenced playing.

The enemy marched into Bexar, and took possession of the town, a blood-red flag flying at their head, to indicate that we need not expect quarters if we should fall into their clutches. In the afternoon a messenger was sent from the enemy to Colonel Travis, demanding an unconditional and absolute surrender of the garrison, threatening to put every man to the sword in case of refusal. The only answer he received was a cannon shot, so the messenger left us with a flea in his ear, and the Mexicans commenced firing grenades at us, but without doing any mischief. At night Colonel Travis sent an express to Colonel Fanning at Goliad, about three or four days' march from this place, to let him know that we are besieged. The old pirate volunteered to go on this expedition, and accordingly left the fort after nightfall.

February 24. Very early this morning the enemy commenced a new battery on the banks of the river, about three hundred and fifty yards from the fort, and by afternoon they amused themselves by firing at us from that quarter. Our Indian scout came in this evening, and with him a reinforcement of thirty men from Gonzales, who are just in the nick of time to reap a harvest of glory; but there is some prospect of sweating blood before we gather it in. An accident happened to my friend Thimblerig this afternoon. He was intent on his eternal game of thimbles, in a somewhat exposed position, while the enemy were bombarding us from the new redoubt. A three ounce ball glanced from the parapet and struck him on the breast, inflicting a painful but not dangerous wound. I extracted the ball, which was of lead, and recommended to him to drill a hole through it, and carry it for a watch seal. "No," he replied, with energy, "may I be shot six times if I do; that would be making a bauble for an idle boast.

No, Colonel, lead is getting scarce, and I'll lend it out at compound interest. —Curse the thimbles!" he muttered, and went his way, and I saw no more of him that evening.

February 25. The firing commenced early this morning, but the Mexicans are poor engineers, for we haven't lost a single man, and our outworks have sustained no injury. Our sharpshooters have brought down a considerable number of stragglers at a long shot. I got up before the peep of day, hearing an occasional discharge of a rifle just over the place where I was sleeping, and I was somewhat amazed to see Thimblerig mounted alone on the battlement, no one being on duty at the time but the sentries. "What are you doing there?" says I. "Paying my debts," says he, "interest and all." "And how do you make out?" says I. "I've nearly got through," says he; "stop a moment Colonel, and I'll close the account." He clapped his rifle to his shoulder, and blazed away, then jumped down from his perch, and said, "That account's settled; them chaps will let me play out my game in quiet next time." I looked over the wall, and saw four Mexicans lying dead on the plain. I asked him to explain what he meant by paying his debts, and he told me that he had run the grape shot into four rifle balls, and that he had taken an early stand to have a chance of picking off stragglers. "Now, Colonel, let's go take our bitters," said he; and so we did. The enemy have been busy during the night, and have thrown up two batteries on the opposite side of the river. The battalion of Matamoras is posted there, and cavalry occupy the hills to the east and on the road to Gonzales. They are determined to surround us, and cut us off from reinforcement, or the possibility of escape by a sortie.—Well, there's one thing they cannot prevent; we'll still go ahead, and sell our lives at a high price.

February 26. Colonel Bowie has been taken sick from over exertion and exposure. He did not leave his bed to-day until twelve o'clock. He is worth a dozen common men in a situation like ours. The Bee hunter keeps the whole garrison in good heart with his songs and his jests, and his daring and determined spirit. He is about the quickest on the trigger, and the best rifle shot we have in the fort. I have already seen him bring down eleven of the enemy, and at such a distance that we all thought it would be waste of ammunition to attempt it. His gun is first-rate, quite equal to my Betsey, though she has not quite as many trinkets about her. This day a small party sallied out of the fort for wood and water, and had a slight skirmish with three times their number from the division under General Sesma. The Bee hunter headed them, and beat the enemy off, after killing three. On opening his Bible at night, of which he always reads a portion before going to rest, he found a musket ball in the middle of it. "See here, Colonel," said he, "how they have treated the valued present of my dear little Kate of Nacogdoches." "It saved your life," said I. "True," replied he, more seriously than usual, "and I am not the first sinner whose life has been saved by this book." He prepared for bed, and before retiring he prayed, and returned thanks for his providential escape; and I heard the name of Catherine mingled in his prayer.

February 27. The cannonading began early this morning, and ten bombs were thrown into the fort, but fortunately exploded without doing any mischief. Provisions are becoming scarce, and the enemy are endeavoring to cut off our water. If they attempt to stop our grog in that manner, let them look out, for we shall become too wrathy for our shirts to hold us. We are not prepared to

submit to an excise of that nature, and they'll find it out. This dis-
covery has created considerable excitement in the fort.

February 28. Last night our hunters brought in some corn
and hogs, and had a brush with a scout from the enemy beyond
gun-shot of the fort. They put the scout to flight, and got in
without injury. They bring accounts that the settlers are flying in
all quarters, in dismay, leaving their possessions to the mercy of
the ruthless invader, who is literally engaged in a war of extermination, more brutal than the untutored savage of the desert could
be guilty of. Slaughter is indiscriminate, sparing neither sex, age,
nor condition. Buildings have been burnt down, farms laid waste,
and Santa Anna appears determined to verify his threat, and con-
vert the blooming paradise into a howling wilderness. For just
one fair crack at that rascal, even at a hundred yards distance, I
would bargain to break my Betsey, and never pull trigger again.
My name's not Crockett if I wouldn't get glory enough to appease
my stomach for the remainder of my life. The scouts report that a
settler, by the name of Johnson, flying with his wife and three little children, when they reached the Colorado, left his family on
shore, and waded into the river to see whether it would be safe
to ford with his wagon. When about the middle of the river he
was seized by an alligator, and, after a struggle, was dragged
under the water, and perished. The helpless woman and her babes
were discovered, gazing in agony on the spot, by other fugitives
who happily passed that way, and relieved them. Those who fight
the battles experience but a small part of the privation, suffering
and anguish that follow in the train of ruthless war. The cannonading continued, at intervals, throughout the day, and all
hands were kept up to their work. The enemy, somewhat imbold-

ened, draws nigher to the fort. So much the better.—There was a
move in General Sesma's division toward evening.

February 29. Before daybreak we saw General Sesma leave
his camp with a large body of cavalry and infantry, and move off
in the direction of Goliad. We think that he must have received
news of Colonel Fanning's coming to our relief. We are all in
high spirits at the prospect of being able to give the rascals a fair
shake on the plain. This business of being shut up makes a man
wolfish.—I had a little sport this morning before breakfast. The
enemy had planted a piece of ordnance within gun-shot of the
fort during the night, and the first thing in the morning they
commenced a brisk cannonade, point-blank, against the spot
where I was snoring. I turned out pretty smart, and mounted the
rampart. The gun was charged again, a fellow stepped forth to
touch her off, but before he could apply the match I let him have
it, and he keeled over. A second stepped up, snatched the match
from the hand of the dying man, but Thimblerig, who had followed me, handed me his rifle, and the next instant the Mexican
was stretched on the earth beside the first. A third came up to the
cannon, my companion handed me another gun, and I fixed him
off in like manner. A fourth, then a fifth, seized the match, who
both met with the same fate, and then the whole party gave it up
as a bad job, and hurried off to the camp, leaving the cannon
ready charged where they had planted it. I came down, took my
bitters, and went to breakfast. Thimblerig told me that the place
from which I had been firing was one of the snuggest stands in
the whole fort, for he never failed picking off two or three stragglers before breakfast, when perched up there. And I recollect,
now, having seen him there, ever since he was wounded, the first

thing in the morning, and the last at night,—and at times, thoughtlessly playing at his eternal game.

March 1. The enemy's forces have been increasing in numbers daily, notwithstanding they have already lost about three hundred men in the assaults they have made upon us. I neglected to mention in the proper place, that when the enemy came in sight we had but three bushels of corn in the garrison, but have since found eighty bushels in a deserted house. Colonel Bowie's illness still continues, but he manages to crawl from his bed every day, that his comrades may see him. His presence alone is a tower of strength. The enemy becomes more daring as his numbers increase.

March 2. This day the delegates meet in general convention, at the town of Washington, to frame our Declaration of Independence. That the sacred instrument may never be trampled on by the children of those who have freely shed their blood to establish it, is the sincere wish of David Crockett. Universal independence is an almighty idea, far too extensive for some brains to comprehend. It is a beautiful seed that germinates rapidly, and brings forth a large and vigorous tree, but like the deadly Upas, we sometimes find the smaller plants wither and die in its shades. Its blooming branches spread far and wide, offering a perch of safety to all alike, but even among its protecting branches we find the eagle, the kite, and the owl preying upon the helpless dove and sparrow. Beneath its shade myriads congregate in goodly fellowship, but the lamb and the fawn find but frail security from the lion and the jackal, though the tree of independence waves over them. Some imagine independence to be a natural charter, to exercise without restraint, and to their fullest extent, all the energies, both physical and mental, with which they have been endowed; and for their individual aggrandizement alone, without regard to the rights of others, provided they extend to all the same privilege and freedom of action. Such independence is the worst of tyranny.

March 3. We have given over all hopes of receiving assistance from Goliad or Refugio. Colonel Travis harangued the garrison, and concluded by exhorting them, in case the enemy should carry the fort, to fight to the last gasp, and render their victory even more serious to them than to us. This was followed by three cheers.

March 4. Shells have been falling into the fort like hail during the day, but without effect. About dusk in the evening, we observed a man running toward the fort, pursued by about half a dozen Mexican cavalry. The Bee hunter immediately knew him to be the old pirate who had gone to Goliad, and, calling to the two hunters, he sallied out of the fort to the relief of the old man, who was hard pressed. I followed close after. Before we reached the spot the Mexicans were close on the heel of the old man, who stopped suddenly, turned short upon his pursuers, discharged his rifle, and one of the enemy fell from his horse. The chase was renewed, but finding that he would be overtaken and cut to pieces, he now turned again, and, to the amazement of the enemy, became the assailant in his turn. He clubbed his gun, and dashed among them like a wounded tiger, and they fled like sparrows. By this time we reached the spot, and, in the ardour of the moment, followed some distance before we saw that our retreat to the fort was cut off by another detachment of cavalry. Nothing was to be done but to fight our way through. We were all of the same mind. "Go ahead!" cried I, and they shouted, "Go ahead, Colonel!" We dashed among them, and a bloody conflict ensued.

They were about twenty in number, and they stood their ground. After the fight had continued about five minutes, a detachment was seen issuing from the fort to our relief, and the Mexicans scampered off, leaving eight of their comrades dead upon the field. But we did not escape unscathed, for both the pirate and the Bee hunter were mortally wounded, and I received a sabre cut across the forehead. The old man died, without speaking, as soon as we entered the fort. We bore my young friend to his bed, dressed his wounds, and I watched beside him. He lay, without complaint or manifesting pain, until about midnight, when he spoke, and I asked him if he wanted any thing. "Nothing," he replied, but drew a sigh that seemed to rend his heart, as he added, "Poor Kate of Nacogdoches!" His eyes were filled with tears, as he continued, "Her words were prophetic, Colonel"; and then he sang in a low voice that resembled the sweet notes of his own devoted Kate,

"But toom cam' the saddle, all bluidy to see,
And hame cam' the steed, but hame never cam' he."

HE SPOKE NO more, and, a few minutes after, died. Poor Kate, who will tell this to thee!

March 5. Pop, pop, pop! Bom, bom, bom! throughout the day.—No time for memorandums now.—Go ahead!—Liberty and independence forever!

GLORIA

ANZALDÚA

— — — —

People Should Not Die in June in South Texas

PRIETITA SQUEEZES THROUGH the crowd of mourners and finds a place near the coffin. She stand there for hours watching relatives and friends one after the other approach the coffin, kneel beside it. They make the sign of the cross, bow slowly while backing away. Even a few Anglos come to pay their respects to Urbano, loved by all. But after two and a half days, her father has begun to smell like a cow whose carcass has been gutted by vultures. People should not die in June in south Texas.

Chicana poet and short story writer GLORIA ANZALDÚA teaches at the University of Texas. Her razor-sharp tales have appeared in numerous publications. Anzaldúa penned "People Should Not Die in June in South Texas" in 1992.

Earlier that day Prietita and her mother had gone to the funeral home, where in some hidden room someone was making a two-inch incision in her father's throat. Someone was inserting a tube in his jugular vein. In some hidden room *una envenenada aguja* filled his *venas* with embalming fluid.

The white undertaker put his palm on the small of her mother's back and propelled her toward the more expensive coffins. Her mother couldn't stop crying. She held a handkerchief to her eyes like a blindfold, knotting and unraveling it, knotting and unraveling it. Prieta, forced to be the more practical of the two, said, "Let's take that one or this one," pointing at the coffins midrange in price. Though they would be in debt for three years, they chose un *cajón de quinientos dólares.* The undertaker had shown them the backless suits whose prices ranged from seventy to several hundred dollars. *Compraron un traje negro y una camisa blanca con encaje color de rosa.* They bought a black suit with a white shirt with pink. "Why are we buying such an expensive suit? It doesn't even have a back. And besides, it's going to rot soon," she told her mother softly. Her mother looked at her and burst out crying again. Her mother was either hysterical or very quiet and withdrawn, so Prieta had to swallow her own tears. They had returned in the hearse with the coffin to a house filled with relatives and friends, with tables laden with *comida* and buckets overflowing with ice and *cerveza.*

Prietita stands against the living room wall watching the hundreds of people slowly milling around. "*Te acompaño en el pesar,*" *dice la tía* as she embraces her. The stench of alcohol enters her nostrils when male relatives pay their condolences to her. *Prieta se siente helada y asfixiada al mismo tiempo.* She feels cold, shocked, and suffocated.

"*Qué guapa. Es la mayor y se parece mucho a su mamá,*" she hears a woman say, bursting into tears and clutching Prietita in a desperate embrace. Faint whiffs of perfume escape from the women's hair behind their thick black mantillas. The smells of roses and carnations, *carne guisada*, sweat and body heat mingle with the sweet smell of death and fill the house in Hargill.

Antes del cajón en medio de la sala aullando a la virgen su mamagrande Locha cae de rodillas persinándose. But Prieta does not cry, she is the only one at the *velorio* who is dry-eyed. Why can't she cry? *Le dan ganas, no de llorar, pero de reír a carcajadas.* Instead of crying she feels like laughing. It isn't natural. She felt the tightness in her throat give way. Her body trembled with fury. How dare he die? How dare he abandon her? How could he leave her mother all alone? Her mother was just twenty-eight. It wasn't fair. *Sale de la casa corriendo,* she runs out of the house, *Atravesó la calle,* she crosses the street, *tropezándose en las piedras,* while stumbling over rocks. *Llegó a la casa de Mamagrande Ramona en donde estaba su hermanito, Carito, el más chiquito.* She reached her grandmother's house, where her little brother was hiding out. His bewildered face asks questions she cannot answer.

Later Prietita slips back into the house and returns to her place by the coffin. Standing on her toes, she cocks her head over the casket. What if that sweet-putrid smell is perfume injected into his veins to fool them all into thinking he is dead? What if it's all a conspiracy? A lie? Under the overturned red truck someone else's face had lain broken, smashed beyond recognition. The blood on the highway had not been her father's blood.

For three days her father sleeps in his coffin. Her mother sits at his side every night and never sleeps. *Oliendo a muerte, Prietita duerme en su cama,* Prieta sleeps in her bed with the smell of death. *En* sus sueños, in her dreams, *su padre abre los ojos al mirarla*, her father opens his eyes. *Abre su boca a contestarle;* he opens his mouth to answer her. *Se levanta del cajón*, he rises out of the coffin. On the third day Prieta rises from her bed vacant-eyed, puts on her black blouse and skirt and black scarf, and walks to the living room. She stands before the coffin and waits for the hearse. In the car behind the hearse on the way to the church Prietita sits quietly beside her mother, sister, and brothers. Stiff-legged, she gets out of the car and walks to the hearse. She watches the pall bearers, *Tío David, Rafael, Goyo, el compadre Juan*, and others, lift the coffin out of the hearse, carry it inside the church, and set it down in the middle of the aisle.

El cuerpo de su padre está tendido en medio de la iglesia. Her father's corpse lies in the middle of the church. She watches one woman after another kneel before la *Virgen de Guadalupe* and light a candle. Soon hundreds of votive candles flicker their small flames and emit the smell of burning tallow.

"Et Misericordia *ejus a progenis timentibus eum*," intones the priest, flanked by altar boys on both sides. His purple gown rustles as he swings his censors over her father's body and face. Clouds of frankincense cover the length of the dark shiny coffin.

At last the pall bearers return to the coffin. Sporting mustaches and wearing black ties, con *bigote y corbata negra*, they stand stiffly in their somber suits. She had never seen these ranchers, farmers, and farm workers in suits before. In unison they take a deep breath and with a quick movement they lift the coffin. Her mother holds Carito's hands and follows the coffin while Prieta, her sister, and brother walk behind them.

Outside near the cars parked in the street, Prieta watches the church slowly emptying, watches the church become a hollowed-out thing. In their black cotton and rayon dresses, following the coffin with faces hidden under fine-woven mantillas, the women all look like *urracas prietas*, like black crows. Her own nickname was Urraca Prieta.

From her uncle's car en route to the cemetery, Prieta watches the billows of dust rise in the wake of the hearse. Her skin feels prickly with sweat and something else. As the landscape recedes, Prietita feels as though she is traveling backwards to yesterday, to the day before yesterday, to the day she last saw her father. Prieta imagines her father as he drives the red truck filled to the brim with cotton bales. One hand suddenly leaves the wheel to clutch his chest. His body arches, then his head and chest slump over the wheel, blood streaming out through his nose and mouth, his foot lies heavy on the gas pedal. The red ten-ton truck keeps going until it gets to the second curve on the east highway going toward Edinburg. "Wake up, Papi, turn the wheel," but the truck keeps on going off the highway. It turns over, the truck turns over and over, the doors flapping open and then closing and the truck keeps turning over and over until Prieta makes it stop. Her father is thrown out. The edge of the back of the truck crushes his face. Six pairs of wheels spin in the air. White cotton bales are littered around him. The article in the newspaper said that according to the autopsy report, his aorta had burst. The largest artery to the heart, ruptured.

She had not seen the crows, *las urracas prietas*, gather on the *ébano* in the backyard the night before that bright day in June. If they had not announced his death then he couldn't be dead. It was a conspiracy, a lie.

Ya se acabó; ¿qué pasa? Contemplad su figura
la muerte le ha cubierto de pálidos azufres
y le ha puesto cabeza de oscuro minotauro.

Is it over? What's happening?
Reflect on his figure.
Death has covered him with pale sulfurs
and has given him a dark Minotaur head.

The *padrinos* place the coffin under the ebony tree. People pile flower wreaths at her father's feet. Prietita shuffles over to her father lying in the coffin. Her eyes trace the jagged lines running through his forehead, cheek, and chin, where the undertaker had sewn the skin together. The broken nose, the chalky skin with the tinge of green underneath is not her father's, *no es la cara de su papi.* No. On that bright day, June 22, someone else had been driving his truck, someone else had been wearing his khaki pants, his gold wire-rimmed glasses—someone else had his gold front tooth.

Mr. Leidner, her history teacher, had said that the Nazis jerked the gold teeth out of the corpses of the Jews and melted them into rings. And made their skin into lampshades. She did not want anyone to take her *papi's* gold tooth. Prieta steps back from the coffin.

The blood in the highway could not be her father's blood.

¡Qué no quiere verla!
Dile a la luna que venga,
que no quiero ver la sangre

I don't want to see it.
Tell the moon to come
that I don't want to see the blood

As she watches her father, a scream forms in her head: "No, no, no." She thinks she almost sees death creep into her father's unconscious body, kick out his soul and make his body stiff and still. She sees *la muerte's* long pale fingers take possession of her father—sees death place its hand over what had been her father's heart. A fly buzzes by, brings her back to the present. She sees a fly crawl over one of her father's hands, then land on a cheek. She wants him to raise his hand and fan the fly away. He lies unmoving. She raises her hand to crush the fly then lets it fall back to the side. Swatting the fly would mean hitting her *papi*. Death, too, lets the fly crawl over itself. Maybe the fly and death are friends. Maybe death is unaware of so inconsequential a thing as an insect. She is like that fly trying to rouse her father, *es esa mosca.*

She stands looking by the coffin at her own small hands—fleshy, ruddy hands—and forces herself to unclench her fists. A beat pulses in her thumb. When her hands are no longer ruddy nor pulsating she will lie like him. She will lie utterly still. Maggots will find her hands, will seek out her heart. Worms will crawl in and out of her vagina and the world will continue as usual. That is what shocks her the most about her father's death— that people still laugh, the wind continues to blow, the sun rises in the east and sets in the west.

Prieta walks away from the coffin and stands at the edge of the gaping hole under the ebony tree. The hole is so deep, *el poso tan hondo,* the earth so black, *la tierra tan prieta.* She takes great gulps of air but can't get enough into her lungs. Nausea winds its way up from the pit of her stomach, fills her chest and becomes a knot when it reaches her throat. Her body sways slowly back and forth. Someone gently tugs her away. *Los hombres* push a metal apparatus over the hole and *los padrinos* place the coffin over it.

Under the *ébano*, around the hole, a procession forms. The small country cemetery, with Mexicans buried on one side and a few Anglos on the other, is now bulging with hundreds of cars *y miles de gente y miles de flores.*

Prieta hears the whir of the machine and looks back to see it lowering her father into the hole. Someone tosses in a handful of dirt, then the next person does the same, and soon a line of people forms, waiting their turn. Prietita listens to the thuds, the slow shuffle of feet as the line winds and unwinds like a giant serpent. Her turn comes, she bends to pick up a handful of dirt. She loosens her clenched fist over the hole and hears the thud of *terremotes* hit her father's coffin. Drops fall onto the dust-covered coffin. They make little craters on the *cajón's* smooth surface. She feels as though she is standing alone near the mouth of the abyss, near the mouth slowly swallowing her father. An unknown sweetness and a familiar anguish beckon her. As she rocks back and forth near the edge, she listens to Mamagrande's litany: "*Mi hijo, mi hijo, tan bueno. Diosito mío, ¿por qué se lo llevó? Ay mi hijo.*"

Next Sunday the whole family has to go to mass, but Prieta doesn't want to attend. Heavily veiled women dressed in black kneel on the cement floor of the small church and recite the rosary in singsong monotones. *Llorosas rezaban el rosario,* hands moving slowly over the beads. "*Santa María, madre de Dios, ruega por nosotros* . . . Holy Mary, mother of God, pray for us now and at the hour of our death." Her mother and Mamagrande Locha dedicate Sunday masses to her father, promising *la Virgen* a mass a week for the coming year. They pay a small fee for each—all for a man who had never entered church except for the funeral mass of a friend or relative.

Her mother wears *luto*, vowing before a statue of *la Virgen de Guadalupe* to wear black for two years and gray for two more. In September when school resumes, her mother tells Prieta and her sister that they are to wear black for a year, then gray or brown for another two. At first her classmates stare at her. Prieta sees the curiosity and fascination in their eyes slowly turn to pity and disdain. But soon they get used to seeing her in black and drab-colored clothes and she feels invisible once more, and invincible.

After school and on weekends her mother shushes them when they speak loudly or laugh, forbids them to listen to the radio and covers the TV with a blanket. Prieta remembers when her father bought the TV. The other kids had been envious because hers had been the first Mexican family to have such an extravagant luxury. Her father had bought it for them saying it would help his *hijitos* learn to speak English without an accent. If they knew English they could get good jobs and not have to work themselves to death.

Pasa mucho tiempo. Days and weeks and years pass. *Prieta espera al muerto.* She waits for the dead. Every evening she waits for her father to walk into the house, tired after a day of hard work in the fields. She waits for him to rap his knuckles on the top of her head, the one gesture of intimacy he allowed himself with her. She waits for him to gaze at her with his green eyes. She waits for him to take off his shirt and sit bare-chested on the

floor, back against the sofa watching TV, the black curly hair on
the back of his head showing. Now she thinks she hears his footsteps on the front porch, and turns eagerly toward the door. For
years she waits. *Four years* she waits for him to thrust open the sag-
ging door, to return from the land of the dead. For her father is a
great and good man and she is sure God will realize he has made
a mistake and bring him back to them. *En el día de los muertos,* on
the day of the dead, *el primero de noviembre,* on the first of
November, *ella lo espera,* she waits for him. *Aunque no más viniera a vis-*
itarlos, even if he only came to visit. *Aunque no se quedara,* even if he
didn't stay—she wants to see him—*quiere verlo.* But one day, *four*
years after his death, she knows that neither the One God nor her
father will ever walk through her door again.

> *pero nadie querrá mirar tus ojos*
> *porque te has muerto para siempre . . .*
> *como todos los muertos de la Tierra.*

> but no one will want to look at your eyes
> because you have died forever . . .
> like all the dead on Earth.

M O L L Y
I V I N S

Texas Observed

THE CLEAN CRAPPER BILL

THE REST OF the country is in future shock and in Texas we can't get Curtis's Clean Crapper bill through the Legislature. Curtis Graves is a state representative from Houston who introduced a bill to provide minimum standards of cleanliness for public restrooms in this state. It was defeated. Solons rose on the floor of the House to defend dirty johns. The delights of peein' against the back wall after a good whiskey drink were limned in excruciating detail. In New York City, Zero Mostel gets up on a stage and prances around singing "Tradition!" while the audience

MOLLY IVINS is the author of a stack of best-selling books, mostly culled from her spicy newspaper columns. "Texas Observed" is from her 1991 best-seller, Molly Ivins Can't Say That, Can She?

wets itself with nostalgia. In America, the rate of change shifts from arithmetic to geometric progression. In Texas, where ain't nothin' sanitized for your protection, we still peein' against the back wall.

What this country really needs, along with a new government, is a stiff dose of Texas. Things still are the way they used to be down here, and anybody who thinks that's quaint is welcome to come dip into the state's premier product. Like Johnny Winter sings, "They's so much shit in Texas/you bound to step in some."

WHY THE SKY IS BIGGER IN TEXAS

I LOVE THE state of Texas, but I regard that as a harmless perversion on my part and would not, in the name of common humanity, try to foist my pathology off on anyone else. Texas is a dandy place, in short spells, for anyone suffering from nausée de Thruway Hot Shoppe. It is resistant to Howard Johnson, plastic, interstate highways, and Standard Television American English. But the reason it's resistant to such phenomena is because it's cantankerous, ignorant, and repulsive.

The reason the sky is bigger here is because there aren't any trees. The folks here eat grits because they ain't got no taste. Cowboys mostly stink and it's hot, oh God, it is hot. We gave the world Lyndon Johnson and you cowards gave him right back. There are two major cities in Texas: Houston is Los Angeles with the climate of Calcutta; to define Dallas is to add a whole new humongous dimension to bad.

Texas is a mosaic of cultures, which overlap in several parts of the state and form layers, with the darker layers on the

bottom. The cultures are black, Chicano, Southern, freak, subur-
ban, and shitkicker. (Shitkicker is dominant.) They are all rotten
for women. Humanism is not alive and well in Texas. Different
colors and types of Texans do not like one another, nor do they
pretend to.

Shitkicker is pickup trucks with guns slung across the
racks on the back and chicken-fried steaks and machismo and
"D-I-V-O-R-C-E" on the radio and cheap, pink, nylon slips, and
gettin' drunk on Saturday night and goin' to church on Sunday
morning, and drivin' down the highway throwin' beer cans out
the window, and Rastus-an'-Liza jokes and high school football,
and family reunions where the in-laws of your second cousins
show up.

You can eat chili, barbecue, Meskin food, hush puppies,
catfish, collard greens, red beans, pink grapefruit, and watermelon
with Dr. Pepper, Pearl, Lone Star, Carta Blanca, or Shiner's, which
tastes a lot like paint thinner but don't have no preservatives in it.
People who eat soul food here eat it because they can't afford
hamburger. Since last year, you can buy a drink in some bars, but
a lot of folks still brown-bag it 'cause it's cheaper, and Chivas and
Four Roses look alike comin' out of a brown bag.

WHAT TO WATCH IN TEXAS

THE FRONTIER IS what John Wayne lived on. Most Texans are
Baptists. Baptists are civilized people. Beware of Church of Christers.

Once when Ronnie Dugger was being poetic he said, "To
a Texan, a car is like wings to a seagull: our places are far apart
and we must dip into them driving . . . the junctions in the highways and the towns are like turns in a city well known." It's true,

Texans are accustomed to driving three hours to see a football game or 150 miles for a movie.

Texas is an un-self-conscious place. Nobody here is embarrassed about being who he is. Reactionaries aren't embarrassed. Rich folks aren't embarrassed. Rednecks aren't embarrassed. Liberals aren't embarrassed. And when did black folks or brown folks ever have time to worry about existential questions? Lobbyists, loan sharks, slumlords, war profiteers, chiropractors, and KKKers are all proud of their callings. Only Dallas is self-conscious; Dallas deserves it.

Texas is not a civilized place. Texans shoot one another a lot. They also knife, razor, and stomp one another to death with some frequency. And they fight in bars all the time. You can get five years for murder and 99 for pot possession in this state—watch your ass.

ENVIRONMENTAL ADVANCES

THE ONLY THING that smells worse than an oil refinery is a feedlot. Texas has a lot of both. Ecology in Texas started with a feedlot. So many people in Lubbock got upset with the smell of a feedlot there that they complained to the city council all the time. The city council members didn't act like yahoos; they took it serious. After a lot of hearings, it was decided to put an Air-wick bottle on every fencepost around the feedlot. Ecology in Texas has gone uphill since then.

The two newest members of the Air Pollution Control Board were up for a hearing before a state senate committee this June. E. W. Robinson of Amarillo told the committee that he was against allowin' any pollution that would prove to be very harmful to people's health. A senator asked him how harmful was very harmful. Oh, lead poisonin' and such would be unacceptable, said Robinson. What about pollution that causes allergies and asthma? Well, you don't die of it, said Robinson. While the air of Texas is entrusted to this watchdog, the water is in good hands, too. Not long ago, the director of the Texas Water Quality Board was trying to defend what the Armco Steel Company is dumping into the Houston Ship Channel. "Cyanide," he said, "is a scare word."

THEY SAID IT WAS TEXAS KULCHER/BUT IT WAS ONLY RAILROAD GIN

ART IS PAINTINGS of bluebonnets and broncos, done on velvet. Music is mariachis, blues, and country. Eddie Wilson, who used to be a beer lobbyist, started a place in Austin, in an old National Guard armory, called Armadillo World Headquarters. Willie Nelson, Freddie King, Leon Russell, Ravi Shankar, the Austin Ballet, the AFL-CIO Christmas Party, the Mahavishnu Band, and several basketball teams have held forth in this, the southwest's largest country-western bohemian nightclub.

Kinky Friedman and the Texas Jewboys cut a single recently with "The Ballad of Charles Whitman" on the one side and "Get Your Biscuits in the Oven and Your Buns in the Bed" on the flip. Part of the lyrics of "The Ballad" go like this: "There was rumor/Of a tumor/nestled at the base of his brain . . ." Kinky lives on a ranch in Central Texas called Rio Duckworth, reportedly in a garbage can.

There is a radio station just across the border from Del Rio, Texas. It plays hymns during the day and broadcasts religious advertisements at night. They sell autographed pictures of Jesus to all you friends in radioland. Also prayer rugs as a special gift for all your travellin' salesmen friends with a picture of the face of Jesus on the prayer rug that glows in the dark. And underneath the picture is a legend that also glows in the dark; it's written, "Thou Shalt Not Commit Adultery."

Texas is not full of rich people. Texas is full of poor people. The latest count is 22 percent of the folks here under the federal poverty line—and the feds don't set the line high. The rest of the country, they tell us, has 13 percent poor folks, including such no-account states as Mississippi. Because Texas is racist, 45 percent of the black folks and the brown folks are poor.

Onliest foreign thang that approaches Texas politics is Illinois politics. We ain't never left it lyin' around in shoeboxes, elsewise, we got the jump on everybody.

Texans do not talk like other Americans. They drawl, twang, or sound like the Frito Bandito, only jolly. Shit is a three-syllable word with a *y* in it.

Texans invent their own metaphors and similes, often of a scatological nature, which is kind of fun. As a group, they tell good stories well. The reason they are good at stories is because this is what anthropologists call an oral culture. That means people here don't read and write much. Neither would you if the *Dallas Morning News* was all you had to read.

Texas—I believe it has been noted elsewhere—is a big state. Someone else can tell you about the symphony orchestras and the experimental theaters and those Texans who are writing their Ph.D. theses on U.S. imperialism in Paraguay and seventeenth-century Sanskrit literature. I'm just talking about what makes Texas Texas.

A N O N Y M O U S

— — — —

The Judge Roy Bean

I. ROY BEAN

COWBOYS, COME AND hear the story of Roy Bean in all his glory,
 "All the law west of the Pecos," read his sign;
We must let our ponies take us to a town on lower Pecos
 Where the High Bridge spans the cañon thin and fine.

He was born one day near Toyah, where he learned to be a lawyer,
 And a teacher and a barber and the Mayor.

"The Judge Roy Bean" was first collected in the 1927 omnibus Frontier
Ballads. "Roy Bean," a popular saloon ditty from the 1880s, was sung to
the tune of "Tramp, tramp, tramp, the boys are marching!" "Necktie
Justice" survives from the same period.

He was cook and old-shoe mender, sometimes preacher and bartender,
    And it cost two bits to have him cut your hair.

He was right smart of a hustler, and considerable a rustler,
    And at mixing up an eggnog he was grand;
He was clever, he was merry, he could drink a Tom and Jerry,
    On occasion at a round-up took a hand.

Though the story isn't funny, there was once he had no money,
    Which was for him not very strange or rare;
So he went to help Pap Wyndid, but he got so absent-minded
    That he put his RB brand on old Pap's steer.

As Pap was right smart angry, old Roy Bean went down to Langtry,
    Where he opened up an office and a store.
There he'd sell you drinks or buttons, or another rancher's muttons,
    Though the latter made the other feller sore.

Once there came from Austin City a young dude reported witty,
    Out of Bean he sort of guessed he'd take a rise;
And he got unusual frisky as he up and called for whisky,
    Sayin', "Bean, now hurry up, goldurn your eyes."

Then a-down he threw ten dollars, which the same Roy quickly collars,
    Then the same Roy holds to nine and hands back one;
So the stranger gave a holler, as he saw that single dollar,
    And at that began the merriment and fun.

The dude he slammed the table just as hard as he was able,
    That the price of whisky was too high, he swore
Said Roy Bean, "For all that fussin' and your most outrageous cussin'
    You are fined the other dollar by the law.

"On this place I own a lease, sir, I'm the Justice of the Peace, sir.
    The law west of the Pecos all is here,
And you've acted very badly." Then the dude he went off sadly
    While down his lily cheek there rolled a tear.

One fine day they found a dead man who in life had been a redman,
    So it's doubtless he was nothing else than bad.
They called Bean to view the body, first he took a drink of toddy,
    Then he listed all the things the dead man had.

For a redman he was tony, for he had a pretty pony,
    And a dandy bit and saddle and a rope;
He'd a fine Navajo rug and a quart within his jug
    And a broncho that was dandy on the lope.

So the find it was quite rare-O, for he'd been a "cocinero,"
    And his pay day hadn't been so far away.
He'd a bran'-new fine white Stetson and a silver Smith and Wesson,
    While a purse of forty dollars jingled gay.

Said Roy Bean, "You'll learn a lesson, for you have a Smith and Wesson,
    And to carry implements of war is very wrong.
Forty dollars I will fine you, for we couldn't well confine you,
    As already you've been laying round too long."

So you boys have heard the story of Roy Bean in all his glory,

    He's the man who was the Justice and the Law;

He was handy with his hooks, he was orn'ry in his looks,

    And just now I ain't a-telling any more.

NOTE: The striking events related will carry this song to a successful end no matter how it be sung.

II. NECKTIE JUSTICE

"HEAR YE! HEAR ye! The honorable court's now in session; and if any galoot wants a snort afore we start, let him step up to the bar and name his pizen. Oscar, serve the gentlemen." Thus did Judge Bean open court to try one Carlos Robles, an opening typical of his original procedure.

"Carlos Robles," he said solemnly after witnesses and hangers-on had downed their liquor, "it is the findin' of this court that you are charged with a grave offense against the peace and dignity of the law West of the Pecos and the State of Texas, to wit: cattle-rustlin'. Guilty or not guilty?"

Not being able to speak or comprehend English, Robles merely grunted.

"Court accepts yore plea of guilt. The jury will now deliberate; and if it brings a verdict short of hangin' it'll be declared in contempt. Gentlemen, is yore verdict ready?"

The twelve nondescript citizens cleared their throats in unison. "It is, your honor," several spoke.

"Thank you, gentlemen. Stand up, Carlos Robles, and receive your sentence. You got anything to say why judgment shouldn't be passed on you in this court?"

Of course Carlos had not, in view of the fact that he had only the vaguest idea of what was transpiring.

"Carlos Robles," Judge Roy continued, his voice almost quaking with the solemnity of the occasion, "you been tried by twelve true and good men, not men of yore peers, but as high above you as heaven is of hell; and they've said you're guilty of rustlin' cattle.

"Time will pass and seasons will come and go; Spring with its wavin' green grass and heaps of sweet-smellin' flowers on every hill and in every dale. Then will come sultry Summer, with her shimmerin' heat-waves on the baked horizon; and Fall, with her yeller harvest-moon and the hills growin' brown and golden under a sinkin' sun; and finally Winter, with its bitin', whinin' wind, and all the land will be mantled with snow. But you won't be here to see any of 'em, Carlos Robles; not by a dam' sight, because it's the order of this court that you be took to the nearest tree and hanged by the neck till you're dead, dead, dead, you olive-colored son-of-a-billy-goat!"

The Law West of the Pecos could be cruel in administering his brand of justice; but he was cruel only when he deemed the accused and the crime fully warranting such cruelty. He more frequently tempered justice with his own peculiar brand of mercy, especially if there was any means by which he could profit by that mercy.

One afternoon several ranchmen brought in a twenty-year old boy accused of horse-stealing. They demanded that he be tried and dealt with according to the enormity of the crime.

Judge Bean duly opened court. He appointed six men as jurors, the actual number meaning nothing to him and depending entirely upon men available. He would not appoint just any citizens to jury duty. They must be good customers of the liquid bar at the other end of the shack during intermissions, or their services as jurors no longer were desirable or acceptable. Every transaction must be made to return the utmost in profit, and non-drinking jurors were strictly dead timber.

"Hear ye! This honorable court is again in session. Anyone wishin' a snort, have it now. This here prisoner is charged with the grave offense of stealin' a horse and Oscar, where are the witnesses?" The Law West of the Pecos opened. He appreciated his own sense of humor in varying his court openings to relieve the monotony; but he seldom varied to the extent of omitting the invitation to participate in a snort at the other bar.

"We caught him in the act of stealin' the animal," the ranchman testified. "He admitted his intentions."

"That right, young feller? You was stealin' the cayuse?"

The young prisoner dropped his head, unruly red hair tumbling down over his high forehead. "Yes, your honor," he mumbled.

"Gentlemen of the jury," His Honor instructed, "the accused pleads guilty to horse theft. You know as well as I do the penalty. I'm ready for yore verdict." And it was promptly forthcoming.

Gravely the judge passed sentence. "If there's any last word, or anything, I'll give you a few minutes," he told the pale Easterner, thus extending an infrequent favor.

"I would like to write a note—to my mother back in Pennsylvania," the doomed prisoner mumbled with obvious emotion. "Thank you."

"Oscar, fetch the prisoner a piece of wrappin' paper and a pencil. I think we got a pencil back there behind that row of bottles." Bean gently handed the convicted thief these writing facilities, got up and tendered him the beer barrel and rickety table from which sentence had just been passed. Then he took a position directly behind the boy so that he could watch over his shoulder at what he wrote.

The victim wrote at length in apology for the grief and trouble he had caused his mother and earnestly sought her forgiveness. "In small part perhaps I can repay you for the money I have cost you in keeping me out of trouble. Enclosed is $400, which I've saved. I want you—."

Judge Bean started, cleared his throat, cut in at this point. "By gobs!" he exclaimed, "gentlemen, I got a feelin' there's been a miscarriage of justice, in this case. I hereby declare it re-opened. Face the bar, young man."

The prisoner removed himself from the beer keg and stood erect in front of the judicial bench, befuddled at this sudden turn.

"After all, that wasn't much of a cayuse the lad tried to steal; and he didn't actually steal him. So I rule it's a finable case. I hereby fine the accused three hundred dollars and get to hell outer this country afore I change my mind!"

The boy gladly enough paid three hundred of his four hundred dollars and assured the court that the next setting sun would find his brow well beyond El Rio Pecos.

Practically every cattleman and law-abiding citizen of the Bean bailiwick had an indefinite appointment as deputy constable to the Law West of the Pecos. Thus any citizen who apprehended any person in the act of committing a crime or suspected of any crime had authority to bring him on forthwith for trial. Bean consistently encouraged such co-operation, for the more business they brought before the court, the greater the financial returns for the whole establishment. Naturally it was understood that such arresting constables did not in any manner participate in the fee accruing from such cases created by them. This doubtless was the only justice court in the State of Texas wherein only one official received all fees collected by the office.

Under authority as deputy constable, Reb Wise, Pecos rancher, brought in a cattle rustler on a hot August afternoon when business at the refreshment counter was exceptionally brisk. It was all both Roy and Oscar could do to handle the trade. Consequently Bean looked up with sour expression when Deputy Constable Wise approached the bar and informed the judge that a prisoner was awaiting attention at the bar of justice.

"What's he charged with, Reb?" Roy asked, opening another foaming bottle of Triple-X beer.

"Cattle-rustlin', yuhr honor," Reb replied.

"Whose cattle?"

"Mine."

"You positive he's guilty, Reb?"

"Positive? Say, Judge, I caught him with a runnin' iron on one of my finest calves!" the rancher replied with emphasis.

For the first time Roy glanced up at the scowling prisoner. He noticed blood dripping from his left ear. "Who plugged his ear?" he inquired.

"I did, yuhr honor, when he wouldn't stop."

"You ought'n shot at his head, Reb. You could 'a' killed

him; and that would 'a' been bad, because he wouldn't have been saved for the punishment he deserves. You real shore he's guilty?"

"Didn't I say, Judge, I caught him runnin' a brand on my stuff?"

"All right then," the judge said. "What'll it be for you, feller?" to a newcomer at the bar, ". . . All right then. The court finds the accused guilty as charged; and as there ain't no worse punishment I know of right handy, I hereby sentence him to be hung. Reb, I'm busy's hell here. You and some of yore compadres take him out and tie his neck to some handy limb—some place where his cronies'll be positive to see him; and that's my rulin'. Court's adjourned and what'll it be for you down there, Slim?"

JOHN STEINBECK

- - - -

Texas Ostentation

WHEN I STARTED this narrative, I knew that sooner or later I would have to have a go at Texas, and I dreaded it. I could have bypassed Texas about as easily as a space traveler can avoid the Milky Way. It sticks its big old Panhandle up north and it slops and slouches along the Rio Grande. Once you are in Texas it seems to take forever to get out, and some people never make it.

Let me say in the beginning that even if I wanted to avoid Texas I could not, for I am wived in Texas and mother-in-lawed and uncled and aunted and cousined within an inch of my

---

American novelist JOHN STEINBECK's legendary tomes include Tortilla Flat, Cannery Row, and The Grapes of Wrath. "Texas Ostentation" is from Travels with Charley (1962), his amusing account of a cross country journey with his aging poodle.

life. Staying away from Texas geographically is no help whatever, for Texas moves through our house in New York, our fishing cottage at Sag Harbor, and when we had a flat in Paris, Texas was there too. It permeates the world to a ridiculous degree. Once, in Florence, on seeing a lovely little Italian princess, I said to her father, "But she doesn't look Italian. It may seem strange, but she looks like an American Indian." To which her father replied, "Why shouldn't she? Her grandfather married a Cherokee in Texas."

Writers facing the problem of Texas find themselves floundering in generalities, and I am no exception. Texas is a state of mind. Texas is an obsession. Above all, Texas is a nation in every sense of the word. And there's an opening covey of generalities. A Texan outside of Texas is a foreigner. My wife refers to herself as the Texan that got away, but that is only partly true. She has virtually no accent until she talks to a Texan, when she instantly reverts. You would not have to scratch deep to find her origin. She says such words as yes, air, hair, guess, with two syllables—yayus, ayer, hayer, gayus. And sometimes in a weary moment the word ink becomes ank. Our daughter, after a stretch in Austin, was visiting New York friends. She said, "Do you have a pin?"

"Certainly, dear," said her host. "Do you want a straight pin or a safety pin?"

"Aont a fountain pin," she said.

I've studied the Texas problem from many angles and for many years. And of course one of my truths is inevitably canceled by another. Outside their state I think Texans are a little frightened and very tender in their feelings, and these qualities cause boasting, arrogance, and noisy complacency—the outlets of shy children. At home Texans are none of these things. The ones I

know are gracious, friendly, generous, and quiet. In New York
we hear them so often bring up their treasured uniqueness. Texas
is the only state that came into the Union by treaty. It retains the
right to secede at will. We have heard them threaten to secede so
often that I formed an enthusiastic organization—The American
Friends for Texas Secession. This stops the subject cold. They want
to be able to secede but they don't want anyone to want them to.

Like most passionate nations Texas has its own private
history based on, but not limited by, facts. The tradition of the
tough and versatile frontiersman is true but not exclusive. It is for
the few to know that in the great old days of Virginia there were
three punishments for high crimes—death, exile to Texas, and
imprisonment, in that order. And some of the deportees must
have descendants.

Again—the glorious defense to the death of the Alamo
against the hordes of Santa Anna is a fact. The brave bands of
Texans did indeed wrest their liberty from Mexico, and freedom,
liberty, are holy words. One must go to contemporary observers
in Europe for a non-Texan opinion as to the nature of the tyranny
that raised need for revolt. Outside observers say the pressure was
twofold. The Texans, they say, didn't want to pay taxes and, second, Mexico had abolished slavery in 1829, and Texas, being part
of Mexico, was required to free its slaves. Of course there were
other causes of revolt, but these two are spectacular to a
European, and rarely mentioned here.

I have said that Texas is a state of mind, but I think it is
more than that. It is a mystique closely approximating a religion.
And this is true to the extent that people either passionately love
Texas or passionately hate it and, as in other religions, few people

dare to inspect it for fear of losing their bearings in mystery and paradox. Any observation of mine can be quickly cancelled by opinion or counter-observation. But I think there will be little quarrel with my feeling that Texas is one thing. For all its enormous range of space, climate, and physical appearance, and for all the internal squabbles, contentions, and strivings, Texas has a tight cohesiveness perhaps stronger than any other section of America. Rich, poor, Panhandle, Gulf, city, country, Texas is the obsession, the proper study and the passionate possession of all Texans. Some years ago, Edna Ferber wrote a book about a very tiny group of very rich Texans. Her description was accurate, so far as my knowledge extends, but the emphasis was one of disparagement. And instantly the book was attacked by Texans of all groups, classes, and possessions. To attack one Texan is to draw fire from all Texans. The Texas joke, on the other hand, is a revered institution, beloved and in many cases originating in Texas.

The tradition of the frontier cattleman is as tenderly nurtured in Texas as is the hint of Norman blood in England. And while it is true that many families are descended from contract colonists not unlike the present-day braceros, all hold to the dream of the longhorn steer and the unfenced horizon. When a man makes his fortune in oil or government contracts, in chemicals or wholesale groceries, his first act is to buy a ranch, the largest he can afford, and to run some cattle. A candidate for public office who does not own a ranch is said to have little chance of election. The tradition of the land is deep fixed in the Texas psyche. Businessmen wear heeled boots that never feel a stirrup, and men of great wealth who have houses in Paris and regularly shoot grouse in Scotland refer to themselves as little old country boys. It would be easy to make sport of their attitude if one did not know that in this way they try to keep their association with the strength and simplicity of the land. Instinctively they feel that this is the source not only of wealth but of energy. And the energy of Texans is boundless and explosive. The successful man with his traditional ranch, at least in my experience, is no absentee owner. He works at it, oversees his herd and adds to it. The energy, in a climate so hot as to be staggering, is also staggering. And the tradition of hard work is maintained whatever the fortune or lack of it.

The power of an attitude is amazing. Among other tendencies to be noted, Texas is a military nation. The armed forces of the United States are loaded with Texans and often dominated by Texans. Even the dearly loved spectacular sports are run almost like military operations. Nowhere are there larger bands or more marching organizations, with corps of costumed girls whirling glittering batons. Sectional football games have the glory and the despair of war, and when a Texas team takes the field against a foreign state, it is an army with banners.

If I keep coming back to the energy of Texas, it is because I am so aware of it. It seems to me like that thrust of dynamism which caused and permitted whole peoples to migrate and to conquer in earlier ages. The land mass of Texas is rich in recoverable spoil. If this had not been so, I think I believe the relentless energy of Texans would have moved out and conquered new lands. The conviction is somewhat borne out in the restless movement of Texas capital. But now, so far, the conquest has been by purchase rather than by warfare. The oil deserts of the Near East, the opening lands of South America have felt the thrust. Then there are new islands of capital conquest: factories in the Middle West, food-processing plants, tool and die works, lumber and pulp. Even publishing houses have been added to the legitimate twentieth-century Texas spoil. There is no moral in these observations, nor any warning. Energy must have an outlet and will seek one.

In all ages, rich, energetic, and successful nations, when they have carved their place in the world, have felt hunger for art, for culture, even for learning and beauty. The Texas cities shoot upward and outward. The colleges are heavy with gifts and endowments. Theaters and symphony orchestras sprout overnight. In any huge and boisterous surge of energy and enthusiasm there must be errors and miscalculations, even breach of judgment and taste. And there is always the non-productive brotherhood of critics to disparage and to satirize, to view with horror and contempt. My own interest is attracted to the fact that these things are done at all. There will doubtless be thousands of ribald failures, but in the world's history artists have always been drawn where they are welcome and well treated.

By its nature and its size Texas invites generalities, and the generalities usually end up as paradox—the "little ol' country boy" at a symphony, the booted and blue-jeaned ranchman in Neiman-Marcus, buying Chinese jades.

Politically Texas continues its paradox. Traditionally and nostalgically it is Old South Democrat, but this does not prevent its voting conservative Republican in national elections while electing liberals to city and county posts. My opening statement still holds—everything in Texas is likely to be canceled by something else.

Most areas in the world may be placed in latitude and longitude, described chemically in their earth, sky and water, rooted and fuzzed over with identified flora and peopled with known fauna, and there's an end to it. Then there are others where fable, myth, preconception, love, longing, or prejudice step in and so distort a cool, clear appraisal that a kind of high-colored magical confusion takes permanent hold. Greece is such an area, and those parts of England where King Arthur walked. One quality of such places as I am trying to define is that a very large part of them is personal and subjective. And surely Texas is such a place.

I have moved over a great part of Texas and I know that within its borders I have seen just about as many kinds of country, contour, climate, and conformation as there are in the world saving only the Arctic, and a good north wind can even bring the icy breath down. The stern horizon-fenced plains of the Panhandle are foreign to the little wooded hills and sweet streams in the Davis Mountains. The rich citrus orchards of the Rio Grande valley do not relate to the sagebrush grazing of South Texas. The hot and humid air of the Gulf Coast has no likeness in the cool crystal in the northwest of the Panhandle. And Austin on its hills among the bordered lakes might be across the world from Dallas.

What I am trying to say is that there is no physical or geographical unity in Texas. Its unity lies in the mind. And this is not only in Texans. The word Texas becomes a symbol to everyone in the world. There's no question that this Texas-of-the-mind fable is often synthetic, sometimes untruthful, and frequently romantic, but that in no way diminishes its strength as a symbol.

The foregoing investigation into the nature of the idea of Texas is put down as a prelude to my journeying across Texas with Charley in Rocinante. It soon became apparent that this stretch had to be different from the rest of the trip. In the first place I knew the countryside, and in the second I had friends and relatives by marriage, and such a situation makes objectivity practically impossible, for I know no place where hospitality is practiced so fervently as in Texas.

But before that most pleasant and sometimes exhausting human trait took hold, I had three days of namelessness in a beautiful motor hotel in the middle of Amarillo. A passing car on a gravel road had thrown up pebbles and broken out the front window of Rocinante and it had to be replaced. But, more important, Charley had been taken with his old ailment again, and this time he was in bad trouble and great pain. I remembered the poor incompetent veterinary in the Northwest, who did not know and did not care. I remember how Charley had looked at him with pained wonder and contempt.

In Amarillo the doctor I summoned turned out to be a young man. He drove up in a medium-priced convertible. He leaned over Charley. "What's his problem?" he asked. I explained Charley's difficulty. Then the young vet's hands went down and moved over hips and distended abdomen—trained and knowing hands. Charley sighed a great sigh and his tail wagged slowly up from the floor and down again. Charley put himself in this man's care, completely confident. I've seen this instant rapport before, and it is good to see.

The strong fingers probed and investigated and then the vet straightened up. "It can happen to any little old boy," he said.

"Is it what I think it is?"

"Yep. Prostatitis."

"Can you treat it?"

"Sure. I'll have to relax him first, and then I can give him medication for it. Can you leave him for maybe four days?"

"Whether I can or not, I will."

He lifted Charley in his arms and carried him out and laid him in the front seat of the convertible, and the tufted tail twittered against the leather. He was content and confident, and so was I. And that is how I happened to stay around Amarillo for a while. To complete the episode, I picked up Charley four days later, completely well. The doctor gave me pills to give at intervals while traveling so that the ailment never came back. There's absolutely nothing to take the place of a good man.

I do not intend to dwell long on Texas. Since the death of Hollywood the Lone Star State has taken its place at the top for being interviewed, inspected, and discussed. But no account of Texas would be complete without a Texas orgy, showing men of great wealth squandering their millions on tasteless and impassioned exhibitionism. My wife had come from New York to join me, and we were invited to a Texas ranch for Thanksgiving. It is owned by a friend who sometimes comes to New York, where we give him an orgy. I shall not name him, following the tradition of letting the reader guess. I presume that he is rich, although I have never asked him about it. As invited, we arrived at the ranch on the afternoon before the Thanksgiving orgy. It is a beautiful ranch, rich in water and trees and grazing land. Everywhere bulldozers had pushed up earth dams to hold back the water, making a series of life-giving lakes down the center of the ranch. On well-grassed flats the blooded Hereford grazed, only looking up as we drove by in a cloud of dust. I don't know how big the ranch is. I didn't ask my host.

The house, a one-story brick structure, stood in the grove of cottonwoods on the little eminence over a pool made by a dammed-up spring. The dark surface of the water was disturbed by trout that had been planted there. The house was comfortable, had three bedrooms, each room with a bath—both tub and shower. The living room, paneled in stained pine, served also as a dining room, with a fireplace at one end and a glass-fronted gun case against the side. Through the open kitchen door the staff could be seen—a large dark lady and a giggleful girl. Our host met us and helped carry our bags in.

The orgy began at once. We had a bath and on emerging were given scotch and soda, which we drank thirstily. After that we inspected the barn across the way, the kennels in which there were three pointers, one of them not feeling so well. Then to the corral, where the daughter of the house was working on the training of a quarter horse, an animal of parts named Specklebottom. After that we inspected two new dams with water building slowly behind them, and at several drinking stations communed with a small herd of recently purchased cattle. This violence exhausted us and we went back to the house for a short nap.

We awakened from this to find neighboring friends arriving, they brought a large pot of chili con carne, made from a family recipe, the best I have ever tasted. Now other rich people began to arrive, concealing their status in blue jeans and riding boots. Drinks were passed and a gay conversation ensued having to do with hunting, riding, and cattlebreeding, with many bursts of laughter. I reclined on a window seat and in the gathering dusk watched the wild turkeys come in to roost in the cottonwood trees. They fly up clumsily and distribute themselves and then suddenly they blend with the tree and disappear. At least thirty of them came in to roost.

As the darkness came the window became a mirror in which I could watch my host and his guests without their knowledge. They sat about the little paneled room, some in rocking chairs and three of the ladies on a couch. And the subtlety of their ostentation drew my attention. One of the ladies was making a sweater while another worked a puzzle, tapping her teeth with the eraser of a yellow pencil. The men talked casually of grass and water, of So-and-So who had bought a new champion bull in England and flown it home. They were dressed in jeans of that light blue, lighter and a little frayed at the seams, that can be achieved only by a hundred washings.

But the studied detail did not stop there. Boots were scuffed on the inside and salted with horse sweat, and the heels run over. The open collars of the men's shirts showed dark red lines of sunburn on their throats, and one guest had gone to the trouble and expense of breaking his forefinger, which was splinted and covered with laced leather cut from a glove. My host went to the extreme of serving his guests from a bar which consisted of a tub of ice, quart bottles of soda, two bottles of whisky and a case of pop.

The smell of money was everywhere. The daughter of the house, for example, sat on the floor cleaning a .22 rifle, telling a sophisticated and ribald story of how Specklebottom, her stallion, had leaped a five-bar corral gate and visited a mare in the next county. She thought she had property rights in the foal, Specklebottom's blood line being what it was. The scene verified what we have all heard about fabulous Texas millionaires.

I was reminded of a time in Pacific Grove when I was painting the inside of a cottage my father had built there before I was born. My hired helper worked beside me, and neither of us being expert we were well splattered. Suddenly we found ourselves out of paint. I said, "Neil, run up to Holman's and get a half-gallon of paint and a quart of thinner."

"I'll have to clean up and change my clothes," he said.

"Nuts! Go as you are."

"I can't do it."

"Why not? I would."

Then he said a wise and memorable thing. "You got to be awful rich to dress as bad as you do," he said.

And this isn't funny. It's true. And it was true at the orgy. How unthinkably rich these Texans must be to live as simply as they were.

I took a walk with my wife, around the trout pool and over against the hill. The air was chill and the wind blowing from the north had winter in it. We listened for frogs, but they had shacked up for the winter. But we heard a coyote howl upwind and we heard a cow bawling for her late weaned bairn. The pointers came to the wire mesh of the kennel, wriggling like happy snakes and sneezing with enthusiasm, and even the sickly one came out of his house and fleered at us. Then we stood in the high entrance of the great barn and smelled at the sweetness of alfalfa and the bready odor of rolled barley. At the corral the stock horses snorted at us and rubbed their heads against the bars, and Specklebottom took a kick at a gelded friend just to keep in practice. Owls were flying this night, shrieking to start their prey, and a nighthawk made soft rhythmic whoops in the distance. I wished that Able Baker Charley Dog could have been with us. He would have admired this night. But he was resting under sedatives in Amarillo curing his prostatitis. The sharp north wind clashed the naked branches of the cottonwoods. It seemed to me that winter, which had been on my trail during the whole trip, had finally caught up with me. Somewhere in our, or at least my, recent zoologic past, hibernation must have been a fact of being. Else why does cold night air make me so sleepy? It does and it did, and we went in to the house where the ghosts had already retired and we went to bed.

I awakened early. I had seen two trout rods leaning against the screen outside our room. I went down the grassed hill, slipping in the frost to the edge of the dark pool A fly was ready fastened on the line, a black gnat, a little frayed but still hairy enough. And as it touched the surface of the pool the water boiled and churned. I brought in a ten-inch rainbow trout and skidded him up on the grass and knocked him on the head. I cast four times and had four trout. I cleaned them and threw the innards to their friends.

In the kitchen the cook gave me coffee and I sat in an alcove while she dipped my fish in corn meal and fried them crisp in bacon fat and served them to me under a coverlet of bacon that crumbled in my mouth. It was a long time since I had eaten trout like that, five minutes from water to pan. You take him in your fingers delicately by head and tail and nibble him from off his backbone, and finally you eat the tail, crisp as a potato chip. Coffee has a special taste of a frosty morning, and the third cup is as good as the first. I would have lingered in the kitchen discussing nothing with the staff, but she cleared me out because she had to stuff two turkeys for the Thanksgiving orgy.

In the mid-morning sunshine we went quail-hunting, I with my old and shiny 12-bore with the dented barrel, which I carried in Rocinante. The gun was no great shakes when I bought it second-hand fifteen years ago, and it has never got any better. But I suppose it is as good as I am. If I can hit them the gun will pull them down. But before we started I looked with a certain longing through the glass door at a Luigi Franchi 12-gauge double with a Purdy lock so beautiful that I was filled with covetousness. The carving on the steel had the pearly gleam of a Damascus blade, while the stock flowed into lock and lock into barrels as though they had grown that way from a magic planted seed. I'm sure that if my host had seen my envy he would have loaned me the beauty, but I didn't ask. Suppose I tripped and fell, or dropped it, or knocked its lovely tubes against a rock? No, it would be like carrying the crown jewels through a mine field. My old beat-up gun is no bargain, but at least anything that can happen to it has, and there's no worrying.

For a week our host had noted where the coveys were gathering. We spread out and moved through brush and thicket, down into water, out, and up, while the spring-steel pointers worked ahead of us and a fat old bitch pointer named Duchess with flame in her eyes outworked them all, and us too. We found quail tracks in the dust, quail tracks in the sand and mud of stream beds, bits of quail-feather fluff in the dry tips of the sage. We walked for miles, slowly, guns up and ready to throw shot at a drumming flight. And we never saw a quail. The dogs never saw or smelled a quail. We told stories and some lies about previous quail hunts, but it did no good. The quail had gone, really gone. I am only a reasonable quail shot but the men with me were excellent, the dogs were professional, keen, hard, and hard-working. No quail. But there's one nice thing about hunting. Even with no birds, you'd rather go than not.

My host thought my heart was breaking. He said, "Look. You take that little 222 of yours this afternoon and shoot yourself a wild turkey."

"How many are there?" I asked.

"Well, two years ago I planted thirty. I think there are about eighty now."

"I counted thirty in the band that flew up near the house last night."

"There's two other bands," he said.

I really didn't want a turkey. What would I do with it in Rocinante? I said, "Wait a year. When they top a hundred birds, I'll come down and hunt with you."

We came back to the house and showered and shaved and because it was Thanksgiving we put on white shirts and jackets and ties. The orgy came off on schedule at two o'clock. I'll skip through the details quickly in order not to shock the readers, and also I see no reason to hold these people up to scorn. After two good drinks of whisky, the two brown and glazed turkeys were brought in, carved by our host and served by us. We said grace and afterward drank a toast all around and ate ourselves into a proper insensibility. Then, like decadent Romans at Petronius's board, we took a walk and retired for the necessary and inevitable nap. And that was my Thanksgiving orgy in Texas.

Of course I don't think they do it every day. They couldn't. And somewhat the same thing happens when they visit us in New York. Of course they want to see shows and go to night clubs. And at the end of a few days of this they say, "We just don't see how you can live like this." To which we reply, "We don't. And when you go home, we won't."

And now I feel better for having exposed to the light of scrutiny the decadent practices of the rich Texans I know. But I don't for one moment think they eat chili con carne or roast turkey every day.

T E X A N S

Interviews

ROSA R. GUERRERO: *Dancing Up from the Barrio*

El Paso, TX, Born 1934

MY GRANDMOTHER WAS born in San Juan near Jalisco and she always worked very, very much as a young girl, as an adult, as a *viejita*. Her household responsibilities were unlimited. She just went on and on. I never saw her sick until I found out that she was dead. She used to cure herself like my mother does, with *hierbas*, home remedies. She never saw a doctor. She never in her life stepped into a beauty shop. She

---

These self-portraits are excerpted from Texans: Oral Histories from the Lone Star State. *The book, edited by* RON STRICKLAND, *is a collection of interviews with seventy modern-day Texans, from bankers to bootmakers.*

never saw most of what we call "civilization" because she was very, very much at heart a traditional Indian and was afraid of escalators and airplanes.

My grandmother followed Pancho Villa during the Revolution. She wanted to really follow the footsteps of what he believed in, and she was a cook and nurse for him. Later on, in the forties, she evolved to be the cook for the president, Manuel Avila Camacho.

The *mole* that my grandmother made was the most authentic *mole* I have ever tasted because she used to get on her hands and knees and start from scratch. There was no Doña María, no jars at that time. There was the *ajonjolí*, and different types of chiles: chile chipotle, chile colorado, and chile *de esto y el otro*. And *cacahuate*, chocolate—mix it all up. I remember doing it. When I tried, I used to smash my fingers with the *metate*, but what a beautiful experience. I was so proud!

I wanted to imitate Grandmother. I remember wanting to make *tortillas de maíz* and they used to come out crazy, longer or fatter, funny or whatever. But at least I said "*Yo quiero aprender, abuelita. Yo quiero aprender.*"

I always wanted to learn. Whether it was the kitchen or whether it was history or language, I was always wanting to learn. More than anybody in my family.

I am still seeking that. I guess I will die learning.

Mi *abuelita* because she was such a good cook also worked outside the home in restaurants. And that's how she was elevated to be the cook for presidente Avila Camacho in the forties. President Camacho used to call her Doña Rosa. My dad also used to call *me* Doña Rosa.

Since my father worked for the railroad, we could go to Mexico every summer and be with the family over there[1]. It was a very beautiful treat to go to Mexico City and be with my grandmother, and go to Jalapa, Veracruz, and be with my grandfather where he had a *sombrerería*, a hat factory. I remember my grandmother getting up at five in the morning and watering the patio and the *hierbas* and all the *plantas* and starting her soups and *frijolitos* and tortillas and the *comal* being ready by six!

I was born in El Paso, Texas, and my mother says I was about eight months old when she first took me to Mexico, so that was about 1935. My relatives still live in Mexico City and Veracruz and Aguascalientes and Torreon, where some of my husband's family are now.

What I liked to do with my mother and father was fiesta. Always, always fiestas. It was a way of life. So much poverty yet so much happiness, too! I can't remember our family ever not going to Juárez every Sunday. Ciudad Juarez was our life. We would go to the bullfights. I remember seeing the greatest of toreros. I saw Manolete. I saw Silverio Perez. I saw David Liciaga. I saw the beautiful Carlos Arruza. On and on and on. I even saw Cantinflas three or four times. I saw Conchita Cintrón, *la Regionadora*, beautiful bullfighter, on horseback.

Whenever they killed a bull, I turned around and hid my eyes. But I loved the art and the *olé* and the music and the *tan tara ta tan*, when the *clarín* came out and announced that the bull was going

---

[1] My childhood was very exciting because we would go to Mexico and immerse immediately in the culture every summer. Sometimes Mother would even take us out of school during Lent because in Aguascalientes were the *Ferías de las flores*. We had to go to the *Ferías de las flores*. The heck with school! Ours was an education that was different. What we learned out of school was as important as what we learned in school.

to be dedicated to the mayor or to whomever. That was exciting, though I love animals too much now to attend bullfights any more.

But that period was when I was starting to get confused inside 'cause I didn't know if I was Spanish or Indian or Mexican because I liked all types of music. The Indian in me would come out when the Matachines would dance. The Spanish would come out when the pasos dobles would play. And the Mexican would come out when the Jarabes would play.

In my childhood, I remember my mother telling me all these stories when she used to get our *piojitos* out, looking for lice in our hair—which is part of the culture, too, whether we like it or not. She used to tell us stories about La Llorona and *cuentos de Pedro de Urdimalcas y las historias de diferentes fantasías románticas de bellas artes.* Things like Cinderella, Sleeping Beauty, the Seven Dwarfs, the beautiful Snow White, *La Blancanieves.* I immediately started stereotyping white as being very beautiful at that time and I wanted to be white like the *Americanas* and like Snow White. Also like Betty Grable and Ginger Rogers—how wonderful it would have been to have been very blond and white! But I had *piojitos* and I did not remember Snow White having them. She was too beautiful to have lice.

I thought I had very poor but very exciting parents. That was a kind of beautiful pride because the school would teach us everything about American history and the Pilgrim colonists and all the time I asked myself about my own ancestry. I would do a comparison in my mind between American history and where my grandparents came from and what they had done. What my grandmother had done in the Revolution and about how she had suffered and how people had died and about how she had come to Juarez and then eventually to El Paso.

So I was confused. I said, "What am I?" I remember the great newspaper writer Ruben Salazar's words, "A stranger in our own land." And here I was in the United States, Lord have mercy! Confusion and schizophrenia. I tell my students now that when God made a Mexican, He got an Indian and a Spaniard and mixed them and made delicious guacamole.

But as a kid I loved all music and nobody was going to tell me what was right or wrong. I loved going with my mother and father to la fiesta taurina, the bullfights. From there we would go out and eat. I remember my father eating the huachinango, un pescadote riquísimo. A huge fish and my father would just leave the skeleton. I thought then that eating a pescado in such a beautiful way was an art in itself.

From the restaurante we used to go to exclusive nightclubs like the Lobby, the Tivoli, or the Casanova. The Casanova was one of the most elegant places in Juarez. My parents would take me because I loved the dancing and because at that time Juarez was very culturally known. It had the greatest musicians and concert pianists and opera singers and zarzuelas and operettas. I saw Veloz and Yolanda do the beautiful ballroom dancing—tango and paso dobles. I saw the greatest flamenco dancers in the world, Carmen Amaya and Antonio Triana. I loved them! They danced with all that Spanish glory! I wanted to be just like Carmen Amaya—with fire, feeling, and spirit.

During the Second World War our whole life-style changed because my four brothers were taken to war. Juarez and El Paso were full of American soldiers and the Red Cross invited adults and us little children to give danzas regionales de México to make them happy, like the Bob Hope caravan.

My mother was still very much a fiestera.

She still is one today! She's going to be eighty-nine on March the nineteenth and she is so alive. She's like an eighteen-year-old. She feels like one and she acts like one. She's Indian, *pata rajada*, strong and determined and that will never change. I adore her for it. I think that the more years that pass, the more I adore her. There were times in high school when I was ashamed of my mom because she didn't know English and was so uneducated. I saw so many faults in her. How stupid I was!

My mother had to work as domestic help because she didn't know English and she didn't have an education as such. She met my father here in El Paso and married him. Consequently all of us seven children grew up and were educated in the United States.

My father was unique. From him I learned about the culture, the dance, the music, and the language (*el Castellano, el Español* was my father's pride and joy). The *escuelita* he gave me at home. We would sit and conjugate verbs in Spanish just for the love of it. We would go over geography, history, dances, opera. Just a beautiful Socratic man. He would just ask me questions and I loved it.

None of my family was like me. I loved relating with my dad because I thought he was the smartest man in the world. Even though my dad drank a lot, I didn't judge him for that. I loved him. When you love somebody, you don't judge. You love and you forget and you forgive.

My mother had been a *hierbera* and a *curandera* and a *cartomanciana*, a fortune-teller. Later on in life I was very confused with that because being brought up a Catholic, I always thought magic was a no-no. That fortune-telling was the Devil's doing. I talked to a priest several years back at a retreat and he said, "You do not judge your mother. God will judge if she is helping people. Let her be!"

So I'm letting her be. She's a beautiful person. She has a different gift from God, to psychoanalyze people, to question them, and through her cards and her way she helps them. That's what she has been doing for a long time. She brought us up and she gave us food from that. I cannot judge and I cannot condemn. She is my mother and she is a very gifted lady. Very gifted.

She worked outside the home. For a dollar a week, I remember she used to boil and scrub all the linen. After Mother got married, she continued working because the Depression came and then my dad didn't have a job. She was the one that worked and my father stayed at home. He was the one that made us *sopita* and *frijolitos* and *arrocito*, and gave us delicious *capirotada*, and played El Papalote and *valero con nosotros. Nos enlazaba; sacaba la soga de Aguascalientes*, the *Lasso y nos enlazaba como si fuéramos los animalitos en el rancho, las canicas, el Juan Pirulero; a todos los jueguitos. ¡Pero iqué padre! Tan hermoso.* He was the first Mr. Mom, because he had to take the part of the woman 'cause there were no jobs during the Depression. Everybody in the neighborhood of Santa Fe Street wore these relief-type striped overalls. Everybody. It looked like the whole prison was there.

We lived at 620 North Santa Fe twenty years. Right in front of the old Providence Memorial Hospital. It's about three blocks from the Civic Center. We used to walk downtown to the library and to the Colon Theater to dance lessons. I started teaching dance at ten, tutoring little four- and five-year-olds. I was a born teacher!

The movies had taught me how to dance, speak, communicate, learn the good and the bad—'cause we saw some filthy movies, too! I remember seeing *Fiesta* twenty-five times with Ricardo Montalbán and Cyd Charisse because they were such great dancers.

We grew up with those movies. We saw some funny ones with Cantinflas the idol, Tin-Tan, and the beautiful movie stars. That was our growing-up time at the Colon Theater, where they used to have *variedades*, musicians and actors and singers, beautiful cultural programs Saturdays and Sundays. They had three shows, at three o'clock, at six o'clock, and at nine o'clock. And we had to go see one of those shows or to go see Cisco Kid and Flash Gordon episodes for five cents a movie at El Alcazar. That theater smelled like an old sock and its rats and bugs were part of the show, too!

Mi mamá trabajó con una viejita que se llamaba Elizabeth Lee Griswald, who was our granny. She was my godmother and a very wealthy woman that lived in Sunset Heights in one of the old colonial homes on Upson. From her my mother learned everything of social amenities: how to set the table, the different ways to dress, the entire fashion. And even though Mama was a domestic, working with her, she was treated as part of the family. Mrs. Griswald was related to General Robert E. Lee. She was from Kentucky and had lost all her plantation home with the slaves in her grandparents' time during the Civil War. In Texas her husband lost everything in the Depression. I remember her saying how she hated the Yankees!

I still have heirlooms of her Early American linens, crystal, and china. They go well with my *metate* and my *molcajete* and are very traditional and very beautiful. But why didn't our history books tell us that our pre-Hispanic heirlooms are *older* than those "Early American" things?

Mi Mamá learned so much with Granny Griswald that to this day she still communicates with the sons and grandsons of the lady! They love my mother. Josefina, they call her.

She used to live in an apartment in the basement on Upson. Later she moved to north El Paso Street and then I was born on 620 North Santa Fe. (Everybody was born at home because we didn't even know what a hospital was like.) There were seven of us. I don't remember really having a lot of chores as a child 'cause I was my father's favorite. My brother Bill and my brother George used to wash dishes and used to do this and used to do that. I loved to clean and to volunteer to do things. To this day I love to help people. I love to please people, please my students, please my educators, my colleagues, my parents, my friends.

My four older brothers didn't have an easier time than I at all because they were given more responsibilities than I 'cause I was the first girl after the four boys. I was *la consentida de mi papá y de mis hermanos*. And I learned how to play all the boys' games and I enjoyed it. I loved my family!

We were very poor materially, though. We had only one bathroom and we had to share it with about thirty people and everybody was constipated!

I used to think anything with tile was Hollywood! I do not take a bathroom for granted. I just thank the Lord for my bathroom now. I thank the Lord for hot water. I thank the Lord for detergents to wash the dishes. I don't mind washing them because I remember not even having soap. And hot water! What a luxury. And a shower! Oh Lord have mercy, to have a shower and tile is like a movie star!

So I think I'm very rich. Rich in many, many things because I never had those wonderful things that I thought were really for *gente rica*, rich people.

Yeah, there were arguments in the family, especially when my father drank.

I used to take care of my father when he was drunk, *pobrecito*. I used to sing to him and take care of him. And I was the only one who could guide him. Mother would get mad with him because he would spend the whole check.

It is a very sad thing in *la cultura mexicana* that the machismo element is there and is so evident *en la borrachera* (which I hated with a passion!). I can still see it around me today, the cycle of poverty, the borracheras, the machismo. It's terrible but it's still here with us today. The only way out of this cycle of poverty, ignorance, illiteracy, and oppression of our women is education. I try to instill this idea in our Hispanic women everywhere I go.

Yeah, my family was different from our neighbors. Very much so because my mother was a fortuneteller and people used to look at her. And so my home was not a regular home. It used to be like Grand Central Station, everybody visiting my mother. And all her friends, patients, *clientas* to see her. It was never really a home that I could see. Just a. . . . I never had my own room. Never, never until I got married because I had to wait until the *clientas* left and then the sofa was made into a bed. It was kind of sad because we didn't have the right studying facilities or anything like that. How we made it in school I don't know. By the help of the Lord, I guess, and a lot of hard work and desire.

I remember that one of my friends, Carmen Rodríguez, said to me, "My mother doesn't want me to play with you."

"Why not?" I said.

"Because your mother's a witch. A fortune-teller and a witch."

"No," I said. I had just seen The Wizard of Oz. "My mother's not a witch and if she's a witch, she's a good witch. She's a beautiful lady and she's my mother and she won't hurt you."

So that was sad. I remember those little things that people would say. Now I cry about it and can't imagine how we all survived. The system and cruel humanity was so bad!

My favorite childhood memory, of course, is my father and dancing with him, getting on his feet, dancing the corridos, dancing the pasos dobles, dancing the mazurkas, the varsovianas, waltzes, and schottisches.

I used to get on his feet and dance and I thought I was tremendously great. What a cultural education before kindergarten! And they used to call me culturally deprived!

And then seeing my mother and father dance, that was such a joy. Everyone used to make a circle around them. No one could dance the pasos dobles like Pedro y Josefina Ramirez, my parents!

At the very beginning I was kind of fearful of school. Speaking Spanish was a no-no! How we were punished for speaking that "dirty language"! So I became determined to know both English and Spanish so that no one could step on me.

Unfortunately, we didn't have any Spanish at all in grammar school, but my dear Spanish teacher Marie Stamps in high school was so great in Spanish that I used to wonder how she could speak Spanish better than I could and still be an Anglo.

I liked reading even though I knew I had an accent and my chs were horrible. Twenty-five years ago I started trying to get a better articulation of my English language, but it was still horrible. My own kids correct me now, especially in writing. How I wish I could have learned how to write well!

There were many, many teachers that I liked. Miss Robinson, the art teacher, was gorgeous and wonderful and funny. And Miss Hignett, my gosh, I learned English with that beautiful Mary Hignett in my homeroom class in the sixth and seventh grades. My gosh, what a teacher! She used to teach every part of speech in English. She was just drilling it to us. And that's why I learned good English grammar, because of her.

Some of the teachers, Miss Eason, I didn't like her. She used to hit me with a ruler for speaking Spanish and hide me behind the closet. And I know she hated Mexicans 'cause I used to see her talking to Miss Hanna and other teachers, "These typical Mexican girls, they stink, blah, blah, blah." You know, we didn't dare say anything back because whatever the teacher said was right, whatever it was. I wish they could see this "dirty Mexican" now!

Nowadays the kids don't have any respect for themselves or for each other, and that's hard for me as an educator and as a person who struggled for so long to get an education.

My parents did not push any of us to graduate from high school because survival was first to them. Yet my dream from when I was a little girl was to graduate from *college*.

My little sister and I were the only ones in the family that did graduate from college. I just wanted to prove to myself and to my family that I could do it. At college in the 1950s in Denton, hundreds of miles away from El Paso, I used to cry sometimes because of the racism but I was determined to prove myself to the world. One of my counselors told me that I was too bossy; I temporarily went into a shell after that, because the kids from East Texas did not like bossy girls.

Some of my classmates had the same background as me.

Unfortunately, I don't see them any more. A lot of them became immediately assimilated. Too assimilated in the American way. They don't dare speak Spanish any more. Some of them changed their names. Many were Anglo-white Hispanic. We just don't have any values, any ideas, anything in common any more. It's very sad because they mistake money for God and I don't care for materialism. I'm a very down-to-earth person.

I never have stopped going to school. I want to go back and I want to study this and I want to study that. I want to take languages and I want to take. . . . I always wanted to get my doctoral degree but I never wanted to be more educated than my husband. My husband is a very beautiful man. Very intelligent. He could have gotten any Ph.D., I'm sure. But he was never guided into that and he's not one of these opportunist guys. He's a very beautiful man: a teacher and a coach and a wonderful, respectable guy.

I got married in 1954 and continued at the university till I graduated in fifty-seven. I got pregnant in my senior year and had to practice-teach and even referee and play basketball while I was pregnant and nursing the baby. I don't want to remember some of those hard experiences, but hard work taught me a lot. I think that to sacrifice and to suffer a little bit, you appreciate life more.

People in El Paso have a tendency to forget their roots of poverty. And for a long time I forgot, too. You know why? Because I felt that everybody had probably gotten out with me, struggling through hard work.

Eventually I forgot that I had lived at the Alamito Projects in the forties with my sister-in-law Minnie when my brother was overseas in France. I forgot that I had thought that the projects were Hollywood because they had had tiles and running water and hot water. God, the first time I had seen hot water! You surely forget very soon. Once you're comfortable you don't want to be reminded how poor you were.

I don't want to be reminded that they have called me every label under the book. They have called me Chicana-honky. They have called me Tía Taco. They have called me Coconut. They have called me radical, militant, anti-American. From both the conservative and the liberal, I have had it.

And I went through a period of horrible, horrible depression and suffering and I even was saying, "Hey, I don't think there's a God. He's not listening to me." But there *was* a God. I was just too impatient with Him. I was not really devout in my faith, so God was testing me. Since then I have learned a lot from some students of mine. For instance, I had four older ladies from the barrio that didn't know how to read or write. They come and apologize to me. "*Señora Guerrero, no sé escribir*—I don't know how to write."

I say, "*Qué le hace, señora.* But look at your children and learn with them."

One has had twenty-three children. I call her my rabbit. Mi *coneja*. [Laughter] But now she is trying to learn. She just lost her husband last year and she's trying to get herself together. This is the first time in her life she can take classes in human relations, English, citizenship, even *folklórico*. I had my *viejitas* dancing *folklórico* down there. And so I made them feel good.

I told them, "It doesn't matter if you don't know how to read and write. It's not a sin. But here is the opportunity that we're teaching. Now take it by the horns and do it. I laugh and say that it is a sin *not* to do something about learning to read and write."

Soon I heard some of them saying "*Ay, Señora Guerrero, usted habla tan bonito.*"

They thought I was so intelligent, but I said "No, you are inspiring me. I don't talk pretty."

They felt that I'm such a scholar. "I'm nothing," I say. "I don't care how many degrees I may have acquired. I am down here trying to help you."

And that's the thing. I don't want to forget my poverty. I don't want to forget where I came from. I don't want to forget my ethnicity. Being proud of my heritage has made me a stronger human being. It helps me to tell others that they are all terrific, too!

I don't want to forget that there is a potential renaissance in all of us, whoever we are.

CLEM MIKESKA: Mr. Texas Barbecue
Temple, TX, Born 1929

I USE THE straight live-oak wood. I think it is a slower-burning, hotter-burning fire and it has a lot cleaner-looking smoke. And it does not have that *diesel aftertaste* like mesquite wood does.

I believe that beef is the best thing for you. It has a lot of protein, a lot of vitamins, and it is just good solid food. You eat good beef and you make it through the day without any problems.

I don't think it will hurt you. It hasn't hurt me as long as I've been living. I think it does me *a lot of good!*

The best thing in Texas to eat is beef. Texas beef! As long as you eat it, you will live a long time.

I've seen a lot of this crap on TV that beef is full of cholesterol. But it isn't. What they did was, they was knockin' the beef so that they could promote fish. I'm not goin' to knock fish or anything like that, but I eat a fish that big and thirty minutes later I'm hungry. It's a real light food and the fish industry people, they are like politicians. They will go out here and knock beef. Now the beef people, they got to come out with some kind of a promotion to get back into the saddle.

Here in Bell County we have a strong youth fair and livestock show operation. The kids raise these calves, hogs, or whatever for their projects to show. I have been buying the grand champion steer for the past many years. We go ahead and send him back home with the boy and have the boy feed him for another thirty days to settle him down. These steers are nervous and excited. Then we bring him to the slaughterhouse.

Yes, we do slaughter him! We do barbecue the parts of the steer that we can and the rest we grind up and make our own sausage out of it.

The kid who raised the steer is tickled to death that he won the grand champion ribbon. He feels good about it and he gets quite a bit of money for him, so he is happy. He goes home and puts the money in the bank for future days. Most of them put up enough money to go to college with. I'm proud of them for finishing this steer out. They make a pretty good profit out of it and they are happy. They just turn the steer loose to me and that's the way it is.

I myself raised animals at my father's farm.

My father, John Mikeska, came from Czechoslovakia when he was nine years old and was a farmer around Temple, Texas, for a long time. In 1936 he started a beef club for about thirty or forty Czech families. He was in charge of slaughtering an animal every Saturday morning and dividing it up so that each family in the club could have fresh meat every week. There was no money involved but he kept records of how many pounds of meat each family had received and what animals they had contributed. So if you didn't have refrigeration, at least you would have fresh meat once a week and then whatever was left over you would preserve it the best way you knew how.

All six of us, my father's sons, helped slaughter every Saturday morning. That gave us the experience. We learned right there with him. When I was about ten years old, we were all learning together.

Around 1939 the beef clubs were discontinued because electricity became available and everybody was able to afford it. And then people began to be able to go to town daily and buy fresh meat whenever they wanted it.

After my father married my mother in 1913, he had gotten interested in the meat business because it was hard to make a living farming. My father was quite aggressive about the business and we learned to be that way, too.

What I'm trying to say is, you just got to hustle. You just got to make it work one way or the other. If one thing don't work, try something else to provide for the family. You don't set back and let it happen. You got to make it happen!

Eventually we brothers each owned our own meat markets in different cities and we got the idea "Why not cook some of this meat on a barbecue pit?" It sounded like a good idea to all of us, so we built barbecue pits in the back ends of our meat markets and started cooking beef, chicken, and sausage. We had a dining area for people to come in and eat or to take out.

That went over real good because the food was good and people got used to the idea of not having to cook. We made potato salad, beans, and everything else. Done a complete meal for everybody!

Times change all the time and you have to change with it. Slowly but surely we got out of the fresh meat end of it and just started cooking and selling the barbecue.

I'll tell you, barbecue is good any time of the day: morning, noon or night. It is better for breakfast than Post Toasties or bacon and eggs, that's for sure. It has a lot of power to it.

Yeah, I eat barbecue every day and enjoy it. When my brothers and I get together, we usually cook steaks on a pit in the back yard at my mother's home in Bastrop and compare notes about our barbecue businesses. We just have a hell of a good time discussing barbecue and everybody pitches in to prepare the picnic. We all have a hand in it, like we are all authorities on it— which we are—and each of us pushes his own opinion on how to barbecue the steaks. But we all agree that when you get out of Texas, you get out of barbecue.

I think Temple is the barbecue capital of Texas and I am glad to be here in Temple. Of course, other cities in the state have good barbecue people, too, and Temple may not be the biggest and it may not be the best. But I'll tell you one thing, whoever is the biggest and the best, we got them nervous!

LOUIS RAWALT: *Beachcomber*
Padre Island, TX, Born 1899

WE LEFT KINGSVILLE on a sunny September morning. Behind me were the years of war, the hospital corridors, the waiting rooms, and the operating tables. I kept the doctor's grim predictions from my mind as much as possible.

Keeping the wheels of the Model T on the parallel planks of the causeway demanded all my attention, but every few moments Viola would cry out over some strange bird flying over Laguna Madre. There were white pelicans by the thousands, snowy egrets, roseate spoonbills, herons, ducks and gulls and terns. Mullet leaped and played in the water, shining like silver in the bright morning sun.

We left the causeway and followed a winding path through the dunes to the Gulf side of Padre. At the beach we turned left and drove along the surf to Corpus Christi Pass, where we set up camp. The pass was open then, and the islands of Padre and Mustang were divided. I don't know what time we reached the pass; we took no clock with us. I didn't want time measured out to me in minutes and hours.

We gathered lumber the rest of that day to build a floor for the tent. Viola did most of the labor, for there was little strength left in my body. When the sun was high in the heavens, we stopped long enough to eat the lunch Mother had packed for us. It had been many months since food had tasted so good, and if the fried chicken was seasoned with a little Padre Island sand, neither of us noticed—or cared.

By nightfall we were snug and secure. We ate a supper of bacon and pork and beans by the glow of our Coleman lantern. Viola had made a table from a small hatch cover the tide had carried in; our chairs were two nail kegs. She stacked some apple boxes, one above the other, to make a cupboard for our supplies. The cots were set up, side by side, at one end of the tent. We turned out the lantern, brushed some of the sand from our bare feet and crawled between the covers. I listened to the pound of the surf a moment before sleep overtook me. From the dunes behind us coyotes howled.

I awoke that first morning feeling refreshed and eager to face the day. I raised the flap of the tent to see the splendor of early morning on the Gulf. Nature was outdoing herself in artistry. The sky, the water, and the clouds along the horizon were all tinted with color—mauve, rose, and copper seeping through the gray. As I watched the sun break through to make a golden path across the water, Viola came softly on bare feet to stand beside me. I had everything. But for a limited time only. That day and the ones following it flowed by; the hours came and went like the waves that broke against the sand, unmeasured and unrecorded. We ate when we were hungry. When we were tired, we rested; and when the time came for sleep, we slept like exhausted children. For the most part, Viola busied herself about the camp, but sometimes she came and dropped down beside the camp chair where I sat for hours at a time fishing with my cane pole.

Gradually the sun and the salt air worked their healing magic, and before many weeks passed I felt the beginnings of strength returning to my body. The aches and pains lessened. The shadow of death lingered, but grew fainter.

Our appetites were enormous. In spite of all the fish we ate, our supplies disappeared rapidly. Neither of us looked forward to the trip to town after more. Fish were plentiful in those days and would strike at anything—even a bare hook. I saw schools of redfish a mile long, their color like a river flowing through the Gulf. There were many other species of fish, and I think I caught some of them all. There were the redfish, trout, drum, pompano, pike, mackerel, golden croaker, whiting, and many less important fishes. The bottom of the lagoon was thick with flounder which we gigged at night by lantern light.

One cool night in October I caught five hundred pounds of redfish on my trotlines. Early morning found us chugging across the causeway with our load. The fish sold for twenty-five dollars; then we bought supplies and more line and hooks and hurried back to our island as fast as the Ford would take us. After that, I fished commercially.

When the first norther' whistled down across the dunes, we realized we would have to have a stove to keep the tent warm. So the next trip to town we bought some stovepipe, a chisel, and some hinges. I took an oil drum and chiseled out a door on one side and hinged it on. For the pipe, I cut criss-crosses and flanged them out to fit snugly. We filled the drum about a fourth of the way up with sand for insulation on the bottom, ran the pipe up through a hole in the tent, and there was our stove. Wood was no problem. The tide took care of that, but cutting it became my chore. Viola tried it once, but swore off tearfully after a stick of wood flew up and hit her in the eye.

Winter passed. A short spring merged into a long summer. By the next October, I realized that I had borrowed six months over my allotted time to live, and by leave of the Almighty I meant to borrow as many more as I could. I was strong again and seldom felt the touch of pain. Fishing was good, and if the proceeds in those days were not astounding, there was always enough for the things we really needed. Island living agreed with Viola. She was brown and healthy and active as a ground squirrel.

We moved our camp to the edge of Big Shell the next year, thirty-five miles down the beach. This time we had a shack to live in. A place loaned us by Major Swan, one of the old-timers of the island. I bought a surf net and a used Model A to replace the rust-eaten Model T. We converted the Ford into a pick-up. Viola helped me with the net until I found a fishing partner.

One morning when we were hauling in the net, something kept leaping against it with the force of a huge shark or a porpoise. We couldn't bring it in, so I staked one end of the net into the sand, and hooked onto the other end with the car. Slowly, I pulled in the net until the creature lay in the edge of the surf. Incredible: It was an eighteen-foot sawfish. When some fishermen came by later that day and found me beside the sawfish with a cane pole—no net in sight—they assumed I had caught it on the pole. I didn't enlighten them, and this tall fish story was told about Corpus Christi for years. The sawfish, I regret to say, became food for the packs of coyotes that roamed the wild stretches of Big Shell.

We seldom saw other human beings there, but coyotes prowled close to our shack at night, and in the early mornings and evenings we saw them on the beach searching for fish, which were the mainstay of their diet. I learned by experience just how clever and crafty they were. I have seen them fishing in the surf for mullet and catching them! Many times I saw these lean, hungry animals watching me from over the rim of the dunes. Once I left the beach, they would sneak down and pick up my discards. Sitting on the porch that I had added to our shack one early morning after I had set out my trotlines, I saw two big coyotes slink down to the water's edge and begin dragging one of the lines in to shore. I was too amazed and curious to move. They pulled the line all the way in; then bit the fish off the hooks and trotted with them back to their habitat in the dunes. Many persons doubted the truth of this, but I saw the same thing happen time and again.

One night Viola nudged me awake. "There's something in the kitchen," she whispered.

Listening, I heard the faint rattle of the tin plates we had left on the table. I got up and edged toward the kitchen. The moonlight streamed through the open door and outlined the gaunt, gray form of a coyote. He was on the table licking up the remains of our supper. He sensed my presence and leaped for the door, but slipped on the greasy plate and somersaulted into the center of the room. I gave a swift kick to the astonished animal and sent it rolling down the back steps. Tail down, it trotted up a nearby dune and sat on its haunches barking with venom. As I looked closer, I saw the forms of four or five puppies, joining in the harsh chorus. They continued to bark until I got my shotgun; then they vanished into the night.

During a big run of redfish one night, I caught ninety, averaging in weight from five to fifteen pounds. I kept them on stringers alive in the surf until I was too tired to fish any more; then, nearing midnight, I started to ice them down in the pick-up. There was no ice. I hastily loaded the fish and hauled them back of the dunes, where I put them in a pond. We could net them in the morning easily and hurry them in to market. This catch would bring seventy or eighty dollars which we needed for supplies.

Satisfied with the night's work, I tumbled into bed and slept until dawn. With the first light of morning, I hurried to the pond. I stared in amazement at what I saw: Scattered around the bank of the pond were the headless carcasses of ninety redfish. The coyotes has outwitted me. Their tracks formed a network around the pond and trailed into the sand hills in every direction. They ate a hearty supper; but what were we going to eat?

I drove in to town that day for a new supply of ice, which was all I could buy. The next night the redfish were still running—so we got our groceries and gasoline after all.

Coyotes weren't the only problem we had to cope with on the beach. In any season, but especially during vernal and autumnal equinoxes, the Gulf might change from peace to violence. We lived in the Devil's Elbow, the bend on the long arm of Padre. It was strewn with the accumulated wreckages of the years, from shrimp boats and freighters to Spanish galleons dating back to the time of Cortez. Salvage from these boats helped us to improve our daily living conditions, and some old coins and jewelry I found at the site of one of the wrecks made interesting additions to our treasure trove of beachcombings.

Some of the castoffs of the waves were unusual and astonishing. One afternoon Viola and I stopped to examine a five-gallon can that had washed up on the beach. I pried the lid off with my fishing knife. The can was filled with clean, white lard. We put it into the pick-up, and before the day was over, we had salvaged more than a hundred cans. There were a lot more damaged cans that we left lying on the beach. The Coast Guard told us later that a Mexican freighter had been torn to pieces by a sudden tumult in the Gulf. She was carrying a cargo of lard; it made a profitable load of salvage for us and a grease bath for the beach. For a long time after that the sand was saturated with lard. The island coyotes grew fat from feasting on it. Even the sand crabs acquired a new look of sleekness.

It was about the same time when the British smuggler I'm *Alone* was shelled and sunk by the Coast Guard cutter in Sigsbee's Deep near the southern tip of Padre. The ship was spotted off New Orleans where she expected to land her contraband cargo of whiskey. The cutter chased her along the coast, finally closing in on her. The captain refused to surrender. He jettisoned the cargo before the Coast Guard cutter blasted the ship full of holes.

I received word by the island grapevine to be on the lookout for liquor, so I started down the beach in the pick-up, searching the incoming waves and the tideline for bottles of the amber elixir. I didn't see anything that looked like whiskey but noticed a full gunnysack imbedded in the sand. I could check it later, so I drove on, but when I saw several more similar sacks, I stopped to investigate. The sack I opened contained a dozen sealed tin cans. I pried the lid from one of the cans. Inside, was a bottle of "Old Hospitality" Bourbon whiskey. During the day, I salvaged one hundred and ten sacks. I stashed this horde behind the dunes, filled a duffel bag with seventy-two bottles, and headed for Port Isabel. The ferryboat took me across the channel. The captain's suspicions were aroused by the weight of the duffel bag. I had to explain what I had found and make a gift of a few bottles. It is enough to say that I disposed of the remainder in Port Isabel.

When I returned to the island, a comforting feeling of cash in my pockets and the prospect of more, I met the captain of the ferryboat and one of his crew. They were driving a pick-up with the bed loaded with bulging gunnysacks. I followed their tracks, as they had, from all appearances, followed mine, to my cache in the dunes. Of all my loot, there wasn't even a bottle left!

For weeks the beach was combed by thirsty men all the way from Port Isabel to Port Aransas. At Port Aransas, one boatman got more of the "drink" than he counted on. He spotted a sack and headed his craft toward it. As he reached over the side for the bobbing burlap bag, he tumbled into the water. He was five miles from shore, and his boat was circling away. He kept afloat by using the liquor as a lifebuoy. The boat swung in a circle, finally coming back to him. He grasped the side and struggled aboard. Evidently the thoughts that raced through his brain as he floundered in the water, with drowning almost a certainty, sobered him greatly, for when he got back to town he sold his boat and other possessions and moved inland.

So the days flowed into weeks, and the weeks became months and years. I had grown steadily stronger and seldom gave a thought to the fact that I wasn't even supposed to be alive. I could walk for miles without tiring, and many nights I slept on the sand with only a piece of tarpaulin around me when I was fishing away from the camp. It was one of the times when I had gone alone to a spot thirty-five miles below our shack that the car stalled. No amount of coaxing or tinkering could get a sound out of it. There was nothing to do but start walking. It was seventy miles to Corpus Christi Pass where someone lived who had a car. The tide was exceptionally high, and I had little hope that any fishermen would be venturing down the beach that day.

It was early morning when I started out. A little before sunset I reached our shack. Viola was visiting my people in Kingsville at the time, so the place was still and empty-feeling. I ate, drank coffee, and rested for a few moments before starting again. The tide was rising rapidly. It looked as though a storm might be brewing in the Gulf. If I didn't get the car up out of the reach of the water, I wouldn't have a car. This thought kept my bare feet plodding through the sand all night. It was dark as pitch. Sudden squalls blew in, keeping me drenched most of the time. But with the first gray light of morning, I could see by the familiar outlines of the dunes that I was only a few miles from the pass.

Bill White, another fisherman, was cooking breakfast in his tar-paper shack when I knocked at his door. I was too tired to eat, but as I gulped down scalding cups of coffee, I couldn't help crowing over the fact that four years before I had been doomed. In the last twenty-four hours I had walked seventy-five miles!

During the next year I acquired a fishing partner. We called him "Shorty," and if he had any other name, we never knew it. He was a good man on the end of a net. It relieved Viola from some pretty hard work, too. She had found a bale of cotton washed up on the beach and subsequently launched into a quilting project. Shorty set up his tent a little beyond our shack, and until the hurricane of that year [1933], we had a pleasant and profitable partnership.

That was the year the Gulf staged a real shindig. We had several scares that September. Viola kept most of our valued and important possessions packed in boxes against the time we might have to evacuate. The Friday before the storm hit on Monday was one of the most perfect of island days. The water was flat and blue. The skies clear and the southwest wind warm and gentle. Shorty was expecting weekend guests, and Viola, thinking they would perhaps visit us, too, had unpacked the boxes and made the house cozy and neat.

I was fishing early Saturday morning when I noticed that the swells were coming over the beach in an erratic rhythm. Far out over the water, the sky had an ominous look; wildlife had deserted the beach. A squall hit with sudden intensity. I pulled in my line and went into the shack. Viola was still sleeping. I wakened her and told her to get ready to go to town, that I thought there was a storm on the way. Sleepily, she started pulling on her jeans and shirt, mumbling about repacking everything. I walked to the porch and looked out. The tide had risen so fast that it was already hazardous to travel the beach.

"You won't have time for that," I told her. "We'll have to go now, or not at all."

Shorty came in then. He had seen the signs. There was no need of telling him. Another squall hit as we were getting into the pick-up, where we squeezed up together in the seat. The beach was almost impassable where the long sweeps crowded us up into the soft sand and shell. But the Model A came through, and in the late afternoon we reached the house of some friends in Corpus Christi.

I checked with the weather bureau and found that there was, indeed, a storm in the Gulf. It was one of exceptional force and was headed straight toward the Texas coast. They expected the storm to hit Monday. After getting Viola more or less safely settled, Shorty and I began to talk about returning to the island and going down to the beach on low tide that night to get some of our equipment. We decided to go, and over Viola's protests we refueled the Ford and drove back over the causeway to Padre.

The island was a place of darkness and fury that night. It rained incessantly and the wind blew in gusts that threatened to blow the pick-up over. We had only gone a mile or two down the beach when we both had to admit that it was hopeless to try to go farther until daylight. So we drove the Ford up into the edge of the dunes and sat there all night trying to sleep, our legs cramping and the water reaching nearer with every heave of the Gulf.

When morning came the rain let up a little. We shoved and shoveled our way through the dunes and to the grasslands in the center of the island. It took all day to reach the shack driving over the rough terrain and through the pools of water left by the night's deluge. It still rained and the wind blew.

WE LEFT THE truck behind the dunes and walked over to the house. The water was running under it so deep it was over our knees as we waded up to the steps. We estimated that the tide was four or five feet above normal. I knew that unless some miracle happened, the shack was not going to stand much longer. I went inside, and dumping a pillow out of its case, started grabbing some of our valuables and putting them into it. I tossed in a box containing several old coins I had found around the wreckage of an old ship, a rust-encrusted lavaliere I had picked up at the site of the Balli mission-ranch. Then there were the stem-wind gold watches I had found in a wooden box on the beach and my collection of arrowheads and spearpoints.

I was looking around at all the rest of our furnishings and equipment, wondering how much to take, when a giant roller hit the shack with terrifying force. I felt the floor sway and buckle under my feet. The water was running up through the cracks when I went out the back door with a pillow case in one hand.

The steps had washed away. As I jumped off the porch into the water that was now over waist-deep, I caught sight of a can of gasoline that I was counting on to use for the return trip to town. I caught the can as it floated by me and waded out of the melee. Shorty, having finished collecting his belongings from the tent, was waiting for me in the truck.

I put the gasoline in and looked back at the house. It had toppled and was being beaten to pieces by the waves. When I started to place the pillow case on the seat, I discovered that I had grabbed the wrong one—I had salvaged only a pillow and a can of gasoline which might not even be enough to get us back to town. Darkness was coming down fast. The storm grew in intensity. We would be lucky if we got out of it with our lives.

Fortune was kind to us that night. By following our recently made tracks back up the center of the island we laboriously made our way to the north end of Padre. There we found the waters of the Laguna Madre lapping over the plank troughs of the causeway. Could we make it? The choice had to be made quickly. We would try. So I nosed the Model A onto the planks, and we inched our way over the water. Wind tore at us and rain poured down in torrents.

It was daylight by then. A liquid, gray daylight in which everything blended and wavered like the scenes in an underwater film. At the ship channel we found that the swing bridge had been torn partly loose. The ends of it were two feet higher than the planks of the causeway. A barge was anchored nearby with several men aboard. They came to our rescue. Climbing from the barge to the causeway, they lifted the Ford and set it on the bridge; then they set it down at the other end. Thus we finally reached the comparative safety of the mainland.

Later we found that during the next hour the causeway was reduced to a total wreck. The planks were torn loose and flung through the air. Some of them were found weeks later in the mesquite forests of the million-acre King ranch, twenty miles away.

That hurricane left devastation everywhere it moved. Much of Corpus Christi was a shambles. Padre Island was cleared of everything for a hundred miles. The contours of the beach were changed and there were thirty channels cut all the way from the Gulf of Mexico to the Laguna Madre.

Within a week after the storm we were back on the island. We got there by loading our car on an improvised raft and poling it across Laguna Madre. Driving the beach was hazardous. It was striped with deep ruts and covered with logs and debris. The passes were filling up with sand, and we were able to drive through them, although we went through water two feet deep at times.

At the site of our former shack there was nothing. Nothing, that is, except an old icebox half sunk in the sand. Shorty's tent had caught around the icebox, and on examination showed its only damage to be a small dent. In searching about the campsite, he found all the things he had left with the exception of a small stew kettle. Viola and I found, as I have said, nothing. Out of all the supplies, the equipment, the bedding, the clothing, and what we regarded as our treasures, there absolutely was not a sign of anything. And Shorty had found everything he owned but a thirty-five-cent kettle!

The ways of the sea are strange. They say that whatever it takes away from you, it brings back. I'm inclined to think that it does. The next few months the tide carried in the lumber and piling for us to build a bigger and stronger house sixty-five miles from the north end of Padre.

Now, many years after the doctors predicted my imminent death, I still roam the wilds of my unsubdued island.

GENARO GONZALEZ

— — — —

Un Hijo del Sol

NACER: AL AMANECER

ADÁN AS A child had an ability to remain unnoticed. Not withdrawn: he merely accommodated himself to the campesino environment to become a part of it. While his *jefitos* harvested a stranger's crops, Adán milled through the fields, scroungy, chocolate. A misplaced Mexican mirage in the backroads of Michigan, a boy-creature shimmering in heat. He picked the harvest only when it betrayed a strain of overabundance, a cow whose swollen teats must be milked. He spent his nights in El Norte smearing firefly glow on his body or sometimes in an abandoned car feeling up a little girl his own age whose name he

Native Texan GENARO GONZALEZ is a psychology teacher in the tiny town of Edinburg. He is the author of a novel, Rainbow's End, *and a collection of short stories,* Only Sons.

never knew or later forgot. When playing *las escondidas* behind tents and trucks, someone inevitably glimpsed a woman in white or heard a whistling *lechuza*, and that was enough to break up the games for the night. Bedding on the floor, veiled by a surplus-store mosquito net, Adán often pretended to be a spider waiting behind its web for insects, although he wouldn't have known what to do after actually catching one, being that spiders were very mysterious about this. Adán did not consciously regard his life as free and happy; he lived it out of a continuous necessity. Today his only real appreciation of that life comes from remembering that he used to lie on a cotton-filled truck bed and gaze at an imposing sky while his parents drove through a temperatureless night. Adán hoisted himself up the side of a wooden panel, to be thrust back by the wind onto a sinking sea of silent cotton, impossible to walk on. Just stretch out and breathe in the smells, covered up snugly by a huge cotton body-muff. Not warm, just unable to conceive of differences such as heat or cold.

Adán went back to McAllen to begin the process of growing up, of growing old. He discovered freedom (natural, not the castrate freedom of societies) by having it taken away. Attendance in kindergarten forced and sporadic, fiasco. Assignment: Acculturation Process, Lesson I. Stand up in front of the class and deliver a mutilated version of simple songs in English. Adán swaggers through "Aquí está el águila negra." Someone missed the boat! No, no, Adán. You must sing in English now. So he just stopped attending kindergarten.

CIRCOS Y SELVAS

ADÁN COULD RECALL having seen a robin in El Valle only once during his entire childhood. Robins and other northern birds supposedly migrated southward in search of warmth, but to Adán's knowledge, only shriveled snowbirds roosted here in winter. The snowbirds, or *turistas*, were valued more than whooping cranes for the golden eggs they laid unto other capitalist birds of prey; they were protected under the auspices of the local chamber of commerce. (In spite of the traffic problems their cumbersome vehicles cause in winter, the *turistas* were repaid in kind: the summer months saw families of Valle migrants in El Norte, temporarily invading the land—an appropriate cultural exchange program to rival the best of colleges.)

The South is known for its whitewashed "southern hospitality." But the hospitality-handout is a phenomenon peculiar to El Valle, wherein wintering snowbirds strew crumbs among the natives. Apparently the tourist trade, regarded as a sacred sort of foreign aid to El Valle's poor, cannot be stressed strongly enough. In school Adán would be led to believe it was a symbiotic ass-kiss-ass process (i.e., "They buy more oranges, thus creating more jobs for orange pickers"), but for him their lives crossed only when the *turistas* slummed through the barrios ("Here but for the grace of God live I") or lost their way, in the utmost arrogance honking to break up and glide through interrupted street games. Their bewildered stares at the surrounding motley *bandidos* only broadened the vacuum between the simple sweltering streets and their elaborate world. The car/tomb. Antiseptic. Shielding. Plush in its doctor's office chill. One day Prieto had enough and hurled a stone at a black Cadillac (to him they all drove Cadillacs). Not as an act of chosen insurrection but as the natural way to destroy an antithesis. The glass screams, a gust of cold sterile air escapes from within, giving Adán a pee-chill. Too lifeless, too unlike the surrounding heat he knew. The withered mummies inside startle from their death, the opened tomb vomits a cold, foreign air onto the torrid barrio streets. *Las viejitas*—the caked putrid faces, sexless, haunted at themselves. No life: anti-sensual. They come here to die. El Valle: an elephant graveyard hidden from the outside world. An empty nightmare that recurs.

LABORES

THAT SCHOOL VACATIONS were during summer seemed no accident: *how else* could the cotton be gleaned and the ripe tomatoes raped from the vines, if not for the *jefitas* with their miniature children-hordes marching across the jungle fields of El Valle? A few of the more fortunate families would leave for El Norte and return with tales of a campesino Cibola, where one merely rustled the cherry-laden limbs for the fruit to fall heavily onto his hands. Best of all, they said, the *patrones* are considerate and "understand us." Adán could not figure out how it was possible for a *patrón* to "understand" his workers and remain their *patrón*. Adán tried to recall his life, his *other* life in El Norte, but could only remember having known *things*—air, trees, soil, streams—not people (maybe people as *objects* that blended into the soil).

Instead Adán would find himself in El Valle, transported at odd intervals to a new "*campo*," there to spend his time, keep out of trouble and even make some money. Besides, no *vatos* stayed on the streets during the day, they all put in their time somewhere. Cover up, "no te vayas a poner prieto." Decked out in faded shirt and jeans (the cotton-picker jumpsuit), the shirt several sizes too small and belonging to another era, sleeves through vanity rolled up two and a half times, but otherwise ideal for *la pisca*.

Sunrise. *Vamos a piscar.* Cool morning with cotton moisture-heavy. Straddled over plants—jean legs wet with dew—alarm clock for rabbits and snakes. Showdowns of cotton boll battles trusting no one within fifty feet, old women ducking stray shots, screaming some philosophy about might-as-well-throw-away money. "La cagan, rucas," Adán philosophized back. Eventually Don Ernesto, the sweat-patched truck driver, came to squelch the free-for-all, warning the "bastardos huevones" that he had but to contact some border patrolmen on his truck telephone (an old disintestined radio). These officers, he explained, were his intimate friends and had agreed to deport any troublemakers from his camp; then an old man who flirted with girls replied that Don Ernesto did indeed attract special attention from *la migra:* whenever patrolmen checked the camp for wetbacks, they always corralled Don Ernesto first due to his suspicious, outlaw looks. Finally Don Ernesto flatly threatened to leave the *chavalos* in the field to walk back home if they kept fighting. His peculiar diplomacy won.

Adán moves on, dragging his sack like a huge, stuffed albino serpent. He inspects his hands, smudged with leaf stains and squashed caterpillars, perfumed with pesticide. He stands up, sees his shadow almost gone. *Hora de comer,* or just about . . . Adán hammocks his sack under the trailer; he reclines Roman-style, feasting on *tacos de frijoles y papas,* lukewarm pale red Kool-Aid, and sometimes a soft splotchy banana almost turned to pudding. Over such cuisine he discusses the day's work with an elite group of young goldbrickers who have retired for brunch. The *patrón* drops by in his pickup, a pained, crowsfeet expression around the eyes, a snarl around the mouth, a bulge around his belt. He climbs up the trailer. Taking a sample of picked cotton in one hand, he stares at the *piscadores*, scans the field in utter disgust, as if seeking whoever picked *that* particular handful of shitty cotton. And liquid, bedroom eyes lazily looked out from the pickup: the *patrón's* teenage daughter smiles in Cleopatra lust from her Nile River pickup-barge. *Los vatos*, their theories on *gavacha* promiscuity rekindled, mutter back and huddle around the pickup. What his friends saw in the plump, slackmouth girl—necklaced in prickly heat rash—was beyond Adán; it seemed not so much lust as a method to hit the *patrón* through his daughter. (Christ, those *chicanitos calientes* would proposition any girl outside their immediate family!; *los bordos*, levees outside McAllen notorious as makeout places for their older brothers, were already legendary in their conversations.)

Again the drag of *pisca . pisca . . pisca . . .* Daydreams border on sunfed hallucinations, eyes and hands automatically discriminate whiteness of cotton from field of vision. *Pisca, pisca.* A girl removes her picking sack and walks off to a deserted patch in the field. Her head bobs down, body bends, she squats, disappears. Macho heads young and old bob up, bodies unbend, they stretch, dissimulate silence of mutual hard-on. Then back to . . . *pisca . pisca.* Sweat and pesticide—nostril nausea. Sweat salt burns his eyes. (For some time Adán thought the sickening odor was a natural by-product of the plants. Only much later did he correlate the airplane dusters with the nausea, that being when a duster once sprayed a field where Adán had wandered chasing a rabbit.) . . . Goddamn, not *one* cloud to cool things off.

TIRED. DEAD. Stand fixedly on a burning dying afternoon. Feel not just a dull backache but *being tired* with: the motionless soil, the meaningless horizons, the lightyear-distant truck—all suffocated and weak in this french-fried heat. Having scorned all

movement and murdered all time. Staring achingly at the peni-
tents in the plastic Purgatorio, bent upon their work, eyes and
minds as one, only the dangling carrot/mirage of the American
cornucopia (Let them eat cotton); expecting in his favor to see
them *all* stand up, gaze contentedly at the bullfight passes of a far-
off airplane duster, then agonized, remove the heavy yoke of the
albatross picking sack from their necks and . . . as One . . . walk
away proud. (Adán yanks off a yet-green cotton boll, an act
tabooed by the *pinche patrón*. He fingers the boll-juicy flesh inside,
unnatural in its pallor. Because of me, Adán reasons, it will never
serve its purpose. Adán then shreds the compact fibers and throws
the ravaged, undeveloped cotton boll away. He turns in the lazy
heat to look at Sylvia, her bent body straining her tight full ass.
Nude Woman picking Cotton, 1959 . . . Then (Lubbock, Tejas . . .
A crude sign: white cotton boll. The sentence: "No niggers, dogs
or meskins allowed."))

LA RAÍZ

AS MAN REVERSING to child to seed to ancestors. And then beyond. Querétaro, México. Dawn through greenglass of bus, past
primitive nonyears. Adán, unable to sleep all night, now sees the
soft countryside with somnambulist eyes, with slowmotion mind
where images bisect and bust in time-war explosions; images
breathe in dull luster of confrontation with senses where artificial
levels—time, maps,—dissolve to yield unique experience.
Marineblue sky he never would have thought possible. Land and
low clouds in serape color and design. Transparent beauty.
Coupled with invisible *indio* presence hangs in revolution atmos-
phere leaps in galvanic-genetic stimulus within Adán. Lucio,

seated in the next row, likewise hypnotized by some kinetic kinship with the peopled land.

Adán continues to stare out. A hunched, burdened figure streaks by in the opposite direction and Adán looks back. Outside the detached bubble of the bus a man dressed in black—his age undetermined—carries a small coffin upon his back. The coffin of a child, deceptively simple—brown and smooth—as the simplicity of a child's life. His gaze is downcast, he strides carefully over rough, plowed ground. Clouds mountains valleys fields provide a sharp immobile background to the plodding man; they seem at once respectfully silent and aloofly indifferent. The man walks slowly, whether because of the coffin's weight or the terrain or perhaps his sorrow, Adán doesn't know. He watches until the man and the coffin fuse into a single blur . . .

Then walking through downtown México, D.F. Trying to merge yet always separate, as oil film on water. Prodigal son transfigured through time and travel, now unrecognized by his family. As Adán seeks a country's life-source he is blitzed by props of lopsided miniskirts, effeminate superheroes, "*clases de inglés.*" People en masse running crawling in the opposite direction, the lost look of lemmings toward cliffs of USA-emulation.

Further down into the barrios with street soccer games religiously played on every block. *Chavalas bien chulas* walk by, baptized by the sprinkling of rain. Children's voices in rhythmic mimicry of barrio slang. *Los locos* under the shelter of awnings, red dreaming eyes entertained by crazy raindrops shooting down like crystal bb's on non-hips. Other *locos* drift with extrovert smile out onto the street among *chavalitos*. *Ojos grifos*, mostly slits in sunlight, now bloom with the cool fascination of single raindrops tapping on their person, wide-eyed that something falling from So High doesn't hurt at all; each raindrop comes as a surprise, like suddenly crashing through chunks of fog in the night. They lift their faces to the sky, perhaps to lingering Aztec spirits of rain and yerba; they offer their minds in sweet sacrifice to herbs. Eyes become rain magnets become the very rain . . .

El sol. An old woman wrinkled within the folds of her shawl sells religious tokens in the name of Christ. Passersby give her looks of disgust for her unchristian hunger. She seems somewhat grateful for the patrons and shade of a cathedral which hangs huge in its background irony. In partial balance a young man of indio features pores with brown eyes over something simply entitled El Che. Adán notes that the indio sits on a bench in the sunlight, away from the shadow of the church. He seems not at all to shy from the steeple's shadow in vampire fright, but is perhaps annoyed that the church is itself a shadow.

It begins to rain again. Lucio walks alone. Adán walks alone. Alone in the company of outsiders and other outlaws. For the moment there is nothing more in his head worth saying aloud. Adán walks in silence through gauze curtains of rain, his face very much alive as cool raindrops burst upon animal warmth then evaporate into *** (He remembers fadedly feels vibrantly as multiple episodes superimpose on his mind. Stained snapshots: a dark boy running from the nowhere heat of smoldered afternoons, slapped softly by wet sheets flapping on laundry lines, hot chocolate chest licked cool by moisture of dampsmelling towels. Simultaneously, he hurries across a scorching street—asphalt brands urgent tingles on bare feet, shock runs up behind his neck and cascades in warm pool of liquid eyes; a whiff of nostril blood, body trembles in heat shivers, he leaps under the neutral shade of a mesquite, his feet become concrete cool become dry-ice cold for an instant; the hot rush from his face sinks to his lungs to his legs out from his toes in total release, as warm shudders of a bursting pee on powder dirt; he stands quietly alone in his triumph over pain, ready to conquer the streets.) He stands quietly alone—

EL MESTIZO Y SU MISTERIO: SIN FIN

A FEELING OF abysses, of canyons, of losing someone to the hungers of time and the universe. Houses—their windows X'd with boards—hung out in El Valle, paralyzed in iron lungs. This feeling within Adán, as of losing someone and finding his own sense of self that much more. Eternity of ghost-town streets, emptiness sweeps a vacuum. Something part air, part fire, and part death surrounds him. Adán breathes the air to live; the fire—burning in his mind—to act; the other stagnates into history and afterthought.

Yet the heat in the fields and barrios of El Valle had fused. A fire had sparked. For Adán, his life proved more demanding, more insistent: it forced him to live with this fire or burn out. A harsher sun enveloped El Valle. Before, it had drowsed Adán, had drained his commitment and his *raza*'s life through centuries of evaporation. Today the sun can not wither Adán, it exposes, it reveals. He can no longer ignore that the sun feeds him fire. *El sol.* Burning timepiece of a burning mestizo. The sun being time. The time being Now.

"Sale a dar la vuelta," suggests 'Milio. "Cirol, 'ta bien agüitado." Roaming the town with the magnetism of Mexico's border towns clutching their minds harder. They decide to give McAllen one last look. *El drive-in. Muerto. El parque. Muerto. El centro. Muerto.* Walking by a store, something catches Adán's attention.

A large wall mirror faces him. He tries to look at the mirror with detached inspection, but his gaze immediately locks him into the mirror. His eyes seem fascinated with themselves, with their mad prophet reflection, at seeing themselves through themselves. In doing so, his eyes alternately become beholder and beheld, beheld and beholder. As if they can only see and know themselves by being *other* eyes, outside eyes which likewise must be seen by what they see. Adán stared . . . stared back . . . stared . . . stared back. Two pairs of eyes—those of himself and of his reflection—mesmerized each other and met at some *distance between* the mirror and Adán. He felt himself as being someplace *outside* his body. Where am *I?* he thought. Space. Spaced out. *Estoy afuera. Yo soy . . . Adán nadA. Adán nadA. Adán nada . . .*

His mind had no recourse but to accept this rebellion, this extreme awareness taking place. Adán realizes that he is para-doxically *more* than himself, that something *within* him is also be-yond him. He is beyond his own understanding.

Later, they decide to go to a rock dance. They enter the building. The heavy bass thumps deep inside their chests like a second heartbeat. Sauntering with almost staged ease to-ward the musicians' platform, they slip through crevices of crushed teenagers. Adán notices a group of Chicanas. Next to them, a large cluster of *gavachas* with characteristic plump-ass-pants/tiny-chiches-shirt had attracted the attention of a few older, foppishly dressed Chicanos, who in turn had attracted the attention of some heavyset *gavachos.* 'Milio was noticeably pissed at the *reglaje* behavior of the older Chicanos, adding that they probably called themselves Spanish-American to boot.

Slowly at first, then steadily, the *gavachos* trickle toward the mismatched crowd of *gringas* and Chicanos, prepared to defend the already torn-down bastion of white female virginity. A scuffle—one of the well-dressed Chicanos falls, bleeding. Adán and several others rush to the small circle. More people, fighting, pushing, running away. Adán looks at the Chicano on the floor; a hard fist is thumped onto his kidneys. Adán moves away, reaches for his knife, turns back to see a shock of blond hair and eyes crying . . . Adán suspends the knife in final decision, weighing the victim versus the act . . . An obsidian blade traces a quick arc of in-stinct—somewhere in time an angry comet flares, a sleeping mountain erupts, an Aztec sun explodes in birth.

A N N

R I C H A R D S

▬ ▬ ▬ ▬

Straight from the Heart

MY DADDY WAS born in a little community called Bugtussle. There are a lot of Bugtussles in Texas, in one place or another, but this one was outside of Lorena, just south of Waco.

Supposedly the community got its name because there was some fellow named Bug—could have been Bugg, for all I know—who caused a problem there. The town was the center of some kind of camp meeting, as they had in the rural South, where people would drive their buggies up and they would hear preaching and they would sing, and they would make a couple of days of it.

In 1989, former Texas Congresswoman ANN RICHARDS published Straight from the Heart, a wild and wooly account of her life in politics. This excerpt recounts her childhood just outside of Waco.

These people had children, and they would stack up brush and make a circle and bed these kids down on quilts—from whence came the expression "Baptist pallet"—and leave them in that circle while they went on about whatever their religious activity was.

It seems that while the children were asleep in their various buggies, Mr. Bug, who was a prankster, switched them from one buggy to another. After the ensuing melee, the town became known as Bugtussle.

I've always thought that was a pretty romantic and ridiculous story, and probably not true. But that's what my Daddy, Cecil, used to tell me.

My Daddy's Daddy was a farmer. Both my parents' folks were farmers. They came from places like Alabama and Tennessee, and they came to Texas like people did from all over the country, because it was a place of opportunity. They were looking for land to farm. In the late 1800s all across the South, there were letters scribbled on doors: "GTT." It meant "Gone to Texas."

My Mama, Iona Warren, was born outside of Hico, which is south of Fort Worth near Glenrose, in a community called Hogjaw. Honest to Pete. They both came from pretty big families, and really poor. Dirt poor. I think my father's pop left the farm and moved into Waco at some point, but my granddaddy on my mother's side, and my grandmother, lived on the Stephenville Highway until they both got too old to live out there and moved into town.

The family stayed close by. Sisters and brothers either lived with their parents even after they were grown and married or they built houses that were very near the home place.

My Mama was the adventurer. She finished what I think is the equivalent of high school and at some point decided to come to Waco. It must have been a very brave thing to do. Both her sisters stayed in Hico, still live there. But Mama was smart and she was ambitious.

It must have been frightening to leave a community where you had grown up, knew everybody, all your family was there, and go off on your own. My uncle I.V. was working in Waco and I guess he encouraged Mama to come. She didn't need much encouraging. She worked in a dry-goods store, selling piece goods and whatever else.

Daddy finished the eighth grade and it became a family necessity for him to go to work. All of the children in that family went to work very young. Even those who got to stay in school skeeted sodas or worked at a drive-in root-beer stand. This wasn't so they could have some spending change, it was so they could bring money home.

They were so poor that at one point the family had got a hold of a whole load of field tomatoes—either got them for nothing or got them for very little—and they peeled those tomatoes and cooked them, canned them, and ate them at every meal for months. My Daddy won't eat stewed tomatoes to this day.

Mama and Daddy met on a blind date. They went to a movie, but either the projector broke down or the film was damaged—anyway, they had to take a rain check, which meant that Daddy asked Mama out again.

When my parents married they bought a little one-bedroom frame house on an acre of land out on the Dallas Highway in Lakeview, about eight miles from Waco. It was just a little country community, didn't have a city council or any kind of government structure. It didn't even have a Main Street. You came into Lakeview off a couple of roads which connected to a highway. One of the roads had a country store and a filling station. There were the Interurban train tracks, which sooner or later led to Dallas, and across from them sat a tiny little grocery store. That was the total commerce of Lakeview.

It wasn't an ugly town, but it was not kept. There were empty lots, and fields where weeds grew. I don't know why in the world it would be called Lakeview; there was no lake to view.

Daddy was working for Southwestern Drug Company, driving a delivery truck, delivering pharmaceuticals and anything you could buy in a drugstore. At one point he had been making $100 a month, but when the Depression hit hardest his salary was reduced to $81.50.

The house cost $700 and my parents paid for it in two years. It seems inconceivable to me that anybody with a salary of $81.50 a month could pay off a mortgage like that so quickly, but they had a big garden and grew everything they ate. They raised chickens, the odd duck or goose, and at one point they had a hog. Everything was grown for food.

It was a little country house, with steps going up to a front porch and a white picket fence around it. There are lots of these frame houses up on hills off the roads of Texas. The main window is in the bedroom over the porch, and the living room always juts out with a big window there too. There are doors off the porch to each room. There's always a swing on the porch.

I was born in the bedroom of that house. Mama went into labor and someone had told her that if she would walk a lot she could make the baby come faster, so she spent most of the day walking up and down the dirt roads in Lakeview. Finally, in the evening, she called old Dr. Beidlespach to come on out from Waco.

I took my time in coming and there wasn't anything anybody could do about it. Dr. Beidlespach went and lay down on the front porch and slept there. He said if they made a bed for him he would never get up when the baby was ready.

I finally arrived at six the next morning.

Mama had gotten a neighbor woman to come in to cook supper for Daddy that night, but the neighbor woman couldn't kill the chicken that she was supposed to cook. My Daddy would be getting home any time now and something had to be done; there's no such thing as maternity leave when you're poor, not even for a moment. My Mama lay on the birthing bed, only hours after I was born, and wrung that chicken's neck so that Daddy would have supper when he got home.

I believe Mama would have liked to have had more children, but times were hard and I was the only one. Daddy had the fear—maybe that fear is indigenous to the Depression generation—that he wouldn't be able to afford all the things he wanted to give me, and he wanted to give me everything he'd never had. So they never had another child.

They were hard-working, thrifty people. My Mama was always trying to figure out how to make a little more money. Not that they were going to spend it on anything; any money we had either went into savings or toward necessities.

My parents never wanted me to have to work as hard as they did. But that was all I ever saw them do, and the message I got was that the only thing of any real value in life is hard work.

It's strange the way things work out.

Mama never wanted me to be frivolous. I always had chores and she always had things for me to do. There were rules, and I was to be responsible. If I went to play with somebody in the neighborhood I could never stay longer than an hour. If I wasn't home by then, Mama would come after me. It always seemed like you just got started playing and you had to go home.

The wallpaper in my bedroom was full of bouquets. If you squinted your eyes just right you could make these little bouquets march at an angle up and down the wall. If you pinched your eyes on each side you could make a triangle of bouquets. I remember trying to concoct that triangle and then trying to make those little bouquets march in and out of it.

The living room was a mystery. It was always dark in there. Mama had gone to Itasca, where they had a big mill, and bought yards and yards of gauzy fabric and made these really elaborate draperies which I thought were terribly exotic. There was a mohair couch and a mohair chair to match, and a coffee table. That coffee table was probably a late addition, but I feel sure we were the only people in Lakeview who had one. I was always puzzled why it would be called a coffee table; no one would ever dare put a cup of coffee on it.

About the only time anybody ever went in the living room was at Christmas or for a meeting of the Home Demonstration Club.

The Home Demonstration Club meeting was an event. Through the extension services of Texas A&M, there was a program in which an agent, usually a woman, would travel around rural communities and teach people how to do things: how to can, how to preserve food, how to quilt. I mean, there wasn't anywhere to go, and everyone would gather and sit around and wear their nicest clothes and listen to the Home Demonstration Lady tell them what new innovative thing was taking place in homemaking.

Mama had an ivy plant that she had trained, maybe tacked it up with some carpet tacks, so it snaked around and covered the whole wall of the porch like a maze. Probably the Home Demonstration Lady taught Mama that milk would make your ivy leaves shine, because one of my jobs was to polish the leaves of that ivy plant with milk. Every dusty leaf on that whole wall needed me and my bottle of milk's particular attention. Oh, I hated to do that job. I thought, "Who cares if those ivy leaves are dusty?!" Lord knows, I didn't.

When pressure cookers came out, we got one. They took a lot of the time out of cooking and made life a tiny bit simpler. There was a little black rubber release valve on the top of the cooker, about the size of a dime. Well, one afternoon I guess my Mama had put on a pot of beans and walked over to the hen-house, when World War II came to our door.

They had built an Army Air Force base right near our little town and there was a lot of talk at school about the wisdom of living near something like that; we were all virtually certain that we were prime targets of the Japanese. Lakeview was in the bombsights and there was a tremendous explosion in our kitchen.

I was absolutely terrified. The Japanese were right overhead! It sounded like Iwo Jima!

What had happened was that the release valve to the pressure cooker had blown off like a mortar and these hard little beans began to blow out of the hole rapidfire and hit the kitchen ceiling.

Well, I didn't know that. I knew we were under attack, the Japanese had found us at last. I ran to the one place in our house that was sanctuary, the place not even the Japanese would dare enter: the living room. I ran in there, hid behind that mohair chair, and wet my pants!

The Home Demonstration Club didn't always bring disaster. They taught sewing and brought patterns. My mother was a skilled seamstress; she made all my clothes. A lot of us wore dresses made out of feed sacks, and in the really old days they said Bewley Mills on them, which was a big flour mill. Everything came in sacks—flour, sugar, feed—so we'd get fed and get a wardrobe at the same time. Then the fabric manufacturers got smart and started making feed sacks with designs on them, little flowers and such.

I always got to play the lead roles in the school plays, or be leader of the rhythm band, because my mother would make the costumes for me. There weren't many women who knew how to do that. I liked stepping out in front, and Mama would buy me the boots with the tassels hanging on the front. No telling how dear those boots were, but she got them.

The Home Demonstration Club was for the women. The men had their own circle. My Daddy, along with our neighbors Boots Douglas and Aubrey Rogers, built what they called a pavilion. I guess we would call it a gazebo today, but to them it was The Pavilion. It had wooden sides about four or five feet high and was screened in above that, and it was just big enough for a domino table. Somewhere Daddy had picked up a slab of marble and they built some kind of base for it, but truthfully I suspect that the games went on out there because there was not a room in anybody's house that was big enough to play dominoes. (They could have played it on our dining room table, but that was re-served for much more special occasions.)

The men used to sit in the Pavilion and play dominoes and the women would sit around and talk. I was supposed to go to bed, but there was kind of a porch off the kitchen that looked out over the back yard to the Pavilion and I can remember sneak-ing out of bed and going and listening to the stories being told and all the men laughing.

My Daddy was then and is now a great storyteller. He was six feet four and a handsome man, and he'd tell these bawdy, raunchy tales. But they were always so funny because of the way Daddy would tell them—he was so gleeful about it! He was so excited when he had a new story to tell. When he started he would back up, like he needed plenty of room to laugh, and he would do this little yarn-spinning dance, take two or three steps backward as he would get into the telling, and as he came to the punchline he would bend over and just laugh all over you. Well, even if the story wasn't funny you would laugh because Daddy's laugh was so infectious.

A lot of things we did for fun were in dead earnest, to get food. If we took an outing and went fishing, it wasn't some kind of sport. You were out there getting fish—to eat. We would set trotlines from one side of the river to the other; at various points we would put a line and hook in place along it, bait the hook, and pray that some big old catfish would come along and like whatever we'd offered.

My Daddy used blood bait. You might be able to buy it at a bait stand, but I can't imagine Daddy buying anything that cost any money. More likely he got it somewhere where they slaughtered animals. Blood bait was just coagulated blood; felt like Jell-O, and the greatest honor in the world would be when my Daddy said, "Hand me a pinch of that blood bait." It was like being cabin boy to the captain of a ship.

You try to run trotlines late at night before you go to bed, and it was always eerie and mysterious. It was dark by the river and you'd have to carry a lantern in the boat as you paddled along the line, pulling the hooks out of the water one by one to bait them. We were forever spooked about snakes. Water moccasins. I don't know whether we thought they were going to jump up into the boat or what, but it was real quiet down there and we were mighty careful.

Snake stories abounded. Once we were staying at a cabin on the Bosque River owned by a family named Whicker, and I was admiring their ingenuity. They had wrapped what looked like a snakeskin around an electric wire and it sure did make a striking impression above the door. I reached up to scratch it and the thing crawled off. Scared the squat out of me.

We went hunting and sometimes we had hunting dogs. There are probably a million hunting-dog stories about how "We had that ol' dog in the back of the truck, and somehow we drove up to the gas station and the dog wasn't in there, and there we were 175 miles from home. And we got home and three days later . . . here comes ol' Rosie." Well, we had one of those stories about one of Daddy's dogs.

If we got an opportunity to go on somebody's deer lease or somebody's farm and kill a deer—that was absolutely wonderful. You could make sausage out of it, you could cure the whole thing and eat for months. It was a great treat.

I loved to go visit my mother's family in Hico. It would be summertime and I would get to ride the Dinky. The Dinky was a small train with an engine that had four or five black and white stripes on it. Chevrons. Looked like a locomotive with four or five mustaches. Some of the boys used to put pennies on the track, that was a big deal. We used to run behind the Dinky and yell, "Freezie, Freezie!" The story was that an engineer would throw used flares to you if you did that, but he never did.

My mother's sisters, my aunts Elta and Oleta, lived in Hico, and they just loved me to death. I don't believe I've been anywhere in my life where I've felt so loved as I did when I was in Hico.

My grandmother and granddaddy loved me too. Granddaddy was a big, big man, somewhere around 250 pounds. They lived out in the country and didn't have electricity until they were in their early seventies, but this was well before then.

My granddaddy was a tough taskmaster; the men were in his time. He would whip those kids with a razor strop and they were afraid of him. He was also a drinker. One time I found all his empty whiskey bottles out in the barn and broke every last one of them. I don't know why. Hico was dry, and if you got anything to drink it wasn't easy to come by.

But my granddaddy was wonderful to me. He could tell stories endlessly, and the kids would just sit around him in rapture. He would tell stories about this critter that came through the country and would kill every farm animal on your place. And this critter, he'd tell us, only left one track. Now that takes some thinking about, right? Nobody's seen it, nobody ever caught it, but they would wake up one morning and all the hogs, all the cows, everything in the barnyard would be stone dead. And this critter just left one track.

My granddaddy let it be known that this critter was still out there on the loose. And, he said, we never know when it will break out and start eating children too.

There was a woman who had a place on the other side of my granddaddy's and he told us that she was so fancy that she had a fan in her outhouse. It wasn't inside the outhouse, it was behind the house—so when she sat down on that hole there would be this cool, cool breeze blowing on her!

And, of course, we'd believe everything he said.

Grandmama and Granddaddy had a storm cellar, just a mound of dirt with a vent pipe stuck in it and a door on it. They had just gone underground and hollowed out a hole, put some stone pavers down on the dirt to form steps going down into it, built some shelves and had themselves a cooling house. They kept smoked meats and canned goods down there.

There was nothing worse than being sent to the storm cellar. You'd be told to go out there and get a jar of peaches or something, and you didn't really want to go. It smelled like a cavern, that musty, mildewy underground smell like you yourself were about to be planted.

And just as you'd get to the door my granddaddy would holler, "Watch out for snakes!" Never failed.

I always thought my grandmama was frail, but she must have been as hardy as an ox. She was all the time cooking for everyone. There were always hot biscuits, two or three different kinds of vegetables, collards and beans; it was always a spread.

The men ate first. Coming in from the fields, definitely, but even if it was a special occasion. We would drive up on Christmas Day and when it came time for the chicken dinner, the men always ate first and the women served. And then, after the men were finished, the women and children ate. But, of course, by the time the men got through there wasn't anything left but wings and necks and gizzards. It would not have occurred to anyone to do anything differently, or to leave something over. The men would eat just what they wanted to eat. And it certainly would not have occurred to the women that it should be done any other way.

Another reason for going to Hico in the summer was for very serious business: I had to get a permanent.

My hair has always been a source of some embarrassment. My Daddy's mother, who I called Nanny, had real thin hair and so did my Daddy's sisters. My Mama had thick, wavy, naturally curly hair, really nice hair. I was a very thin, skinny, scrawny child with thin, skinny, scrawny hair, and Mama always said I had "Willis hair." So in the summer I would go to Hico and a woman named Carmen would give me a permanent.

It probably cost three dollars, and it was one of those big machines where you sat under it and they put these rollers in your head and poured all this crimping solution on it, and then they hooked you up to these heated covers that fit over the rollers and were connected to electrical wires that ran up into a central unit.

It would kind of burn my hair into a squiggly nest and I'd have to live with it. My modified Willis hair would be very tight and unattractive for the first month or two, and then just sort of hang limp the rest of the time. Mama would roll my hair up so that it would "look nice," and then put a hair net on it— not one of those real-hair hair nets like old ladies wear, but one of those heavy hair nets—and then send me off to school.

The net was to keep the hair nice, but no one could see my hair under it. I decided that was foolish. I would take it off before I got to school and put it back on when I was walking down the road on the way home.

When Toni home permanents came out, that was a great breakthrough. Mama said no self-respecting woman would have straight hair once they'd invented Toni home permanents.

I WAS ALWAYS taking lessons. Whatever it was they had to offer, Mama wanted to make sure I took it. If she had anything to say about it, I was going to learn something else besides hard work. I would ride five miles on my bicycle over to Mrs. Glenn's house for piano lessons, and there was a woman who would drive out from Waco to our schoolhouse and teach Expression.

Expression meant you had to memorize some little ditties and poems and then get up and say them at a recital. I was really good at that. I would cut out stories from whatever I could find and paste them in my little book, and then at recital I would shine. I was nothing but a little-bitty first-grader but I was taught early to stand up and say my piece.

My best friend was a girl named Regina Garrett. She had bright red hair and everybody called her Rusty. She was real cute and short and, I thought, popular. I was always kind of weeny, wimpy, and skinny. Mama would follow me around with cod liver oil and everything else in the world, trying to get me to eat.

Lakeview had one paved road. Everybody's mailbox stood on it, but the road to each house was dirt. When Rusty and I would go see each other and play I was allowed to walk only as far as our mailbox with her, then I'd have to turn for home. At my road she and I would walk backwards, waving to each other until we got out of sight.

Across the road from our house was an open field with some oaks, but what I remember best are the chinaberry trees. There was a big one in our backyard. Chinaberry trees are short-lived and brittle; the limbs fall off in the rain. But they bloom a beautiful cluster of amethyst-colored blossoms with a sweet, sweet smell to them. In spring and summer the trees are full of bees, and the smell of chinaberry is everywhere. The blossoms turn into little hard round green berries, which then fall off and turn into squishy yellow berries. We had regular chinaberry wars and chucked the berries at each other.

My other friend was Virginia Lynn Douglas. Virginia Lynn lived across the street from me in her parents' house, which was right next door to her grandmama's and granddaddy's house. I think the Douglases had less money than we did.

They were always reading at the Douglases'. They had all the Nancy Drew books. Virginia Lynn had read the Bible, and her father, Boots, gave her a dollar when she did. I thought that was really remarkable, first that she could read it and second that he would give her a dollar to do it. I had one book growing up: *Heidi*. It's an okay book, but it's not the whole literary world.

Daddy read the *Saturday Evening Post* and the newspaper, and I would borrow books from Virginia Lynn, but growing up reading makes a lot of difference in the appetite you have for it.

Mama was a little impatient when I wanted to read. I think she thought it was a good thing to do in the abstract, but that when it got right down to it, really, it took you away from your work if you were just reading a book. Perhaps it was the denial of books then that makes me such an avid reader now.

I was always the youngest in my class at school. All twelve grades were in one building and I never had more than fifteen kids in my whole grade. My folks didn't really care about my grades—scholarship was not something that mattered all that much to them—but they wanted me to go to college and get an education "just in case."

There wasn't much doing in school. It was just school. I talked out in class a lot and probably drove everybody crazy. I remember more times than once hearing, "Dorothy Ann, if you don't quit talking . . ." (My name was Dorothy Ann Willis. I dropped the Dorothy in high school.)

I loved the plays at school and I wanted to be in every one. I could never carry a tune, so I couldn't be in any of the musicals, and I remember one time we put on a show about Texas history and there were three or four kids who got to dress up like cowboys and sit around the red cellophane fake fire and sing "Cool Water." I wasn't one of them and I was so envious.

The PTA had raised a considerable amount of money to put an intercom system into the school building, the idea being to open each school day with the news of the moment and a prayer. But it was also used for other purposes. Kids were forever getting into trouble, as kids will, and the principal, Mr. Grady Moore, had the brilliant idea to begin Radio Discipline. When a boy needed to be reprimanded for some form of unacceptable be-

havior, Mr. Moore would flip the PA switch in the principal's office and say, "The voice you are about to hear is Charles
Goodall." Everybody in the school would listen and, after a rap
with a ruler, this poor kid would begin to holler.

I don't quite know how it happened, but my Daddy became a member of the school board and created quite a stir. It
seems that a fourth-grade teacher, Mrs. Julian, became pregnant and many members of the board weren't going to let her
continue at her job because it wouldn't be seemly for anyone
who "showed" to teach school to the community's impres-
sionable children.

My father got up and said that that was the most
ridiculous thing he'd ever heard. This woman was married to a
man who was in the service, and she was literally depending
on that income for her livelihood. My Daddy was never a fire-
brand progressive—far from it—but that was pretty amazing.
And the board listened to him. He saved her job and she taught
school that year.

THE CHURCH WAS the center of all religious and social happen-
ings in Lakeview. There was a Baptist church in town and a
Church of Christ, but we were Methodists.

It was nothing romantic—no stained glass, no artifacts,
no relics. Not even Sheetrock. Just whitewashed boards all around
and a bare elevated pulpit. There was a low railing up in front,
and when you joined the church, or when you were called to
Jesus, you would walk up the center aisle to that wood railing.

This was a very poor church. The most valuable item that
church owned was a Shirley Temple cup. It was smoky blue glass-

ware and had Shirley Temple's face and her signature in white across the front of it. That's what they used to baptize you with. Later on, a man with some woodworking skills joined the church and he made a pedestal and a wooden bowl for that purpose, much more uptown-looking, but for the longest time you were introduced to the Lord by Shirley Temple.

It was quiet inside and the floorboards creaked when you walked on them each Sunday. A wooden plaque with removable numbers hung on the wall, telling the number of people in attendance at Sunday school that Sunday, the total number of community church members, and how many people had showed up for church the week before. There weren't many, maybe sixty.

If you went to Sunday school religiously every Sunday you got a sheep to paste on your Jesus picture.

We each had this 8 x 10 picture portrait of Jesus sitting on a stone in the middle of a meadow. One by one you could paste these little sheep on it, and I thought that was wonderful. I wanted the whole flock.

On special occasions there would be a covered-dish event held on the grounds outside the church. We saw this more as getting together with your neighbors than getting next to the Almighty, although I suspect the gatherings were organized to increase interest in the church. I remember my Mama and I cooked a lot of stuff and took it places. There was no such thing as going to someone's house for dinner; people didn't do that. Either you went to an event or you went on a picnic where everybody brought something.

I could never sing in front of people in school, but I could sing with everybody else in the choir and I had a great time at it.

My friend Regina and I used to sit in church and play this

game, "Between the Sheets." I'm sure this was after we got much older and more sophisticated—about ten or eleven. We would read the titles of the hymns and then say, "between the sheets."

"Just as I Am" ("between the sheets").

"Love Lifted Me" ("between the sheets").

And, of course, we'd get real tickled and sit there in church and snicker.

At that time, the preachers who were sent to those little country churches were either older men who had been rejected somewhere else or young men just out of theology seminary and just learning. We got this minister, I think his name was Reverend Craig, and he was into the Holy Ghost. He would preach hellfire and damnation and he would jingle the coins or keys in his pocket, and he got it going pretty good.

There were two sisters in the congregation, the Freeman girls, who were always seized with the Holy Spirit. (That's country language, "the Freeman girls." If people ask about them it would always be "Now let me see, the Freeman girls. Didn't one of them marry the Jones boy?" I was "that Willis girl.")

The Freeman girls' eyes would roll back in their heads and they would get real stiff, they would fall down on the floor and their tongues would hang out of their mouths and they would moan and carry on, and it was really awesome. I'd sit there and watch them, and so would everyone else. The Sunday service became a real show and these two women were monopolizing it.

My Daddy was on the church's board of stewards, and he was extremely impatient with this kind of carrying on. It's one thing to bring people to the light, it's quite another to daze them with it. Daddy thought that this guy was just going a little too far.

There was a big blowout over it. Part of the community was offended by the holy rolling, another part by my Daddy. My Daddy got offended by the whole thing; he resigned from the board and never went back to church. Mama and I went, but Daddy stayed away.

There were lots of events that went on at the church. They may have had Home Demonstration meetings there too. There was always an Easter egg hunt. One year it was held in the lot to the side of the church and all the congregation's children were there.

The prize egg that year, not just any colored egg but the one that if you found it would make you the year's real winner, was made out of crystallized sugar. They showed it around before they hid it and you could look in a little hole at one end and see all kinds of little colors and patterns inside. I wanted it real bad. The elders hid the eggs while we all shuffled and shifted in our Easter finery, and then they let the kids loose.

Where could that egg be? I wasn't much interested in any of the others, I wanted that crystalline sugar egg.

I saw it! Partly hidden halfway up a window ledge, it was perched for the taking. No one else saw it but me! I didn't think of slowly ambling over and picking it off. I made a run for it.

I was running across the church yard when one of the mothers looked at me, looked at my destination . . . and spotted the egg. She called her daughter's name and pointed. The little girl started shouting. She was screaming. "There it is! There it is! I see the Easter egg. I've got it! It's mine!"

Everybody turned around. First they heard her screaming, then they saw me running.

She got the egg.

I clawed and cried and pitched such an almighty fit that my Mama had to take me home. The unfairness of it! I saw it first. Mothers aren't even supposed to be there; it's not their Easter egg hunt, it's ours. That girl never even touched it. She would never have seen it if I hadn't seen it first. She knew that. Her mother knew that. But neither of them said a word. They just took my crystallized sugar egg. I was shouting and struggling and gulping for air all the way home. I believe that was the first time I was really made to see that life is not necessarily fair, that honor does not always triumph, not even in church, and that I shouldn't expect it to.

I HAD SCHOOL shoes, but I only wore them in school. You always took your shoes off, and you didn't have to wait until you got home to do it, because the more you wore them the more you wore them out. The roads in Lakeview were like hot dust in the summer and the first few days you'd be moving around real quick, but after the first couple of weeks your feet would toughen up so you could take it.

I did a lot of walking around barefoot. Well, actually, I can't remember ever walking; I ran everywhere. I fell down a lot; my knees and shins were always scabby. My Daddy said I was a perpetual motion machine, always squirming around like a worm in hot ashes.

I hated naps. Hated them. When I was too young for school, or during the summers, my Mama would make me go in and lie down for a while. I don't know whether she wanted to take a nap herself, or if she was worried that I'd just go *boing* one day like a broken spring, but she did build this midday nap into my routine. I would lie there just as long as I could with my eyes open, determined not to blink because if I blinked I might go out. It seemed like such a waste of time.

But I *was* always getting into something. Rusty and I used to smoke cedar bark. You take the bark from a cedar post, strip it, crumble it, shred it, and roll it up in paper. If you could get ciga- rette paper, that was very exotic; I don't ever remember having any. No, these were stogie-sized operations. The major problem was sneaking the matches to be able to light these things. One time when we did, Rusty and I built a little fire up near Rusty's house and we set the woods on fire. We had to call her granny to come put it out.

I climbed trees. When *Superwoman* comics came out I really believed that I could be her. I got on the roof of the garage with a rope—a magic lariat—and jumped off. I believed I could do anything, and my father encouraged me to believe it. Mama did too, with the caveat that you just had to work at it.

And when you work at it, she told me, you have to do the job right. If I had a chore or task and I didn't do it perfectly, I had to go back and do it again.

Oh, how I hated that. When I shined those ivy leaves, if I missed some I had to go back and do it *all* over again. If I missed a little crumb clinging to the side of the skillet I had to go back and rewash the whole skillet. When I learned to iron, if I didn't iron a blouse right I had to sprinkle it down and go back and iron it again. Mama taught me to sew, and if the stripes didn't match exactly on a seam, well then you had to tear it out and sew it over. It had to be quality or it really wasn't worth anything. You had to be sure that you did it right, and did it right the first time—because that would eat into whatever time you had to play.

I don't want to paint a portrait here that I was some poor little kid who worked all the time. There probably was no child in the world more loved than I was. Mama and Daddy expected something of me, they just didn't know quite what.

THERE WASN'T A whole lot going on around my house. We had a telephone, but there weren't a great number of places to call. And besides, it was a party line; you never knew who might be listening in. One of our neighbors was Miss Lucas, who was known as "Telephone, Telegraph, Tell-A-Lucas," because anything Miss Lucas picked up you could be sure the whole community was going to know.

Up the road a ways there was a man who bred and raised greyhounds. Of course, betting was against the law in Texas, but there were these backwoods events where they would race these dogs, and it was pretty big-time stuff. Dogs are important in Texas.

My Mama hated those greyhounds. They would come down and suck her eggs.

Those dogs would break into her henhouse. First she'd have to worry about them killing the chickens, but if they didn't do that, then they would bite the end out of all the eggs and suck the whites and yolks out of them.

That's right, exactly. People think those expressions are made up. Egg-sucking dogs.

One time when those dogs got into the henhouse, Mama and I scalded those chickens in the washing machine. If you get to the birds quickly enough you can still eat them, and we didn't have enough food to be throwing away chickens. Mama usually scalded them one at a time in an iron pot and then plucked them, but this one time I swear she ran the hot water and threw the whole mess of them into the washer.

IF MY MAMA and Daddy didn't put a lot of stock in scholarship, they greatly valued personality. I was always encouraged to perform, not just by my folks but by the Whickers and the Rogerses, people who were our friends in the neighborhood. I learned early on that people liked you if you told stories, if you made them laugh. People loved my Daddy.

I was nine years old the first time I saw my father cry. World War II had been claiming the local men—a lot of Lakeview's boys were going away and not coming home—and Daddy got drafted into the Navy. Townspeople hung little stars in their windows to serve notice that they had a child in the service, but I was virtually untouched by all that, with the exception of being afraid of the Japanese bombing us. But the night before he left, we were in the back room and my father hugged me and broke down and cried. We were not a touching family, we didn't do a lot of embracing, so I remember the moment when he reached for me as if it were this morning.

Daddy was thirty-five when he was drafted. A month later they stopped drafting men with children. He went through boot camp and pharmaceutical school, and was stationed in San Diego. Mama and I were on our own but she was a resourceful woman. Even before Daddy got drafted she had gone to comptometer school at 4C Business College so that when he did have to go into the military she would have a skill and a way to earn some money.

Mama was a real worker. She got a job at Southwestern Drug, where Daddy had worked, in what was called the sample room, which was glorious. It was filled with toasters and music boxes and toys and all the things people bought as gifts at drugstores, and we could buy things wholesale.

I don't remember too much about the time without Daddy, not even how long it was. I do remember that at some point we moved out to be with him.

We drove.

This was a big adventure, not the kind of thing a woman was supposed to do with any degree of safety or sanity. Mama killed all the chickens and canned them because she knew that things were going to cost a lot in San Diego. We filled the car with canned goods and all of our belongings, strapped Mama's sewing machine into the trunk, gathered a second cousin, Fannabee Fryer, and lit out for California.

Daddy says when we got there we looked like the Joads, straight out of The Grapes of Wrath.

It was wartime and housing in San Diego was so scarce that we lived in one room underneath someone's house. I slept on a cot and the place was so small I had to get up so that Daddy could get out the door in the morning.

Eventually we found an apartment. My parents were scandalized at the thirty dollars a month we had to pay, and my Daddy didn't live there all the time. He lived at the naval base during the week and would come home on the weekends.

There was no demand for my Mama's comptometer skills, and we needed money. I hand-lettered a sign that said "Alterations and Dressmaking," and we put it in front of our apartment at the corner of Avenue A and Hawthorne, and Mama started taking in sewing.

My mother got very sick in California. She had an ectopic pregnancy and was bleeding a lot. The doctors kept telling her that she was going through an early change of life, but later they had to rush her to the hospital. I didn't understand any of this at the time; all I knew was that when she came home she was in bed for a while and I had to be careful, I could upset Mama easily.

But living in San Diego was like looking through binoculars for me. I had grown up in this tiny, tiny place and suddenly the world just opened up. I ate my first doughnut.

I had never seen a doughnut. There were no doughnut shops in Lakeview, and not one deep-fat fryer. Mama baked pies and cakes and biscuits and bread, but doughnuts were a whole new heaven. Doughnut holes especially; I thought they were the greatest things in the world and they cost about three cents.

Mama would send me to this grocery store half a block down the street, which was another shock. Remember, we grew almost everything we ate in Lakeview and all of a sudden we had a grocery store nearby. I would get whatever it was she sent me for and I would take three pennies out of her purse and buy a doughnut hole. I had to gobble down the whole thing before I got home so she wouldn't know I'd done it.

I went to school at Theodore Roosevelt Junior High School, way across town. I'd walk about a block to the bus stop and ride the bus to central San Diego, then change and catch a streetcar that would take me to school. The streetcar went across a high trestle through Balboa Park and you could see a long way down either side and it seemed like a forest.

I thought my school was really pretty. Spanish architecture, tile roofs—it looked like something out of the movies. It was nothing like Lakeview. Neither were my classmates.

This was my first exposure to kids who were Italian and Greek and black and Hispanic. It was a real eye-opener. I can still remember some of their names; Helen Castenada, Josephine Giacalone.

Occasionally I would go to their houses, but it was rare. This was not a neighborhood school; kids came from all over San Diego, and my folks were probably justifiably concerned about me getting around in a big city. I was all of eleven years old and this was a city full of thousands of young sailors and Marines, and God knows they must be wild, or I guess that's what my parents thought.

Going to California at that time was like going to a foreign country. There were kids of different colors who came from different backgrounds but who were just like me. I was never able to understand racial prejudice after that.

There were no blacks living in Lakeview and you'd only see a black person once in a while; they'd come by the house and offer to do day labor, but they didn't live anywhere nearby. There were blacks in Waco, but they lived in East Waco. They had their own high school; there was never any mixing. You would see black people in Waco down on the square.

There was racial prejudice everywhere when I was growing up. Texas was a totally segregated state. About the only black person I met before I went to California was a man named Smoke Munson who worked with my Daddy at Southwestern Drug. The company had a picnic every year and they barbecued vast quantities of chicken and beef, and my Daddy and Smoke Munson did most of the barbecuing. When I would visit Daddy at the loading dock where he and Smoke worked, Smoke would lift me up and they would put me on the scale where they weighed packages, and he would brag about how big I was. My Daddy would always laugh with him and I had the sense that they were great friends.

But there was no question that the general attitude was that blacks were inferior to whites. Blacks, of course, had been forced so long into the most menial, low-paying, low-skilled jobs. Black women rarely had an opportunity to work at anything but cleaning or washing and ironing. In Texas and all over the South, that's the way things worked.

I can remember hearing the expression, "He's a good nigger." Or, "He's one Jew that will give you the shirt off his back," meaning unlike the others. Prejudice is rarely individual, it's always universal. Smoke Munson was a wonderful man, but unfortunately he would have been described as "the exception that proved the rule."

It all stemmed from ignorance, unfamiliarity, and a need to feel superior at the expense of others. It's an unthinking, unreasoned emotional reaction: "I must be okay because there is another whole group of people that I consider inferior to me." Prejudice is such a strange and pathetic form of elevating oneself.

Eleanor Roosevelt came to the Naval Hospital while we were in San Diego and refused to allow her photograph to be made unless there was a "colored man" in the picture. Well, that occupied a lot of conversation, let me tell you. I thought she was bold and exciting. She must have been a remarkable woman.

THE WAR ENDED, and after twenty-two months in the service my Daddy was discharged and we went back to Texas.

I played basketball for the Lakeview Bulldogs. In rural, small-town Texas the competition between schools is really intense. There is very little in terms of entertainment and things that kids can do, so these sports events are a very big thing. I was always so skinny and scrawny that I was not much of a basketball player, but I did get to play. It was particularly ludicrous because a lot of who we played against were these big old strong country girls. I mean, they were stout.

In those days, girls were not allowed to play full court. You either played offense or defense, you weren't allowed to cross the mid-court line, and you weren't allowed to dribble the ball more than three times in a row. The game, like our lives, was pretty restricted.

We had these little uniforms which our parents had saved up dearly to buy for us, and I thought I looked pretty good. There was a boy I knew who went to school at Ross, a little town up near West, Texas, and Abbot (Willie Nelson's hometown), and I knew he was at the game. I had a free throw coming, and just as I was about to take my shot this voice boomed out from high in the bleachers. It was that boy from Ross, and he hollered really loud and clear, "Make that basket, birdlegs!"

I really do feel that most people see themselves pretty much as they did when they were very young. Whatever the world thought of them when they were young kids, they pretty much think of themselves that way now. I certainly do. In my mind's eye I'm probably still that skinny kid trying to make that basket.

I graduated from Lakeview in whatever fashion one graduates from junior high, and, because Mama and Daddy felt that I needed to have a first-class education, we moved into Waco. It must also have been that after they had gone to California, their world had opened up too.

We rented a very small place out on Beverly Drive and Mama began the business of building us a house.

Mama and Mr. Whicker drew up plans for her dream house, she and Daddy bought a parcel of land on North 35th Street, and she started putting it up.

A house costs money, and I'm sure Mama had saved it from every single thing she and Daddy ever did. I mean, it was Waste not, want not, Wear it out and wear it again. She had been putting aside money from Daddy's wages and her sewing. In Waco Daddy had gone back to Southwestern Drug and progressed from delivery driver to salesman, and was probably one of their best.

And I promise you that Mama built that house for half what it would have cost anyone else. She would drive down to the unemployment office, or to the square where the men were hanging out, and she'd name a price and say, "Do you want to work?" Then she would take a carload of men out to the job site.

That house was no small deal. It had two bedrooms at one end, then a den with a fireplace, a living room with another fireplace and a big picture window, a formal dining room, a kitchen, and what was called a breezeway connecting to a double garage with an Austin stone exterior and a big cement patio in the back with a barbecue pit that Daddy used every weekend. It was really a remarkable undertaking.

Somewhere Mama had found a houseful of accessories—mantels and doors, copper doorknobs and door plates, and all kinds of things from some old house—and I spent hours cleaning them before they were installed in our new house. Mama did a lot of the painting herself.

I spent a lot of time alone that year, more time than I was accustomed to, while she was building that house. I would come home from school and she would not be there, and when she and Daddy would come home they'd both be real tired.

As Mama started her house, I started at Waco High School. I was determined to be a new person.

I wanted to be "somebody," and high school was that new beginning where I could prove somehow that I was worth something and that people should like me. Mama and Daddy had high expectations, but exactly what they were neither they nor I knew. I just knew that my standards were way beyond me. Way beyond me. It seems like I was scared all the time.

I guess that I felt that the old me was kind of pathetic and inadequate. I was always afraid I wasn't measuring up. I never thought I was smart enough, I knew I wasn't pretty enough, and whenever I succeeded I thought it was a mistake. When you live like that, you always feel like you're faking it; like sooner or later they will all catch on and that will be the end of you.

The first thing I did was change my name. Dorothy Ann Willis, to me, meant a kind of country girl who couldn't compete in this new big-city sophisticated milieu. I dropped my first name and registered as Ann. And I did not tell my parents that I was going to do it.

My first day, all the freshmen were in study hall going through orientation and I walked around and introduced myself to all these total strangers. No one else did it; it must have been perfectly ridiculous. Rusty had moved to Waco and she was there that morning. I went up to her and laughingly said, "Hi, I'm Ann Willis." She looked up at me and said icily, "How old did you say you are?" It laid me to waste.

Mama was pleased that I was going to Waco High School for another reason: she hoped I would get to know a group of kids who weren't poor. I don't think she cared about me being rich, she just cared about me not being poor. In Lakeview we had probably been as well off as anybody in the community. But in Waco we were definitely not as well off as a lot of the kids with whom I went to high school.

I never thought of us as poor, but in high school I became much more aware of what it took to provide all the accouterments of a higher level of living. Waco was very much a traditional Southern city in terms of its societal structure; there were definitely the Haves and the Have Nots. I'll never forget the first cashmere sweaters I owned. We bought most clothes on sale and then would put them up for next year; we would put a down payment on them and then Mama would pay them out.

Mama knew what I ought to wear. She was still sewing most of my clothes. Most of the other kids had store-bought clothes, but I never minded wearing what Mama made; she made beautiful clothes.

IN HIGH SCHOOL we all had to take the Kuder Preference Test. It asked things like, "Would you rather watch a TV, fix a TV, or sell a TV?" and was supposed to direct you towards a likely profession. I always tested higher in careers with a predilection toward being with people. People skills. I don't think I ever placed any value in that, as if I did it well so it must not be worth much. That's what I carried around with me.

I wasn't much of a student. Anything that I was interested in I could do pretty well, but anything that didn't catch my fancy I simply let go. Math was really difficult for me. I think I nearly flunked trigonometry. But I loved my English classes and I did really well in speech. I liked any class where I got to talk a lot.

The new me always wanted to do everything. If somebody was going to call the roll, I wanted to do it. If somebody was going to pass the paper out, well, I wanted to do that. I had so much energy that sitting still was painful. Do not forget that you are dealing here with a worm in hot ashes.

The best thing that happened in my freshman year was Mattie Bess Coffield's speech class. The class was more than just speech, it was debate. I'm a logical thinker, and that is really what debating is all about. The verbal, oral expression is important, and that's what I did well. We debated both sides of an issue and I had to be sure what my thesis was and be able to make logical arguments for the side I was on.

In Miss Coffield's class I competed in extemporaneous speech, declamation, debate, and acted in one-act and three-act plays. I'd always been able to talk; now I was getting good grades for it.

I liked the idea of competing with other schools. And it was a good excuse to get out of class; if you were in interscholastic league competition you could always get a pink slip to go to Miss Coffield's room to work on something or other, or to the library and avoid whatever studying you were supposed to be doing.

It never occurred to me not to debate. I loved it. My Daddy encouraged me, and I believe it was the first thing I did where Mama really rewarded me. If I went to a speech tournament and we won, I would come home and Mama would cook macaroni and cheese, my favorite. It was her way of saying, "We are glad that you won, and you did a good job."

But debating wasn't the only thing I was introduced to my freshman year. I had my first date that winter.

I was probably fourteen and my parents wouldn't let me have dates. I was always younger than my classmates and I think Mama felt that I would "grow up too fast." Most kids began going to the show together in junior high school, and by ninth grade girls were wearing their boyfriend's ring on a chain. No girl who wanted to be popular was a freshman in high school before she had her first date. So I had a gap in that boyfriend/girlfriend period in which I just didn't learn the skills.

I was befriended by a girl named Janey Baker. Janey had a car. Her parents were divorced and she was allowed to do all kinds of things. I had been asked to a dance and Janey convinced my mother to let me go.

It was a DeMolay Dance (DeMolay is a junior group of the Masons) and I needed a formal dress in a hurry. My mother knew someone who had a dress that would fit me, so I borrowed the dress, got a pair of thong summer sandals, wore my Aunt Juanita's big fur coat—which was totally inappropriate for a fourteen-year-old girl to wear anywhere—and went to the ball.

Well, I didn't know how to dance. It was my first date, I was a nervous wreck, and the poor guy who asked me was not much better. And what made it worse was that we were double-dating with one of the most beautiful girls in the school.

I got in line for punch. Remember, I was going to be new and likable and popular . . . and I threw up all over the girl in front of me, my date, the borrowed dress, and the marble floor.

We loaded into the car to go home and the boy in the backseat lit up a cigarette. There was this terrible buildup of smoke and throw-up all over my clothes, and there was nowhere to hide. I felt certain that my life was over.

I HAD A friend I liked a lot whose name was J. B. Little. J. B. had grown up with the Haves, but he didn't have a car, so he was on the outer fringes of Waco High School society. I always felt behind the rest of the kids in knowing what I was supposed to do and how I was supposed to act.

I didn't understand or have any grasp of the fine art of flirtation. I only knew how to go straight to the heart of a thing. I said what I was thinking; I didn't have any tact. And tact is something you really need when you're a teenage girl. Some people are threatened by that kind of directness, but I figured if you're not going to tell people who you are and what you think, you've done them a disservice. They'll have bought a package of goods and they won't be sure what's in it. So I know in high school I must have been kind of goofy, kind of crazy, just willing to do or say anything. There was no Home Demonstration Lady to show me how to grow up as a teenager.

Mama talked to me a lot about how girls must be very, very careful about their reputations. There were some girls in my school, as in all other schools, who suffered from a "bad reputation"—most of them undeservedly. It's such a tough, vicious, mean time of life.

The social life of the Haves revolved around the Fish Pond Country Club. There was nothing grand about it, but it was the center of that world. My family didn't belong to a country club, but I was usually invited to go play cards by the swimming pool. I never looked like much in a bathing suit, too skinny, so I was never all that comfortable. But I'd go. There'd be the leading socialites—Leta Patton and Barbara Allen and sometimes Kay Coffelt. I'm sure Mama felt it was a big waste of time, but I'd be there at the big umbrella tables learning to play bridge and canasta and samba.

The Fish Pond was where they held all the high school dances, and by the time I was in the eleventh grade I got to go to most of those. There were Valentine's Day dances with construction paper hearts and red crepe paper swirls. All the boys would stand along one wall, and the boys who I wanted to ask me to dance, didn't. Either they didn't dance or they were too shy. I don't think I knew then that boys could be shy.

The band would play "Blue Moon," "Stardust," "Deep Purple." There was one boy named Frank Trapolina who danced with everyone. Frank was a deep dipper, and he was all over the floor. A show-off dancer. Dancing with him was an athletic experience; you'd come away with half the side of your face and head wet with perspiration.

A boy named Morris Warren invited me to dance one day and I came home excited. "Mama," I told my mother, "this darling boy has asked me out!" That was a big mistake. From then on Mama and Daddy wouldn't stop kidding me about that "darling boy." I took a lot of teasing at home about boyfriends. And there was a big thing in high school, if you were going with somebody he would walk you to class, carry your books, and hold your hand. I always felt a little uncomfortable when I had a boy walking me to class, as if everyone was looking at me and making fun.

This is not to tell you that I was some poor pitiful Pearl. I wasn't.

IF I DIDN'T want any attention holding hands in the corridor, I surely didn't mind people listening to me when I talked. My debating had attracted some notice and in eleventh grade I was chosen by the Waco High School counselor, Lulu Strickland, to represent Waco High at Girls State.

Girls State was an annual gathering sponsored by the Women's Auxiliary of the American Legion, in which two representatives from each Texas high school came to Austin for one full week and set up a mock government.

Girls State was run by Frances Goff, who had been in the WACs and was associated with M. D. Anderson Cancer Hospital. She gave her time to the program each summer. Elections were run, bills were passed, and for that week the girls got a taste of what government is really all about. Well, that was pretty thrilling stuff!

The young women at Girls State were supposed to be the cream of the crop. The first thing I did was go around and meet everybody, find out where they were from. I was fascinated. I lived in Central Texas; I didn't know much about the rest of the state. I think I had gone to San Antonio once when I was a kid, and Mama and Daddy had driven me to football games away from home, but this was the first time I had ever met girls from the Rio Grande Valley.

I was hardly even aware that South Texas existed, but they had a wonderful song called "My Valley Home" and I felt a real envy that there were so many girls from these small places and they knew each other's towns. It seemed like a really great kind of community.

Other people might have slipped into a corner and watched the proceedings before diving in, but it was my natural impulse to work the room. If you don't know people, you can't know things. People are my information source, they're the doorway to it all. Unless you are open to them they will never be open to you, you will live in a cocoon. I figured, if you don't meet everybody you won't be able to pick out the ones you choose to be with.

I don't think I was like a Labrador retriever, the kind that jumps up on your shoulders and plants a big wet lick across your face. But let us say that, at the least, I was very outgoing.

At Girls State you could nominate yourself for office. I ran for mayor of my town, then county judge of my county, and then state attorney general.

It was announced that I won! My natural inclination to meet and greet everybody had turned out well. I got to do all the folderol and ceremony of being sworn in. They had a reception for the officeholders at the governor's mansion and Lieutenant Governor Allan Shivers came through and shook hands with each of us. It was a real thrill.

Then I found out I'd lost.

It had been very close, and someone counting the ballots had read a four as a nine. I had actually come in second. I felt terrible for the real winner; I'd shaken hands with the lieutenant governor and gotten all the fun out of it, and she'd actually won the election.

Girls State was fascinating. A lot of elected officials came and spoke with us, such as John Ben Sheppard, who was then attorney general. I was electrified.

Why did I like all this government activity better than I liked anything else? I do not know, but I loved it. I loved it when the men came and explained what they did. It seemed when those men stood up there and talked about their jobs, and talked about serving people, that it must be the finest thing anyone could possibly do.

There wasn't the slightest thought, of course, that I might apply this to my future. Girls simply didn't do that. This was an exercise in learning, it was not an exercise in preparation for a career. That may have been in Frances Goff's mind, but it certainly was not in any of ours.

Even though no one told me, there were certain things that you knew, and the world knew, that women and girls couldn't do. Running the government was one of them. That didn't meant you didn't study or learn about it, it just meant that it didn't apply to you. Any group—blacks, Hispanics, Asians, females—knows that. You know what you're allowed to do and what you're not.

But I didn't consciously think in those terms, I was having such a good time. The following year I went back as a junior counselor, and two more years as a senior counselor.

At the end of the week, two girls were chosen by the counselors and Frances to go to Washington, D.C., to participate in Girls Nation. One of the girls chosen was Mary Garana, who had been elected governor. The other girl was me.

Girls Nation! Even getting there was a treat. We traveled—without a chaperone—by train. I got to sleep in the top bunk and we spent a lot of time staring out the window, watching the states we had only read about roll by. We went down to the dining car to eat dinner, and in those days the service on dining cars was first class. They brought us finger bowls and I had no idea what they were. I don't think I did anything dumb—I didn't drink out of it—but I was truly puzzled.

Girls Nation operated on the same principle as Girls State but on a larger scale. We were taken to the State Department and the Treasury, and met all sorts of dignitaries, including Georgia Neese Clark, Treasurer of the United States, who signed the dollar bills. I thought that was pretty impressive, especially since she was the only female I had seen in any of this business of government.

We went to the White House, into the Rose Garden, and shook hands with President Harry Truman.

Sometime during Girls Nation a group of us delegates were sitting together and had our picture taken. It wasn't any big deal; AP and UPI just had photographers there snapping away. When the photo appeared in the Waco paper it showed me sitting next to a black girl. That's the only thing anybody wanted to know when I came home. Not, How was Girls Nation? or What was it like to meet the president? No. The basic question boiled down to How did this thing happen? and How many black girls were up there? In Waco, young white girls didn't just sit around public places getting their pictures made with black girls. It unfortunately caused a real stir.

ESPINOSA

— — — —

The Expedition of 1709

IN THE NAME of the Most Blessed Trinity, God the Father, the Son, and the Holy Ghost. Here begins the diary of the expedition undertaken in the year 1709 by the Rev. Father Fray Antonio de Olivares, Apostolic Preacher, Commissary of the Holy Cross of Querétaro, accompanied by Father Fray Isidro de Espinosa, Apostolic Preacher and Missionary in charge of the Mission of San Juan Bautista on the Río Grande del Norte, and assisted by Captain Pedro de Aguirre, Commander of the Presidio of Río Grande del Norte and fourteen men from his

---

ESPINOSA was the official diarist of the Espinosa-Olivares-Aguirre Expedition of 1709. Our excerpt finds the expedition just north of the Rio Grande. The diary was translated in 1712 by Rev. Gabriel Tous, a "corresponding member of the commission."

company, agreeable to the orders issued by his Excellency the Duke of Albuquerque, Viceroy, Governor, and Captain General of New Spain, etc.

April 5th. Friday. After midday the whole expedition set out in search of the San Marcos River and after crossing the Río del Norte, which carried much less water than usual, stopped at a place called Cuervo Encampment. There were only [a few] pools of rain water which was brackish and somewhat salty. The expedition travelled this day four leagues.

April 6th. [Saturday.] We travelled on this day in an easterly direction across level ground and some mesquite groves. Here we found a dry arroyo in which there were clumps of oak trees. After crossing a small thicket of mesquites we went over a few low sandy hills covered with good pasture. We came to a small permanent spring where there is an abundance of haddock, catfish, and other fish which temporarily appeased our hunger. The expedition travelled this day eight leagues.

April 7th. Sunday. After we had built a bower of branches to celebrate the Holy Sacrifice of the Mass, a strong wind arose which prevented it, from fear of some irreverence. We continued our march through open country and crossed a small thicket of mesquites. We then descended to the arroyo of Caramanchel whose two branches were dry. There are many ash trees, elms and an abundance of alfalfa. From the arroyo to the Nueces River it is all level ground. The water of this river is fresh and clear. It has many ash trees, elms, and walnuts, and there is an abundance of Cocomecalt, a plant whose thorny nature might bear some relation to the writer's name. [Espinosa means thorny.] There are many fish of which we had some for dinner.

On this day we met three Indians of the Pacuasian nation who were out hunting mice. The other Indians, who made a thick smoke in the woods upon our arrival, did not show themselves again and were lost in the thickness of the woods along the bank. We travelled this day five leagues.

April 8th. Monday. We moved from said place and travelled over level ground for about a league to the east. We then travelled for two leagues through mesquite forest and thorny bushes and thistles, very difficult to cross although there was a path. We came to the crossing of the Nueces, where the abundance and pleasantness of the various trees like mulberries, elms, and oaks enlivened its banks. The river has plenty of good fresh water. After crossing many ravines, or small streams, and sparse mesquite woods we came to a dry arroyo filled with oaks. From here we went to stop on the Sarco River or, as the Indians call it, Río Frío. Here we found some Indians, two Xarames and a number of Pacuasians, about twenty in all. This day the expedition travelled seven leagues.

April 9th. Tuesday. We advanced through a small mesquite flat and over level ground towards the northeast and came to the Hondo River whose bed was filled with pools of water. Continuing through the day in the same direction we arrived at the arroyo of Capa, where there were many sabines, elms and evergreen-oaks, the fields being covered with flowers as in April. After ascending the arroyo for about two leagues to the north we stopped. On the way we hunted for turkeys, the expedition being supplied with meat by seven which were killed. We travelled this day nine leagues.

April 10th. Wednesday. Passing some small valleys filled with mesquite clumps and oak groves we came to the arroyo called Chiltipiquie, which was dry. We then crossed some plains, going about three leagues towards the east, and passed a few holm-oak groves in the same direction, until we came to the arroyo of the Robalos which had a few pools of water. The expedition travelled this day eight leagues.

April 11th. Thursday. We set out from the said place towards the east in search of the Medina River which we reached and crossed. On the opposite bank, in a clearing along the river, we found the ranchería of the Payayas who were not numerous. The river is bordered by walnuts, the daily food of the nations who live along the banks. Along the river are many green and white poplars, elms and a diversity of other trees which beautify it. Here we consulted and planned the route we were to follow in search of the San Marcos. We stopped at this place after travelling five leagues.

April 12th. Friday. We moved on to the east through a plain, and at a distance of three leagues, not far from the river, met some Payaya Indians. Later we met five others of the Pampoa tribe, who were going to the ranchería of the Payayas. Crossing the Medina a second time we continued in sight of it, until we arrived at the ranchería of the said Pampoas, where it was necessary to cross the river a third time, halting on the other bank. Here we inquired about the watering places in order to continue our journey. We took an Indian on horseback as guide, twelve Pampoas accompanying us on foot. We travelled this day five leagues.

April 13th. Saturday. We continued our course towards the east through some ravines filled with holm-oaks, mesquites and some white oaks, until we arrived at the arroyo of Leon, which had running water, and we crossed it about a gunshot from where General Gregorio Salinas crossed it some years before. We crossed a large plain in the same direction, and after going through a mesquite flat and some holm-oak groves we came to an irrigation ditch, bordered by many trees and with water enough to supply a town. It was full of taps or sluices of water, the earth being terraced. We named it San Pedro Spring (agua de San Pedro) and at a short distance we came to a luxuriant growth of trees, high walnuts, poplars, elms, and mulberries watered by a copious spring which rises near a populous ranchería of Indians of the tribes Siupan, Chaulaames and some of the Sijames, numbering in all about 500 persons, young and old. The river, which is formed by this spring, could supply not only a village but a city, which could easily be founded here because of the good ground and the many conveniences, and because of the shallowness of said river. This river not having been named by the Spaniards, we called it the river of San Antonio de Padua. Having distributed tobacco among all of them, we took four Indians to guide us from this ranchería, and after passing a forest of mesquite trees we came to an arroyo of briny water and stopped on the opposite bank. We travelled this day eight leagues.

April 14th. Sunday. The Holy Sacrifice of the Mass was celebrated in a bower. After Mass we went on towards the northeast in search of the River Guadalupe, and crossing over open country except for some mesquites, we came upon a branch of the Guadalupe River, having crossed a deep arroyo with large pools of water. Having heard of the other branch of this river, we set out in search of it going towards the northeast, and at times to the east, through a very dense forest of mesquite clumps and holm-oaks. We came out upon a few bare hills, and continued till we reached the other branch of the said river of Guadalupe. Its banks are very fertile and pleasant. Its waters are abundant, clear and good. On coming to the river, while going along its banks, a soldier's horse suddenly turned and the soldier was thrown into the water unintentionally. He came out drenched and shivering. Two others who went to his rescue also got a bath without intending it. Here there is an abundance of sabines, elms, poplars, willows and other trees. In the river there is a variety of fish that we relished, and alligators have been seen by the Spaniards. Wild turkeys, commonly called *guijolotes*, abound. While hunting them two shots were fired, one of which took effect in the hand of the fowler rather than on the game. We waited here for the Sanac Indians, who were to bring us news of the Tejas nation, whom we had summoned but they did not come. We stopped on the far bank of the said river, having travelled nine leagues.

April 15th. Monday. We left the said river to look for the San Marcos, travelling towards the northeast through some mesquite clumps. We made signal fires to attract the attention of those around. While going over plains and gentle hills we killed two turkeys which appeased our appetite. We soon arrived at the San Marcos. Having crossed right over the hills, we reached the river sooner than we had anticipated. The banks of the river are very pleasant, full of walnut trees, elms, black mulberry trees and very tall poplars. We travelled this day as far as the San Marcos River, six leagues.

April 16th. Tuesday. We crossed the San Marcos River very near its source, the crossing being two arquebus shots from where the river rises. Directing our course eastward through a forest of mesquite clumps and some elms we came, after a distance of about two leagues, to an arroyo with little water which we named San Raphael, Sovereign Prince, to whom we intrusted the success of our journey. This arroyo has many holm-oaks and some elms and is reached by leaving the crest of the hills. Beyond the arroyo mentioned we went on toward some low hills in the direction of the northeast, travelling sometimes to the east. In the center of a plain is a grove of holm-oaks, where there is a small spring of water, not far from said arroyo. After we passed the hills we came to a stream which, because of the many ticks, *garrapatas*, we found there, we called arroyo of the Garrapatas. All of us, though against our will, carried away many of them. We stopped this day at this arroyo. A buffalo which was seen accidentally by an Indian who was with us was killed and though somewhat lean answered our purpose. We travelled this day eight leagues.

April 17th. Wednesday. We went on to the northeast in search of the Colorado River or Espiritu Santo, which is all one, in order to see if we could meet some Indians who could give us information about the Tejas, since the Indians of the Siupan tribe had told us they did not know of them. At a distance of five leagues, when about to reach Espiritu Santo, the guide saw four buffalos. In a little while all four fell into the hands of the soldiers, who, as executioners, put an end to them, providing the expedition with meat. We stopped near this river, having travelled five leagues.

April 18th, Thursday. Having made a thick smoke in order to see if the Indians would respond and not finding any traces or footprints of them, we decided to go on by a marsh on the opposite bank of the river. We set out with the captain and seven soldiers, seven others remaining in the camp we left at the river, with orders that, if they had any news of Indians who might come there, or anything else worth knowing, they should make a smoke that we might repair to camp. We came to the river, which is sheltered on either side by luxuriant trees, walnuts, ash trees, poplars, elms, willows and wild grapes, much higher and larger than those of Castile. The river has sand banks all along its margin, showing the high water mark, and it is a quarter of a league wide. Its water is the best we have found. Just beyond this part of the river is a shady place, about half-a-league, surrounded by trees, where we found an abandoned ranchería, in the shape of a half-moon which had more than 150 circular huts, but large and well made. There, while on our way, we came upon four graves covered with sticks, two of which still gave out an offensive odor and appeared to be fresh. We passed said place and, guided by the Indian, we directed our course towards the east through a forest of oaks for a distance of about six leagues. Looking for Indians we crossed the said river a second time, and continuing our course to the northeast for about two leagues, always in sight of it, we stopped again at some ponds not far from the river, because the forest before us was so dense that we could not penetrate it. We travelled this day nine leagues.

April 19th. Friday. Having suffered much from the cold the preceding night, and being about to decide to cross over to the other bank of the river, which we had not explored, some of the party thought they saw some smoke on the bank of the river we had already explored. We recrossed the river to investigate the smoke, but there was no trace of it nor a footprint of man or beast, only deep tracks and pathways of the buffalo that crossed the river. On both sides we saw many herds of them. This caused us no little surprise, not having found even old tracks of them from the San Marcos River to the Río Grande. Seeing there were no people we returned, avoiding the forest through which we had come, and on the way the soldiers killed three buffalo cows and three calves. They took as much meat as they could carry, and about this time, we saw a thick smoke rising from the spot where we left the camp. While returning to the river aforementioned, we amused ourselves a short while by teasing a buffalo. At sunset, although lost, we got to the river passage, and it was already night before we crossed. On arriving at the camp we found there Captain Cantona, an Indian, who is very well known by the Spaniards. With him were more than forty Indians, most of them of the Yojuan tribe, a few Simonos and a few Tosonibi, who arrived that morning with many others who had returned to the ranchería, seventy-seven persons in all. They came from the river single file, bearing a well wrought *otate* (bamboo) cross before them. The cross-bearer was followed by three other Indians, each one with an image of Our Lady of Guadalupe, two of which were painted, and the other was an old engraving. As they came to where we were, all made manifestations of peace, some bowed, others approached the Spaniards, petted their faces and embraced them as is their custom in showing their joy and high esteem for those they love. There they waited until we, the two religious and the captain, arrived. They then explained themselves in this manner: Two

Indian youths seeing the thick smoke we had made before arriving at the river, came to investigate it, and following our tracks, reached that night the place where our camp was. Suspecting that those in camp were Apaches, they cautiously watched the camp until they saw by the reflections of the fire the red waistcoat of the Alferez. They knew then that they were Spaniards, because they had seen them on another occasion when they entered the province of the Tejas. These two went to inform the ranchería, which was four leagues distant, and on Friday morning all came in the manner already mentioned. They declared that they were very much afraid to approach the camp but finally resolved to do so. As soon as we dismounted from our beasts, the Indians embraced us with many manifestations of joy. We gave them the most affectionate welcome we could and distributed tobacco among them, this being the present most prized by them. They stayed with us that night with much rejoicing, refusing to return to their ranchería in order to be with the Spaniards.

Seeing that our efforts to reach the arroyo of the Otates in the hope of meeting the Tejas had been fruitless, and knowing that the Indian leader of the Yojuanes, called Cantona, frequents the province of the Tejas with his followers, we inquired particularly about the said Indians, and asked if it was true that they had left their territory and had come to settle on the San Marcos River. To this they replied that the Asinai Indians, commonly called Tejas, were in their own country where they had always lived; that they had not moved to the place we inquired about; that only a few were in the habit of going in search of buffalo meat to the Colorado River and its neighborhood. Asked again, if they knew this to be the truth, they maintained what they had said and declared further that Bernardino, a Tejas Indian, who knew Spanish and was very crafty, having lived many years among the Spaniards, was the chief of all the Tejas, and this they knew well. All this caused us sorrow on the one hand, because we wanted to see the Tejas, and [joy] on the other hand, because it relieved us of the uncertainty under which we had labored concerning the whereabouts of the Tejas. The Indians said also that it was a three-day journey from the place where we were to the village of the Tejas. Not having planned to stay any longer, and the Captain of the military expedition not having instructions to go any farther, and having been told by all who knew him that the chief of the Tejas was very adverse to all matters of faith, never having been made to live like a Christian, and that he had escaped from the mission on the Río Grande with some Indian women who had been left there, we decided not to proceed any further. On the day that all this happened we travelled over rough ground covered with oak trees nine leagues.

— — — —

APRIL 23RD. TUESDAY. We left the said place and travelled in sight of the hills, following our tracks to the Salado. We crossed the said river of San Antonio and did not find the people we had left there, because they had moved down the river. From here we crossed the San Pedro, and continued as far as the arroyo of Leon where a thick smoke, made by eight or ten Indians of the Sijames nation who were going to the Medina, was observed. We continued our march to the said Medina river, having travelled this day fourteen leagues.

April 24th. Wednesday. The Pampoa Indians came out to see us as well as the captain of the Paxti nation. We asked for an Indian to guide us so that we could cut across straight through the country, but it happened that instead of guiding us to the west, he took us to the southeast, leading us into such thick woods and sand dunes that were it not for the good luck of being directed by the good sense of our Spaniards we would not have come out of the labyrinth by sunset. From here the captain of the soldiers went ahead of us with two companions. This day was very distressing, because besides being lost, we had no water whatsoever with us as on other occasions, not even a single jar, all of which [circumstances] redoubled our troubles. At sunset the Lord delivered us and we arrived at the arroyo of the Robalos. We travelled this day sixteen leagues according to our time.

April 25th. Thursday. We went on straight through the country directly west, and at four o'clock in the afternoon we reached the arroyo of Chapa, having travelled this day nine leagues.

April 26th. Friday. We left the said arroyo and crossed the Jondo River on our way, and reached the Sarco or Frío River. As the beasts were tired, we stopped here, having travelled eight leagues.

April 27th. Saturday. Having passed a very disagreeable night, because of the rain that poured upon us unhindered, we, two religious accompanied by a soldier and two Indians, went ahead and came within two leagues of Caramanchel spring, where we slept after travelling this day sixteen leagues.

April 28th. Sunday. We did not celebrate Mass, because we had no accommodations for it. We set out for the Río

Grande, after some delays caused by the running away of the saddled horse of our soldier companion. We reached the Río Grande which we crossed though it had more water than when we crossed it before, and with our Lord's grace we arrived at three-thirty in the afternoon at the Mission of San Juan Bautista from where we had set out, with health, success and consolation, for all of which we thanked God to Whom be all glory, honor, and praise forever and ever AMEN. Finis.

Translated by Gabriel Tous, T.O.R.

Jack Kerouac

——

On the Road

"TEXAS! IT'S TEXAS! Beaumont oil town!" Huge oil tanks and refineries loomed like cities in the oily fragrant air.

"I'm glad we got out of there," said Marylou. "Let's play some more mystery programs now."

We zoomed through Beaumont, over the Trinity River at Liberty, and straight for Houston. Now Dean got talking about his Houston days in 1947. "Hassel! That mad Hassel! I look for him everywhere I go and I never find him. He used to get us so hung-up in Texas here. We'd drive in with Bull for groceries and

---

Beat icon JACK KEROUAC is the author of The Dharma Bums, Big Sur, and The Subterraneans. But his real beat brainstorm was cruising coast to coast with Neal Cassady, penning the unique, often copied, On the Road. In this excerpt, the crew lands in Texas.

Hassel'd disappear. We'd have to go looking for him in every shooting gallery in town." We were entering Houston. "We had to look for him in this spade part of town most of the time. Man, he'd be blasting with every mad cat he could find. One night we lost him and took a hotel room. We were supposed to bring ice back to Jane because her food was rotting. It took us two days to find Hassel. I got hung-up myself—I gunned shopping women in the afternoon, right here, downtown, supermarkets"—we flashed by in the empty night—"and found a real gone dumb girl who was out of her mind and just wandering, trying to steal an orange. She was from Wyoming. Her beautiful body was matched only by her idiot mind. I found her babbling and took her back to the room. Bull was drunk trying to get this young Mexican kid drunk. Carlo was writing poetry on heroin. Hassel didn't show up till midnight at the jeep. We found him sleeping in the back seat. The ice was all melted. Hassel said he took about five sleeping pills. Man, if my memory could only serve me right the way my mind works I could tell you every detail of the things we did. Ah, but we know time. Everything takes care of itself. I could close my eyes and this old car would take care of itself."

In the empty Houston streets of four o'clock in the morning a motorcycle kid suddenly roared through, all bespangled and bedecked with glittering buttons, visor, slick black jacket, a Texas poet of the night, girl gripped on his back like a papoose, hair flying, onward-going, singing, "Houston, Austin, Fort Worth, Dallas—and sometimes Kansas City—and sometimes old Antone, ah-haaaaa!" They pinpointed out of sight. "Wow! Dig that gone gal on his belt! Let's all blow!" Dean tried to catch up with them. "Now wouldn't it be fine if we could all get together and have a real going goofbang together with everybody sweet and fine and agreeable, no hassles, no infant rise of protest or body woes misconceptalized or sumpin? Ah! but we know time." He bent to it and pushed the car.

Beyond Houston his energies, great as they were, gave out and I drove. Rain began to fall just as I took the wheel. Now we were on the great Texas plain and, as Dean said, "You drive and drive and you're still in Texas tomorrow night." The rain lashed down. I drove through a rickety little cowtown with a muddy main street and found myself in a dead end. "Hey, what do I do?" They were both asleep. I turned and crawled back through town. There wasn't a soul in sight and not a single light. Suddenly a horseman in a raincoat appeared in my headlamps. It was the sheriff. He had a ten-gallon hat, drooping in the torrent. "Which way to Austin?" He told me politely and I started off. Outside town I suddenly saw two headlamps flaring directly at me in the lashing rain. Whoops, I thought I was on the wrong side of the road; I eased right and found myself rolling in the mud; I rolled back to the road. Still the headlamps came straight for me. At the last moment I realized the other driver was on the wrong side of the road and didn't know it. I swerved at thirty into the mud; it was flat, no ditch, thank God. The offending car backed up in the downpour. Four sullen fieldworkers, snuck from their chores to brawl in drinking fields, all white shirts and dirty brown arms, sat looking at me dumbly in the night. The driver was as drunk as the lot.

He said, "Which way t'Houston?" I pointed my thumb back. I was thunderstruck in the middle of the thought that they had done this on purpose just to ask directions, as a panhandler advances on you straight up the sidewalk to bar your way. They gazed ruefully at the floor of their car, where empty bottles rolled, and clanked away. I started the car; it was stuck in the mud a foot deep. I sighed in the rainy Texas wilderness.

"Dean," I said, "wake up."

"What?"

"We're stuck in the mud."

"What happened?" I told him. He swore up and down. We put on old shoes and sweaters and barged out of the car into the driving rain. I put my back on the rear fender and lifted and heaved; Dean stuck chains under the swishing wheels. In a minute we were covered with mud. We woke up Marylou to these horrors and made her gun the car while we pushed. The tormented Hudson heaved and heaved. Suddenly it jolted out and went skidding across the road. Marylou pulled it up just in time, and we got in. That was that—the work had taken thirty minutes and we were soaked and miserable.

I fell asleep, all caked with mud; and in the morning when I woke up the mud was solidified and outside there was snow. We were near Fredericksburg, in the high plains. It was one of the worst winters in Texas and Western history, when cattle perished like flies in great blizzards and snow fell on San Francisco and LA. We were all miserable. We wished we were back in New Orleans with Ed Dunkel. Marylou was driving; Dean was sleeping. She drove with one hand on the wheel and the other reaching back to me in the back seat. She cooed promises about San Francisco. I slavered miserably over it. At ten I took the wheel—Dean was out for hours—and drove several hundred dreary miles across the bushy snows and ragged sage hills.

Cowboys went by in baseball caps and earmuffs, looking for cows. Comfortable little homes with chimneys smoking appeared along the road at intervals. I wished we could go in for butter-milk and beans in front of the fireplace.

At Sonora I again helped myself to free bread and cheese while the proprietor chatted with a big rancher on the other side of the store. Dean huzzahed when he heard it; he was hungry. We couldn't spend a cent on food. "Yass, yass," said Dean, watching the ranchers loping up and down Sonora main street, "every one of them is a bloody millionaire, thousand head of cat-tle, workhands, buildings, money in the bank. If I lived around here I'd go be an idjit in the sagebrush, I'd be jackrabbit, I'd lick up the branches, I'd look for pretty cowgirls—hee-hee-hee-hee! Damn! Bam!" He socked himself. "Yes! Right! Oh me!" We didn't know what he was talking about any more. He took the wheel and flew the rest of the way across the state of Texas, about five hundred miles, clear to El Paso, arriving at dusk and not stopping except once when he took all his clothes off, near Ozona, and ran yipping and leaping naked in the sage. Cars zoomed by and didn't see him. He scurried back to the car and drove on. "Now Sal, now Marylou, I want both of you to do as I'm doing, disembur-den yourselves of all that clothes—now what's the sense of clothes? now that's what I'm sayin—and sun your pretty bellies with me. Come on!" We were driving west into the sun; it fell in through the windshield. "Open your belly as we drive into it." Marylou complied; unfuddyduddied, so did I. We sat in the front seat, all three. Marylou took out cold cream and applied it to us for kicks. Every now and then a big truck zoomed by; the driver in high cab caught a glimpse of a golden beauty sitting naked with two naked men: you could see them swerve a moment as they vanished in our rear-view window. Great sage plains, snowless now, rolled on. Soon we were in the orange-rocked Pecos Canyon country. Blue distances opened up in the sky. We got out of the car to examine an old Indian ruin. Dean did so stark naked. Marylou and I put on our overcoats. We wandered among the old stones, hooting and howling. Certain tourists caught sight of Dean naked in the plain but they could not believe their eyes and wobbled on.

Dean and Marylou parked the car near Van Horn and made love while I went to sleep. I woke up just as we were rolling down the tremendous Rio Grande Valley through Clint and Ysleta to El Paso. Marylou jumped to the back seat, I jumped to the front seat, and we rolled along. To our left across the vast Rio Grande spaces were the moorish-red mounts of the Mexican border, the land of the Tarahumare; soft dusk played on the peaks. Straight ahead lay the distant lights of El Paso and Juárez, sown in a tremendous valley so big that you could see several railroads puffing at the same time in every direction, as though it was the Valley of the World. We descended into it.

"Clint, Texas!" said Dean. He had the radio on to the Clint station. Every fifteen minutes they played a record; the rest of the time it was commercials about a high-school correspondence course. "This program is beamed all over the West," cried Dean excitedly. "Man, I used to listen to it day and night in reform school and prison. All of us used to write in. You get a high-school diploma by mail, facsimile thereof, if you pass the test. All the young wranglers in the West, I don't care who, at one time or another write in for this; it's all they hear; you tune the radio in Sterling, Colorado, Lusk, Wyoming, I don't care where, you get Clint, Texas, Clint, Texas. And the music is always cowboy hillbilly and Mexican, absolutely the worst program in the entire history of the country and nobody can do anything about it. They have a tremendous beam; they've got the whole land hogtied." We saw the high antenna beyond the shacks of Clint. "Oh, man, the things I could tell you!" cried Dean, almost weeping. Eyes bent on Frisco and the Coast, we came into El Paso as it got dark, broke. We absolutely had to get some money for gas or we'd never make it.

We tried everything. We buzzed the travel bureau, but no one was going west that night. The travel bureau is where you go for share-the-gas rides, legal in the West. Shifty characters wait with battered suitcases. We went to the Greyhound bus station to try to persuade somebody to give us the money instead of taking a bus for the Coast. We were too bashful to approach anyone. We wandered around sadly. It was cold outside. A college boy was sweating at the sight of luscious Marylou and trying to look unconcerned. Dean and I consulted but decided we weren't pimps. Suddenly a crazy dumb young kid, fresh out of reform school, attached himself to us, and he and Dean rushed out for a beer. "Come on, man, let's go mash somebody on the head and get his money."

"I dig you, man!" yelled Dean. They dashed off. For a moment I was worried; but Dean only wanted to dig the streets of El Paso with the kid and get his kicks. Marylou and I waited in the car. She put her arms around me.

I said, "Dammit, Lou, wait till we get to Frisco."

"I don't care. Dean's going to leave me anyway."

"When are you going back to Denver?"

"I don't know. I don't care what I'm doing. Can I go back east with you?"

"We'll have to get some money in Frisco."

"I know where you can get a job in a lunchcart behind the counter, and I'll be a waitress. I know a hotel where we can stay on credit. We'll stick together. Gee, I'm sad."

"What are you sad about, kid?"

"I'm sad about everything. Oh damn, I wish Dean wasn't so crazy now." Dean came twinkling back, giggling, and jumped in the car.

"What a crazy cat that was, whoo! Did I dig him! I used to know thousands of guys like that, they're all the same, their minds work in uniform clockwork, oh, the infinite ramifications, no time, no time . . ." And he shot up the car, hunched over the wheel, and roared out of El Paso. "We'll just have to pick up hitchhikers. I'm positive we'll find some. Hup! hup! here we go. Look out!" he yelled at a motorist, and swung around him, and dodged a truck and bounced over the city limits. Across the river were the jewel lights of Juárez and the sad dry land and the jewel stars of Chihuahua. Marylou was watching Dean as she had watched him clear across the country and back, out of the corner of her eye—with a sullen, sad air, as though she wanted to cut off his head and hide it in her closet, an envious and rueful love of him so amazingly himself, all raging and sniffy and crazy-wayed, a smile of tender dotage but also sinister envy that frightened me about her, a love she knew would never bear fruit because when she looked at his hangjawed bony face with its male self-containment and absentmindedness she knew he was too mad. Dean was convinced Marylou was a whore; he confided in me that she was a pathological liar. But when she watched him like this it was love too; and when Dean noticed he always turned with his big false flirtatious smile, with the eyelashes fluttering and the teeth pearly white, while a moment ago he was only dreaming in his eternity. Then Marylou and I both laughed—and Dean gave no sign of discomfiture, just a goofy glad grin that said to us, Ain't we gettin our kicks anyway? And that was it.

DON
DeLillo
— — —

22 November

AT THE AIRPORT they were standing on baggage carts and clinging to light posts. They were draped over the chain-link fence,
people in raincoats, waving flags, hanging off the sign for Gate
28. Skies were clear now and the 707 swung massively to a stop
on the tarmac. They came running from their cars. They stood at
the edge of the crowd, jumping up and down. Children rode the
shoulders of gangly men. There was a mood rising from the
parked bodies, an eager spirit of assent. Members of the welcom-
ing party edged into place at the foot of the ramp, fussing with

---

DON DELILLO is the author of eight novels, including Great Jones Street,
White Noise, and The Names. In 1985, he received the American
Book Award for White Noise. "22 November" is from his 1988 novel,
Libra.

their clothes and hair. The aft door opened and the First Lady appeared in a glow of rosebud pink, suit and hat to match, followed by the President. A sound, an awe worked through the crowd, a recognition, ringing in the air. People called out together, faces caught in some stage of surprise resembling dazzled pain. "Here" or "Jack" or "Look." The President fingered his lapel, gave a little jacket-adjusting shrug and walked down the ramp. The sound was a small roar now, a wonder. They shook the fence. They came running from the terminal building, handbags and cameras bouncing. There were cameras everywhere, held aloft, a rustling of bladed shutters, with homemade signs poking through the mass.

Welcome Jack and Jackie to Big D.

After the handshakes and salutes, Jack Kennedy walked away from his security, sidestepping puddles, and went to the fence. He reached a hand into the ranks and they surged forward, looking at each other to match reactions. He moved along the fence, handsome and tanned, smiling famously into the wall of open mouths. He looked like himself, like photographs, a helmsman squinting in the sea-glare, white teeth shining. There was only a trace of the cortisone bloat that sometimes affected his face—cortisone for his Addison's disease, a back brace for his degenerating discs. They came over the fence, surrounding him, so many people and hands. The white smile brightened. He wanted everyone to know he was not afraid.

The Lincoln was deep blue, an iridescent peacock gleam, with an American flag and a presidential standard attached to the front fenders. Two Secret Service men in front, Governor Connally and his wife in the jumpseats, the Kennedy's in the rear. The Lincoln moved out behind an unmarked pilot car and five motorcycles manned by white-helmeted city cops showing traditional blank faces. Stretching half a mile behind came the miscellaneous train of rented convertibles, station wagons, touring sedans, Secret Service follow-up cars, communications cars, buses, motorcycles, spare Chevys, Lyndon, Lady Bird, congressmen, aides, wives, men with Nikons, Rolliflexes, newsreel cameras, radiophones, automatic rifles, shotguns, service revolvers and the codes for launching a nuclear strike.

The Lincoln seemed to glow. Sunlight flashed from the fenders and hood, made the upholstery shine. The Governor waved his tan Stetson and the flags snapped and the First Lady held roses in the crook of her arm. The burnished surface of the car mirrored scenes along the road. Not that there was much to collect in the landscape at hand. Airport isolation. Horizontal buildings with graveled rooftops. Billboards showing sizzling steaks. Random spectators, brave-looking, waving, in these mournful spaces. And a man standing alone at the side of the road holding up a copy of the Morning News opened to the page that had everybody talking. *Welcome Mr. Kennedy to Dallas.* An ad placed by a group called the American Fact-Finding Committee. Grievances, accusations, jingo fantasia—not so remarkable, really, even in a major newspaper, except that the text was bordered in black. Nicely ominous. Jack Kennedy had seen the ad earlier and now, with towered downtown Dallas in the visible distance, he turned and said softly to Jacqueline, "We're heading into nut country now."

Still, it was important to be seen in a open car without a bubbletop, without agents on the running boards. Here he was among them in a time of deep division, the country pulled two ways, each army raging and Jack having hold of both. Were there forebodings? For weeks he'd carried a scrap of paper with scribbled lines of some bloody Shakespearean ruin. *They whirl asunder and dismember me.* Still, it was important for the car to move very slowly, give the crowds a chance to see him. Maximum exposure as the admen say, and who wants a president with a pigeon's heart?

And there were friendly crowds ahead. The strays on the outskirts, stick figures, gave way to larger groups, to gatherings. They appeared at intersections. They stood on bumpers in stalled traffic and cried, "Jack-eeee." Signs, flags, surging numbers, people fifteen deep, crowds growing out over the curbstone, craning for a look at the brilliant limousine. The cops astride their Harleys trimmed the ragged edges. There were people backed against building walls who could not see the limousine but only figures gliding by, spirits of the bright air, dreamlike and serene. The crush was massive down near Harwood. It was a multitude, a storm force. The motorcycles rumbled constantly, an excitement in the sound, a power, and the President waved and smiled and whispered, "Thank you."

Advise keep crowds behind barricades. They are getting in the street here.

Street by street the crowd began to understand why it was here. The message jumped the open space from one press of bodies to the next. A contagion had brought them here, some mystery of common impulse, hundreds of thousands come from so many histories and systems of being, come from some experience of the night before, a convergence of dreams, to stand together shouting as the Lincoln passed. They were here to be an event, a consciousness, to astonish the old creedbound fears, the stark and wary faith of the city of get-rich-quick. Big D rising out of caution and suspicion to produce the roar of a sand column twisting. They were here to surround the brittle body of one man and claim his smile, receive some token of the bounty of his soul.

Advise approaching Main go real slow speed.

Into the noontide fires. Twelve city blocks down Main Street, some embers of the melodrama of small towns, of Hallmark and Walgreen and Thom McAn, scattered among the bank towers. The motorcycles came, a steady throttling growl, a tension that bit into the edge of every awareness. The sight of the Lincoln sent a thrill along the street. One roar devoured another. There were bodies jutting from windows, daredevil kids bolting into the open. *They're here. It's them. They're real.* It wasn't only Jack and Jackie who were riding in a fire of excitement. The crowd brought itself into heat and light. A knowledge charged the air, a self-awareness. Here was a new city, an idea that traveled at the speed of sound, pounding over the old hushed heart, a city of voices roaring. Loud and hot and throbbing. The crowd kept pushing past the ropes and barricades. Motorcycles drove a wedge and agents dropped off the running boards of the follow-up car to jog alongside the Lincoln. Was it frightening to sit in the midst of all this? Did Jack think this fervor was close to a violence? They were so damn close, nearly upon him. He looked at them and whispered, "Thank you."

The men in dark glasses were back on the running boards as the motorcade began its swing into Houston Street and the last little dip before the freeway.

THEY RAN TO the birdcage elevators, four young men in the lunch-hour race, horse laughs, jostling at the gates. Lee heard them call to each other all the way down. Dust. Faded white paint on the old brick walls. Stacks of cartons everywhere. Old sprinkler pipes and scarred columns. A layer of dust hovered at a height of three feet. Loose books on the floor. His clipboard already hidden, jammed between cartons near the west wall. Stillness on six.

He stood at the southeast window inside a barrier of cartons. The larger ones formed a wall about five feet high and carried a memory with them, a sense of a kid's snug hideout, making him feel apart and secure. Inside the barrier were four more cartons—one set lengthwise on the floor, two stacked, one small carton resting on the brick windowsill. A bench, a support, a gun rest. The wrapping paper he'd used to conceal the rifle was on the floor near his feet. Dust. Broken spider webs hanging from the ceiling. He saw a dime on the floor. He picked it up and put it in his pocket.

He looked down Houston Street as the motorcade approached, slow and vivid in the sun. There were people scattered on the lawns of Dealey Plaza, maybe a hundred and fifty, many with cameras. He held the rifle at port arms, more or less, and stood in plain view in the tall window. Everything looked so painfully clear.

The President had chestnut hair and the First Lady was radiant in a pink suit and small round hat. Lee was glad she looked so good. For her own sake. For the cameras. For the pictures that would enter the permanent record.

He spotted Governor John Connally in one of the jump seats, a Stetson in his lap. He liked Connally's face, a rugged

Texas face. This was the kind of man who would take a liking to
Lee if he ever got to know him. Cartons stamped Books. Ten
Rolling Readers. Everyone was grateful for the weather.

The white pilot car turned, the motorcycles turned. The
Lincoln passed beneath him, easing left, making the deep turn left,
seeming almost to rotate on an axis. Everything was slow and
clear. He got down on one knee, placed his left elbow on the
stacked cartons and rested the gun barrel on the edge of the carton
on the sill. He sighted on the back of the President's head. The
Lincoln moved into the cover of the live oak, going about ten
miles an hour. Ready on the left, ready on the right. Through the
scope he saw the car metal shine.

He fired through an opening in the leaf cover.

When the car was in the clear again, the President
began to react.

Lee turned up the handle, drew the bolt back.

The President reacted, arms coming up, elbows high and wide.

There were pigeons, suddenly, everywhere, cracking down
from the eaves and beating west.

The report sounded over the plaza, flat and clear.

The President's fists were clenched near his throat,
arms bowed out.

Lee drove the bolt forward, jerking the handle down.

The Lincoln was moving slower now. It was almost dead still.
It was sitting naked in the street eighty yards from the underpass.

Ready on the firing line.

RAYMO GOT OUT of the supercharged Merc in the parking lot
above the grassy embankment a little more than halfway down

Elm. A wooden stockade fence enclosed the parking area, with trees and shrubs set alongside. The rear bumper of the car nudged the fence. There were ten or twelve cars parked nearby, many more in the spaces to the north and west.

Raymo stood a moment, rolling his shoulders. He gave a firm hoist to his balls, three quick jogs with the left hand. The fence was about five feet high, too high for him to brace his left arm comfortably. He went to the rear of the car and stood on the bumper. He looked out over the fence and across a stretch of lawn. The pilot car approached the Elm Street turn.

Frank Vásquez got out of the car on the driver's side. He carried a Weatherby Mark V, scope-mounted, loaded with soft-point bullets that explode on impact. He stood by the rear fender until Raymo extended a hand. Frank gave him the weapon.

He went back to the driver's seat. The car bounced when he got in and Raymo glanced back sharply.

The crowd noise from Main Street was still in the air, faintly, a rustle somewhere overhead, and Frank, with his back to the action, sat at the wheel listening. His view was past the rail-yards to the northwest. Water towers painted white. Power pylons trailing into a flat grim distance. All light and sky. He felt like he could see to the end of Texas.

Raymo stood just west of the point where the two sections of fence form a near-right angle. From the deep shade of the trees he looked out on a sun-dazzled scene. Small groups collecting on the grass on both sides of Elm, families, cameras, like the start of a picnic. The limousine came swinging into the street. People on the north side of Elm, their backs to Raymo, shaded their eyes from the sun. Other people waving, Kennedy waving, applause, sunlight, sharp glare on the hood of the limousine. A girl ran across the grass. The dangling men. Four men dangling from the sides of the follow-up car, only a few feet behind the blue Lincoln.

Dallas One. Repeat. I didn't get all of it.

Leon fired too soon, with the car passing under the tree. The report sounded like a short charge, a little weak, a defect, not enough powder.

Kennedy reacted late, without surprise at first, his arms coming up slowly like a man on a rowing machine.

The driver slowed to half-speed. The driver sat there. The other agent sat there. They were waiting for a voice to explain it.

Pigeons flared past.

Raymo eased the gun barrel out over the fence. He set his feet firmly on the bumper. His left forearm, bracing the weapon, was wedged between the tops of two pickets. He tilted his head to the stock. He waited, sighting through the scope.

ON THE GRASS a woman saw the limousine emerge from behind a freeway sign with the President clutching his throat. She heard a sharp noise, like a backfiring car, and realized it was the second noise she'd heard. She thought she saw a man throw a boy to the grass and fall on top of him. She didn't really hear the first noise until she heard the second. A girl ran waving toward the limousine. The noise cracked and flattened, washing across the plaza. This wasn't making sense at all.

THERE WAS SO much clarity Lee could watch himself in the huge room of stacked cartons, scattered books, old brick walls, bare light bulbs, a small figure in a corner, partly hidden. He fired off a second shot.

He saw the Governor, who was turned right, begin to look the other way, then double up suddenly. A startle reaction. He knew this was called a startle reaction, from gun magazines.

He turned up the handle, drew the bolt back, then drove it forward.

Stand by a moment please.

Okay, he fired early the first time, hitting the President below the head, near the neck area somewhere. It was a foolishness he could dismiss on a certain level. Okay, he missed the President with the second shot and hit Connally. But the car was still sitting there, barely moving. He saw the First Lady lean toward the President, who was slumped down now. A man stood applauding at the edge of the telescopic frame.

Lee jerked the handle down and aimed. He heard the second spent shell roll across the floor.

THERE WERE ROSES on the seat between Jack and Jackie. The car's interior was a nice light blue. The man was so close he could have spoken to them. He stood at curbside applauding. A woman called out to the car, "Hey we want to take your picture." The President looked extremely puzzled, head leaning left. The man stood applauding, already deep in chaos, looking at crumpled bodies, a sense of guns coming out.

Put me on, Bill. Put me on.

Bobby W. Hargis, riding escort, left rear, knew he was hearing gunfire. There was a woman taking a picture and another woman about twenty feet behind her taking the same picture, only with the first woman in it. He couldn't tell where the shots were coming from, two shots, but knew someone was hit in the car. A man threw his kid to the ground and fell on him. That's a vet, Hargis had time to think, with the Governor, Connally, kind of sliding down in the jump seat and his wife taking him in, gathering the man in. Hargis turned right just after noticing a girl in a pretty coat running across the lawn toward the President's car. He turned his body right, keeping the motorcycle headed west on Elm, and then the blood and matter, the unforgettable thing, the sleet of bone and blood and tissue struck him in the face. He thought he'd been shot. The stuff hit him like a spray of buckshot and he heard it ping and spatter on his helmet. People were down on the grass. He kept his mouth closed tight so the fluid would not ooze in.

In the jump seat John was crumpled up. Nellie Connally pulled him over into her arms. She put her head down over his head. She was pretending she was him. They were both alive or both dead. They could not be one and one. Then the third shot sent stuff just everywhere. Tissue, bone fragments, tissue in pale wads, watery mess, tissue, blood, brain matter all over them.

She heard Jackie say, "They've killed my husband."

It could have been Nellie's own voice, someone speaking for her. She thought John was dead. Then he moved just slightly and she thought at the same time that Jackie was out of the car, gone off the end of the car, but now was somehow back. John moved in her arms. They were one heart pumping.

We are hit. Lancer is hit. Get us to Parkland fast.

The car picked up speed and everything went rushing past. Nellie thought how terrible this must be, what a terrible sight for people watching, to see the car speeding past with these shot-up men; what a horror, what a sight.

She heard Jackie say, "I have his brains in my hand."

Everything rushing past.

The man in the white sweater, applauding, saw the stuff just erupt from the President's head. The motorcycles went by. There were guns coming out, a man in the second car with an automatic rifle. The second car went by. A motorcycle went fishtailing up the grassy slope near the concrete structure, the colonnade. Someone with a movie camera stood on an abutment over there, aiming this way, and the man in the white sweater, hands suspended now at belt level, was thinking he ought to go to the ground, he ought to fall right now. A misty light around the President's head. Two pink-white jets of tissue rising from the mist. The movie camera running.

LEE WAS ABOUT to squeeze off the third round, he was in the act, he was actually pressing the trigger.

The light was so clear it was heartbreaking.

There was a white burst in the middle of the frame. A terrible splash, a burst. Something came blazing off the President's head. He was slammed back, surrounded all in dust and haze. Then suddenly clear again, down and still in the seat. Oh he's dead he's dead.

Lee raised his head from the scope, looking right. There was a white concrete wall extending from the columned structure, then a wooden fence behind it. A man on the wall with a camera. The fence deep in shadow. Freight cars sitting on the tracks above the underpass.

He got to his feet, moving away from the window. He knew he'd missed with the third shot. Went wild. Missed everything. Maggie's drawers. He turned up the bolt handle.

Put me on. Put me on. Put me on.

He was already talking to someone about this. He had a picture, he saw himself telling the whole story to someone, a man with a rugged Texas face, but friendly, but understanding. Pointing out the contradictions. Telling how he was tricked into the plot. What is it called, a patsy? He saw a picture of an office with a tasseled flag, dignitaries in photos on the wall.

He drew the bolt back, then drove it forward, jerking the handle down. He walked diagonally across the floor to the northwest end, where the staircase was located. Books stacked ten cartons high. That fragrance of paper and binding.

THE FENDER SIRENS opened up, the guns started coming out.

The girl stopped running toward the car. She stood and looked without expression.

A woman with a camera turned and saw that she was being photographed. A woman in a dark coat was aiming a Polaroid right at her. It was only then she realized she'd just seen someone shot in her own viewfinder. There was bloodspray on her face and arms. She thought, how strange, that the woman in the coat was her and she was the person who was shot. She felt so dazed and strange, with pale spray all over her. She sat down carefully on the grass. Just let herself down and sat there. The woman with the Polaroid didn't move. The first woman sat on the grass, put her own camera down, looked at the colorless stuff on her arms. Pigeons spinning at the treetops. If she was shot, she thought, she ought to be sitting down.

AGENT HILL WAS off the left running board and moving fast.
There was another shot. He mounted the Lincoln from the
bumper step, extending his left hand to the metal grip. It was a
double sound. Either two shots or a shot and the solid impact, the
bullet hitting something hard. He wanted to get to the President,
get close, shield the body. He saw Mrs. Kennedy coming at him.
She was climbing out of the car. She was on the rear deck crawling, both hands flat, her right knee on top of the rear seat. He
thought she was chasing something and he realized he'd seen
something fly by, a flash somewhere, something flying off the
end of the limousine. He pushed her back toward the seat. The
car surged forward, nearly knocking him off. They were in the
underpass, in the shadows, and when they hit the light he saw
Connally washed in blood. Spectators, kids, waving. He held tight
to the handgrip. They were going damn fast. All four passengers
were drenched in blood, crowded down together. He lay across
the rear deck. He had this thought, this recognition. She was trying to retrieve part of her husband's skull.

He held on tight. He could see right into the President's
head. They were doing eighty now.

FLASH

SSSSSSSSSS

       BLOOD STAINEZAAC

KENNEDY SERIOSTY WOUNDED

SSSSSSSSSS

MAKE THAT PERHAPS PERHAPS

SERIOUSLY WOUNDED

Raymo's view was briefly obscured. He had to wait for the right side of the limousine to clear the concrete abutment. He knew Connally was hit. He had time to think, Leon's picking them off one by one. He had a sense of people ducking and scattering even though they weren't in the frame. Now the car moved clear, quartering slowly in. He held on Kennedy's head. The man was leaning left, tight-eyed in pain. A hundred and thirty feet. A hundred and twenty feet. He got off the shot. The man's hair stood up. It just rippled and flew. Raymo stepped off the bumper and got in the back seat. Frank had the car moving. He drove between rows of parked cars behind the Depository. He headed straight for three freight cars marked Hutchinson Northern. Raymo leaned forward. Watch it, man. But he didn't say a word.

See if the President will be able to appear out here. We have all these people that are waiting. I need to know whether to feed them or what to announce out here.

Frank found a lane to the street. He went one block east on Pacific Avenue. He made a left onto Record Street. Warehouses and parking lots. He felt there was someone sitting inside his body making these moves and turns. He tried not to think past the moment. Elevated highway straight ahead. He had a pestering fear about what would happen when they were past the moment of turns and traffic signs. He didn't know how he'd feel when he was back in his body again.

The guns were coming out.

Cops left their Harleys to run up the slope with pistols drawn. In the motorcade the Secret Service men had automatic weapons cocked, sidearms coming out.

Pigeons reversing flight, beating eastward now.

Mackey watched from the south colonnade, across Elm, across Main, across Commerce. There was no one on the lawns or under the trees here. It was the matching half of the plaza, less than a hundred yards from the scene but totally remote, hot and empty in the glare. He stood against a column, arms folded. He let his sunglasses dangle from his right hand.

The sirens opened up. Outside the Book Depository, policemen stood with rifles and shotguns pointing up. Men pointing. People looking up.

```
GET OFF NXR

    BULLETIN

SSSSSSSSSS     ZA SNIPER SERIOUSLY

    WOUNDED

    OFF ALL OF YOU              STAY

OFF AND

    KEEP OFF              GET OFF
```

A small girl stood with a hand over each ear. The motorcade was in collapse, vehicles stopped, others rushing past. Ordinary traffic moved into Elm. Many people running up the steps between the stockade fence and the colonnade. A goddamn mob of people. Figures prone on the grass. A man pounding his fist on the hood of a car. Mackey saw a man get out of another car and fall down. Ragged cries and shouts. People on their knees. Others sitting, with cameras, out of breath and unbelieving.

He saw a fire truck come down Main. It was the dumbest thing he'd seen in twenty years.

SPEAKING AT THE TT

WILL U U PLEASE STAY OFF THIS

WIRE

SSSSSSSSS

STAY OFF   STAY OFF

SSSSSSSSS

ZA SNIPER SERIOUSLY WOUNDED

PRESIDENT KENNEDY

DOWN TOWN DAL LAS TO DAY

PERHAPS FAAATALLY

FROM THIS DISTANCE Mackey wasn't sure whether the people going up the embankment steps looked like a lynch mob or men and women in raw shock, in flight, running with others. He was thirsty and depressed. Strange harsh cries kept sounding from the lawns, from the echoing underpass, a thickness of voice, all desperate effort, like speech of the deaf and dumb.

LEE HID THE rifle on the floor between rows of cartons near the sign for the stairway. They'd find it easy enough. But he still had to hide it, just to do the expected thing, make them believe he didn't want to be identified. It was the same with the clipboard, already hidden, and the unfilled orders that were fixed to it. He wanted to give them something to uncover, a layer to strip away.

He liked the idea of a job that required a clipboard.

He was down the stairs fast and headed for the Coke machine on the second floor. A Coke in his hand would make him feel secure. It was a prop, a thing to carry around by way of saying he was okay. He thought he might need a prop to get him out of the building.

He heard a voice behind him like, "Come here."

It was a cop with a drawn gun rushing into the lunch-room. He had one of those plastic covers on his hat for rainy days. Lee turned and walked slowly at him. He showed a face you'd see on any public transport, anonymous and dreamy. He made it a point not to notice the pistol aimed at his chest.

Roy Truly came in then and the cop said, "Does this man work here?" And Mr. Truly said yes and they both headed out to the stairway. Lee got his Coke and wandered down one flight and out the front entrance, a hole in the elbow of his shirt.

AGENT GRANT STOOD under the canopy at the Trade Mart entrance, just off Stemmons Freeway. He was explaining to two local business leaders how to present themselves to the Kennedys. He heard sirens getting louder. He saw the pilot car, the motorcy-cles, the Lincoln doing maybe eighty, with somebody spread-eagle on the rear deck. Other vehicles following, high speed, the craziest damn scene, a press bus blowing past. He asked one of the businessmen what time he had. Then they all checked their watches, placing the event in a framework they could agree upon.

HE LAAAAAAAAAA

THERE WAS A man holding Mary's arm and she was crying. He had hold of her camera trying to take it with him. He said he was Featherstone of the Times Herald. Mary's friend Jean was saying, "I thought that was a dog on the seat between them. I was saying I could see Liz Taylor or the Gabors traveling with a dog but I can't see the Kennedys on tour with dogs." Mary was not listening to this. She was crying and fighting to keep her camera. This man from the paper would not let go her arm. He was dragging her away toward Houston Street. Jean wasn't able to get to her feet. She sat on the grass trying to finish her train of thought about seeing a dog in the car. She wanted to say to Mary, she did actually say, "I realized finally that little fuzzy thing. It was roses on the seat between them."

FLYING DOWN THAT freeway with those dying men in our arms and going to no telling where. Everything flashing by. A billboard reading, Roller Skating Time.

LEE GOT OFF the bus in stalled traffic and walked to the Greyhound terminal to catch a taxi. The traffic was stalled for pretty obvious reasons, so maybe the bus was not a good idea. He walked south on Lamar, the sirens going all around him, and spotted an empty cab. They were a little removed here from the major congestion.

He got in next to the driver and here is a nice old lady sticking her head in the window looking for a taxi. Lee started getting out. He offered the cab to the lady. But the driver rolled away and Lee gave him an address a few blocks from his rooming house. It was a five- or six-minute ride, going out over the old viaduct. The driver said something about all the squad cars running a code three—lights spinning, sirens going. He wondered what was up.

Lee got out and walked north on Beckley, hearing a jangling in the air, feeling the first nervousness.

What do I look like?

To anybody seeing me, where do I look like I'm coming from?

He checked the numbers on the license plates of parked cars.

Do I look like someone leaving the scene?

His stomach was empty and he had that feeling in the mouth where there's a rusty taste, something oozing from the gums.

That old patchy sadness of this part of Oak Cliff, the room-to-let signs and the trees going bare, the clotheslines, the bare-looking house fronts.

He was wishing he'd taken that Coke along.

The housekeeper was watching TV and it was all over the air waves. She said something but he went right by. In the toilet he pissed and pissed. It just kept coming.

Jangling in the air.

He went to his room and opened the dresser drawer for the .38. It was only common sense. He couldn't go out there without a gun. This was the day of all days when he needed protection.

They'd find the Hidell rifle. He had Hidell documents in Ruth Paine's garage. His wallet was full of Hidell. So it was only common sense to take the Hidell handgun. A dozen layers to strip away. It was everything, together, Hidell.

He scooped the loose cartridges out of the drawer. Bought off the street by Dupard. Would they even go bang?

He'd left his blue jacket at work. He took his gray one. Wherever he'd be spending the night, and the rest of his life, he might need a jacket. Plus it covered up the gun.

The room. The iron bed.

To anybody watching, what do I look like with the bulge at my hip under the jacket?

Unknown white male. Slender build.

He went out the door and down the walk. He was having a little trouble figuring what to do. All the clarity was gone. There was a nervous static in the air.

What do I look like?

Do I stand out in the street, walking?

He went down Beckley figuring there was no choice but to go to the movie house where they were supposed to pick him up. He knew he couldn't trust them but there was nowhere else to go. He had fourteen dollars and a bus transfer. They had him cold. He could be walking right into it. The lurking thought, the idea of others making the choice now. He wanted to believe it was out of his hands.

He saw a police car up ahead, coming this way, and he made a left onto Davis, knowing he'd turned too quick. The streets were nearly empty. He actually saw the cop watching him move down Davis, squeezed eyes peering, although the car was out of sight now.

Okay, he shot him once. But he didn't kill him. To the best of his knowledge he hit him in the upper back or somewhere in the neck area, nonfatally. Then he missed and hit the Governor. Then he missed completely. There are circumstances they don't know about. Are they sure it was him in that window? It could be different than they think. A setup.

Slender white male. Five feet ten.

The car came into view again, down Patton, and he walked halfway along the next block. Then he did an about-face and went back to Patton and walked south. To fake out the car. He figured if he went to where he'd seen the car, it would be somewhere else.

Do I look like a suspect fleeing?

Have they figured out who's missing from the Book Depository?

What is my name if I am asked?

He went down Patton to Ninth Street. Nobody around this time of day. The idea was to make a quick move back to Beckley, across Beckley, down to Jefferson. A dozen old hair-drying machines stood along the curbside. A mattress on a lawn.

He wanted to write short stories about contemporary American life.

At Tenth and Patton he expected to see the car, if at all, moving away from him. But it was cruising east, to his right, coming at him. He crossed the street and began walking east and by this time the car was right behind him, tagging along, going ten to twelve miles an hour, the motorcade speed, teasing.

From the corner of his eye he could see the number on the door. A number ten. The car was marked number ten and this was Tenth Street.

He wasn't sure if he stopped first or the car stopped. It was like they both had the same idea. He went over to the window on the passenger side.

They spoke at the same time. Lee said, "What's the problem, officer?" And the cop, strong-featured, looking maybe one-eighth Indian, said something about "You live around here, buddy?"

Lee stuck his head right in the window, smelling stale cigarettes, and said, "Any reason to want to talk to me?"

"You look to me like you're taking evasive tactics."

"I'm walking in broad daylight."

"To me, you're doing every possible thing to evade being spotted."

There was a voice squawking on the radio.

"I'm just a citizen on foot."

"Then maybe you'd like to tell me where you're going to."

"I don't think I'm required to tell you that. I live in this area, which I'm telling you more than required by law."

He took the position, the attitude, that he was being singled out for harassment. Even if they had a description, from witnesses looking up at the window, how specific could it be?

"I'm saying for your own good."

"I'm only walking on the street."

One other person in sight, a woman approaching the intersection of Tenth and Patton.

"You carrying ID or not?"

"I'm a resident here."

"I'm saying for the last time."

He did not like the way cops, had never liked it when cops sat in their car and you had to approach them with documents, bending all the time, leaning toward their windows.

"I'm only asking what's the reason."

"Better show me some paper real soon."

"I hear you."

"Then do it."

"I'm a citizen on foot."

"I'm saying one last time."

They spoke at the same time again. The cop sat in his Ford getting a little testy. A voice on the radio said, *Disheveled hair.*

We're on Tenth Street and the car is number ten. All the factors converging.

"Look. If I have to get out of this vehicle."

"Harass."

"I want to see your hands."

"This is how we have misunderstandings."

"Hands on the fucking hood."

"I hear you."

"Then fucking do it, pencil-neck."

The cop reached for the door handle on his side, not taking his eyes off Oswald. They were going to another level now.

"I'm only asking what for."

"Hands, *hands*—where I can see them."

"I have a right I'm on the street without harassment."

He began easing out the door. He said something else about "Go real slow," and Lee said, "A man taking a walk in his own city."

Talking at the same time.

The cop was on the other side of the car. A little traffic down the street. Lee pulled the .38 out of his belt and fired four times across the hood, blinking and muttering. Poor dumb cop. Opened his mouth and slid down the fender. Lee saw a woman ninety feet away and their eyes definitely met. She dropped some stuff she was carrying and put her hands in front of her face. He moved in a jog step to Patton and turned south, ejecting empty cartridges from the cylinder and reloading as he went.

Helen took her hands away from her eyes. She was all alone screaming in the street. The policeman's cap was a little ways out from the body. He was on his side gushing blood. She picked up her purse and work shoes and went toward him, calling for help and screaming. She walked bent over, actually screaming at the body.

Then there were some people in the street and a man climbing out of a pickup. Helen approached the body screaming. The man was in the police car saying, "Hello hello hello." Helen saw the blood take oval shape in the street. She moved around the body and put her shoes on the hood of the car. She stood bent over, seeing wounds in the chest and head. She just could not believe the volume of blood.

The Mexican said into the dashboard, "Hello hello hello."

Later there was an ambulance and many police cars with red lights and sirens, cars on the sidewalks and lawns and men taking pictures of the stains in the street. Helen stood in front of a frame house halfway down the block, where she'd somehow ended up, trying to tell a detective what she'd seen. She said she waitressed at the Eat Well downtown and was on her way to the bus stop to go to work. Three or four shots, real rapid fire.

Back at the scene there were two small white canvas shoes on the hood of Patrolman Tippit's car. The men from Homicide stood around wondering. They discussed what these objects could possibly mean.

FREDERICK

LAW OLMSTED

— — — —

San Antonio, 1857

THE PRINCIPAL PART of the town lies within a sweep of the river upon the other side. We descend to the bridge, which is close down upon the water, as the river, owing to its peculiar source, never varies in height or temperature. We irresistibly stop to examine it, we are so struck with its beauty. It is of a rich blue and pure as crystal, flowing rapidly but noiselessly over pebbles and between reedy banks. One could lean for hours over the bridge-rail.

From the bridge we enter Commerce street, the narrow principal thoroughfare, and here are American houses, and the

FREDERICK LAW OLMSTED was a sucessful landscape architect, primarily known for his design of New York's Central Park. In his free time, Olmsted dabbled in travel writing. This excerpt is from his 1857 volume, A Journey Through Texas.

triple nationalities break out into the most amusing display, till we reach the main plaza. The sauntering Mexicans prevail on the pavements, but the bearded Germans and the sallow Yankees furnish their proportion. The signs are German by all odds, and perhaps the houses, trim-built, with pink window-blinds. The American dwellings stand back, with galleries and jalousies and a garden picket-fence against the walk, or rise, next door, in three-story brick to respectable city fronts. The Mexican buildings are stronger than those we saw before but still of all sorts, and now put to all sorts of new uses. They are all low, of adobe or stone, washed blue and yellow, with flat roofs close down upon their single story. Windows have been knocked in their blank walls, letting the sun into their dismal vaults, and most of them are stored with dry goods and gro-ceries, which overflow around the door. Around the plaza are American hotels, and new glass-fronted stores, alternating with sturdy battlemented Spanish walls, and [these are] confronted by the dirty, grim, old stuccoed stone cathedral, whose cracked bell is now clunking for vespers in a tone that bids us no wel-come, as more of the intruding race who have caused all this progress on which its traditions, like its imperturbable dome, frown down.

We have no city except perhaps New Orleans that can vie, in point of the picturesque interest that attaches to odd and anti-quated foreignness, with San Antonio. Its jumble of races, cos-tumes, languages and buildings; its religious ruins, holding to an antiquity for us indistinct enough to breed an unaccustomed solemnity; its remote, isolated, outposted situation, and the vague conviction that it is the first of a new class of conquered cities into whose decaying streets our rattling life is to be infused, combine with the heroic touches in its history to enliven and satisfy your traveler's curiosity.

Not suspecting the leisure we were to have to examine it at our ease, we set out to receive its impressions while we had the opportunity.

After drawing, at the Post-office window, our personal share of the dear income of happiness provided by that department, we strolled, by moonlight, about the streets. They are laid out with tolerable regularity, parallel with the sides of the main plaza, and are pretty distinctly shared among the nations that use them. On the plaza and the busiest streets, a surprising number of old Mexican buildings are converted, by trowel, paintbrush, and gaudy carpentry, into drinking-places, always labeled "Exchange," and conducted on the New Orleans model. About these loitered a set of customers, sometimes rough, sometimes affecting an "exquisite" dress, by no means attracting to a nearer acquaintance with themselves or their haunts. Here and there was a restaurant of quieter look, where the traditions of Paris are preserved under difficulties by the exiled Gaul.

The doors of the cabins of the real natives stood open wide, if indeed they exist at all, and many were the family pictures of jollity or sleepy comfort they displayed to us as we sauntered curious about. The favorite dress appeared to be a dishabille, and a free-and-easy, loloppy sort of life generally seemed to have been adopted as possessing, on the whole, the greatest advantages for a reasonable being. The larger part of each family appeared to be made up of black-eyed, olive girls, full of animation and tongue and glance, but sunk in a soft embonpoint, which added a somewhat extreme good-nature to their charms. Their dresses seemed lazily reluctant to cover their plump persons, and their attitudes were always expressive of the influences of a Southern sun upon national manners. The matrons, dark and wrinkled, formed a strong contrast to their daughters, though, here and there, a fine cast of feature and a figure erect with dignity, attracted the eye. The men lounged in roundabouts and cigaritos, as was to be expected, and in fact the whole picture lacked nothing that is Mexican.

THE STREET-LIFE of San Antonio is more varied than might be supposed. Hardly a day passes without some noise. If there be no personal affray to arouse talk, there is some Government train to be seen, with its hundred of mules, on its way from the coast to a fort above; or a Mexican ox-train from the coast, with an interesting supply of ice, or flour, or matches, or of whatever the shops find themselves short. A Government express clatters off, or news arrives from some exposed outpost, or from New Mexico. An Indian in his finery appears on a shaggy horse, in search of blankets, powder and ball. Or at the least, a stagecoach with the "States," or the Austin, mail, rolls into the plaza and discharges its load of passengers and newspapers.

The street affrays are numerous and characteristic. I have seen for a year or more a San Antonio weekly, and hardly a number fails to have its fight or its murder. More often than otherwise, the parties meet upon the plaza by chance, and each, on catching sight of his enemy, draws a revolver and fires away. As the actors are under more or less excitement, their aim is not apt to be of the most careful and sure; consequently it is, not seldom, the passers-by who suffer. Sometimes it is a young man at a quiet dinner in a restaurant who receives a ball in the head, sometimes an old negro woman returning from market who gets winged. After disposing of all their lead, the parties close to try their steel, but as this species of metallic amusement is less popular, they generally contrive to be separated ("Hold me! Hold me!") by friends before the wounds are mortal. If neither is seriously injured, they are brought to drink together on the following day, and the town waits for the next excitement.

Where borderers and idle soldiers are hanging about drinking-places, and where different races mingle on unequal terms, assassinations must be expected. Murders, from avarice or revenge, are common here. Most are charged upon the Mexicans, whose passionate motives are not rare, and to whom escape over the border is easiest and most natural.

The town amusements of a less exciting character are not many. There is a permanent company of Mexican mountebanks, who give performances of agility and buffoonery two or three times a week, parading before night in their spangled tights with drum and trombone through the principal streets. They draw a crowd of whatever little Mexicans can get adrift, and this attracts a few sellers of whisky, tortillas and tamaules (corn, slap-jacks and hashed meat in corn-shucks), all by the light of torches making a ruddily picturesque evening group.

The more grave Americans are served with tragedy by a thin local company, who are death on horrors and despair, long rapiers and well oiled hair, and for lack of a better place to flirt with passing officers, the city belles may sometimes be seen looking on. The national background of peanuts and yells is not, of course, wanting.

A day or two after our arrival, there was the hanging of a Mexican. The whole population left the town to see. Family parties, including the grandmother and the little negroes, came from all the plantations and farms within reach, and little ones were held up high to get their share of warning. The Mexicans looked on imperturbable.

JAN MORRIS

Where the Worlds Meet

WHICHEVER WAY YOU drive down to Presidio you will pass through classic Texas country—scrub-and-desert country, cow country, buck country, where great trains crawl tentatively across mighty landscapes, and ranch houses stand isolated on apparently unreachable horizons. The little towns along the way proclaim themselves very Texanly. Alpine (population: 6,818) claims to be the Biggest Town in the Biggest County in the Biggest State in the United States; Sierra Blanca (altitude: 4,512 feet) says it has the best climate in the world; Marathon boasts of its all-woman chamber of commerce; the masthead of the *Sanderson Times* is

---

Novelist and essayist JAN MORRIS is renowned for her travel writing, which has appeared in numerous magazines and is collected in six books. This excerpt, written in the 1980s, is from her volume of travel essays, *Locations*.

embellished with an oil rig, a cowboy, and a railway engine—potent Texas symbols every one.

But when you get into Presidio County, and the road heads southward through the emptiest country of all, everything changes. It gets hotter as the road loses altitude, and the scrub becomes strangely speckled with white-blossoming yuccas. Ahead of you there rise mountains, ribbed and sunbaked. The dust seems dustier somehow. The air is certainly sultrier. And when you enter the town of Presidio itself (population: 2,070; altitude: 2,594 feet), you feel yourself to be hardly in Texas at all.

Presidio is a shabby crouched little town with no brag to it. Its low mud-brick buildings include several bars and hardware stores, a bus station, a notary public's office, and a pair of churches. The streets seem to be more or less abandoned, especially if you arrive in the middle of the day, the houses look clamped, those stark mountains loom rather meanly in the background, and a sense of spooky resignation hangs over everything. Ninety-three degrees is the temperature, and a hot wind blows. Keep going through the town though, and before long you will reach a narrow muddy river, crossed by a rickety pole-shored bridge; and here you may feel a frisson of a different kind.

There are a few huts down there, in the shade of the cottonwood trees, and around them a little crowd of brown-skinned people hangs around, as though they are waiting for something. Two bulky men in uniform survey them, chewing gum and leaning against walls in the shade. Rock music thumps from somewhere. Now and then a car comes plunging down the pot-holed track from the bridge. On the far side of the river two horses on the bank flick their tails in the heat, and beyond them is a huddle of brown houses, and a church tower. You may feel that the scene has something obscurely significant to it, some sense of latent power or historical meaning—something allegorical, perhaps.

And you will be right. That modest river is the Rio Grande, and you have reached one of the earth's archetypal frontiers. On this side is the United States, on that side is Mexico. Here the generic North confronts the notional South, and the richest society on earth comes face to face with the Third World.

THERE IS NO pretending that it is a comfortable frontier, or even by and large a beautiful one. The Rio Grande forms the entire southern boundary of Texas, and it runs for about a thousand miles through spectacularly varying terrain—from the great border city of El Paso in the west, commanding the Pass of the North from Old Mexico into New, through remote canyons of Big Bend, past the arable country that Texans call simply the Valley, where the land blossoms into prodigies of fertility and is fallen upon by hordes of elderly Midwesterners in recreational vehicles, to peter out at last in the desolate salt marshes of Boca Chica on the Gulf of Mexico. It is, however, a frontier less than absolute, because thousands upon thousands of people from the south live to the north of it, speaking their own language and preserving more or less their own culture. It reminds me of the place on the beach where the tide turns, leaving behind its long deposit of seaweed, plastic bags, pretty shells, and messages in bottles. Perhaps it is less a frontier really than a kind of no man's land between countries, a transient, blurred, and uncertain place, where you are seldom sure which culture is paramount, which language is more readily understood, or even which nation you are looking at.

Arriving one steamy afternoon at a place called Roma, in Starr County, I felt those cross-bred effects to have reached a bewildering climax. The river there is perhaps a hundred yards across, and very shallow, and on each side is a small town. The two of them seemed to me all but indistinguishable.

I stood upon the Texas bank, but I might just as well have been in Mexico. Whitewashed adobe buildings were on both sides of the stream, on both sides tumbled dwellings hung with washing, snuffled about by pigs and dogs. All was indeterminate and intermingled, and the river seemed less a division than a shared amenity. A cock crowed somewhere, but whether it was a Mexican or an American rooster I could not tell. Someone shouted, but in a throaty indeterminate tongue.

Where was I? I felt I was nowhere in particular, in a frontier limbo. Even as I watched, a small boy on a bicycle rode straight into the river on the Mexico side and splashed merrily across the shallows to a Texas sandbank, raising plumes of spray behind his wheels. When I walked away from the river, back toward US Highway 83, I saw looking out at me from a parked car a swarthy, unsmiling, and dark-spectacled man whom I recognized instantly as a Central American arms salesman, kidnapper, or possible political subversive. 'Adios,' I said as I passed him. 'Have a nice day,' he murmured shyly in reply.

THE TEX-MEX frontier is a pungent place. Everything about it is pungent. Here now sits the Reverend Canon Melvin Walker La Follette, head of the Episcopalian mission in Redford, a river hamlet where the customs men, they tell me, prefer to pursue their investigations in pairs, and where clans who have lived here since before Texas was born maintain their immemorial feuds on both sides of the Rio Grande.

The Reverend Canon Melvin Walker La Follette is unperturbed, for he is the very model of a modern frontier priest. Dressed in T-shirt, jeans, and sneakers, he sits amid the indescribable cheerful confusion of his small house (theological treatises and Greek lexicons spilling all over the floor), showing me on a map the immense and mainly roadless area of his parish, across which he pursues his pastoral missions in a hefty four-wheel-drive truck provided by his bishop. He hardly recognizes the existence of the border, helping people indiscriminately on both sides of the river and ministering to anyone who asks, in any language. In the yard he keeps two goats, some chickens, a quarter horse, and a couple of dogs. He looks like a Welsh rugby player and is officially described as Canon Missioner of the Episcopal Diocese of the Rio Grande.

The frontier is rich in such figures, like characters out of fiction, deposited here as miscellaneous flotsam themselves. Such speculations they arouse! By what romantic route did the blond and smiling Swiss lady, like someone out of a Renoir, come to preside over her breakfast counter in Laredo? What brought to this tangled country the man in the coffee shop who speaks six languages, who has a home in France and another in Italy, who spends four months of each year abroad but who feels most at home along this crude border? Or what about the storekeeper of Garciasville, who combines groceries with taxidermy, whose provisions are grimly supervised by owls, deer, armadillos, a wildcat, and a big black bearskin from the Mexican mountains?

Proper frontier faces abound, Indian faces, Spanish faces, nut-brown faces with Mongolian eyes, hunter's faces, rivermen's faces, and one face in particular that like some rare fauna seems to be unique to this territory: a lizardlike face, this one, not quite Hispanic, not quite Anglo either, rather squashed-up brow to chin, with hard, hollow cheeks and deep-set eyes beneath the statutory Stetson—a predatory face, which catching your eye perhaps over a breakfast plate of biscuits and gravy, breaks into a savage but not immediately threatening smile.

Everywhere one catches pungent cameos, too. Here beneath the bridge at Eagle Pass cluster the weird beehive huts of the Kickapoo Indians, made of skins, cardboard, cane, and assorted tacked-up textiles, with tumbledown roofs and Indians sitting stolidly on benches outside them. Here a wild crew of fieldworkers, almost black with sun, cheer and dance when a man stripped to the waist throws a weighted net into an irrigation canal and to everyone's astonishment pulls out a muddy fish. And always, at every crossing, you see the shifting, ceaseless movement of the frontier traffic: long lines of pedestrians, heavy with shopping bags, labouring back and forth, back and forth, across wire-meshed bridge walkways; slow lines of cars which, seen from a distance crossing the great humped bridges at El Paso, glitter brazenly in a shimmer of heat and exhaust fumes—this way perhaps to hock a family heirloom at La American Pawnshop in Laredo, Established 1884, that way to consult Jesús Aguirre, the well-known and by no means expensive dentist of Nuevo Progreso, who Guarantees Satisfaction and for whom No Appointment Is Required.

San Jacinto Plaza in El Paso is the most pungent paradigm of all. I was sitting there one day watching the passing scene—the clusters of Mexican shoppers comparing blenders or cotton lengths, the twos and threes of weathered old men in their wide hats on the benches, the children playing obscure Hispanic games, the blond scrubbed servicemen from Fort Bliss, the man unenthusiastically selling solid silver necklaces from Juárez, the couple of superannuated hippies with their droopy moustaches and fringed shoulder bags—I was sitting there in the sunshine when I heard music from the little podium on the western side of the square.

Two Anglos in long white robes had struck up a hymn. The man had a straggly white beard, and held a thick stave rather taller than himself. The woman held the hymnbook. Solemnly, earnestly, short-sightedly, altogether ignoring the palm-shaded and exotically peopled scene around them, oblivious to the ding-ding and Spanish cry of the ice-cream vendor on his tricycle down the street, they sang an old hymn straight from the heart of traditional Texas—'Nothing but the blood, nothing but the blood of Jesus.' At their feet they had dropped a hand-painted sign: 'Porqué ir al Inferno? Jesus Can Open the Gates of Hell.' Nobody paid them much attention, but some of those lizardy old men, I noticed, tapped their toes to the beat.

WHEN I WAS there the hand-pulled ferry over the river at Los Ebanos was out of action because of troubles on the frontier—an American anti-drug officer had lately been kidnapped and murdered in Mexico, and the ferry was closed in consequence. The little immigration building was deserted, the ferry barge was tied up at the shore, and in the sleepy heat of the afternoon only the raucous grackles squawked and hooted. On the opposite bank, where a dirt track led to the Mexican village of Diaz Ordaz, I could see the abandoned table of a money-changer beneath a tree labelled 'Cambio.' There was no sign of human life on either side, which suggested to me a frontier closed by war, numbed, boarded up, and ominous.

It is certainly not an easy frontier—never has been. Though the two riparian governments like to make fulsome public gestures of undying amity, in fact this border has seldom been anything but a heap of trouble. Wars, bandit raids, smuggling, kidnappings, illegal entries, skulduggeries of every conceivable kind are fundamental to its ambience, and although the frontier is unfortified, often and again along its length you encounter a structure of embattlement, whether it is one of the little airfields built in the twenties to control the region with blimps or bi-planes, or the nineteenth-century mud fort, perched on a bluff outside Presidio, that looks out across the border wilderness for all the world like a fortress on the Khyber.

Wherever you are on the thousand miles of this bound-ary, you may be quite sure that very close to you somebody, somehow, is violating it. It is a frontier of interminable, uncount-able, uncontrollable mayhem and mischief, from the laundering of drug money to the illegal importation of parrots. 'Smuggling's for the single guy,' a resident of Starr County said to me without a blush. 'I gave it up when I married.' 'Listen,' said another, 'I can make $50,000 in a day, easy, just taking one load of dope up to Houston.' Hardly an issue of any local newspaper, hardly a conversation in any café, fails to mention heroin, wetbacks, com-munist subversion in the south, or coyotes, the scoundrels who prey upon hapless and ignorant illegal aliens. It is a festering fron-tier. It is a great place for the two parked cars, side by side, all alone in the middle of nowhere, or the sudden silence in the room when a stranger walks in. The men of the Border Patrol are inescapable here, bundling manacled people into vans in down-town city streets, checking for unregistered aliens at roadblocks, sitting among crackling radios beside enormous maps in tall-masted border post. Sometimes, when the tensions of the frontier are especially high, the cars waiting to cross the bridges into Texas queue in their hundreds far back into Mexico, while the customs and immigration officers examine every trunk, every purse, every permit, and every face.

An incomprehensible flow of wealth, an unimaginable flow of people, cross this frontier night and day. A little town like Hidalgo, which looks like a semi-permanent prospectors' settle-ment, harbours in its banks and exchange houses hundreds of millions of dollars; along the road in San Benito sixty to seventy refugees from El Salvador are habitually shacked up in the dim-lit, crowded bunkhouse of the Casa Oscar Romero, a sanctuary for political refugees. Look at a labouring line of workers in any Rio Grande field (bent over their hoes, in baseball caps and straw hats, like a row of convicts, or perhaps cotton-pickers of the Old South), and the chances are that half of them are illegal aliens from south of the border—it is illegal to be one, but not illegal to employ one.

Behind all the mayhem, of course, ordinary honest com-munities, happily mixed of race, get on with their lives—farmers and businessmen, mayors and Shriners and ladies' leagues. It is difficult to remember the fact, though, so disturbing are the nu-ances of the frontier, and so dark its cross-currents. Much more characteristic of its sensations, I thought, than any Sunset Mall or

Galleria was a place I came across by chance on the riverbank east of Progreso, in Hidalgo County. Until the fifties a frontier bridge was here, but it was swept away by floods, and now nothing is left but the remains of its immigration buildings and a plethora of faded frontier signs. Even the course of the river itself has changed a little, leaving only a soggy cut-off with a dredger high and dry.

There are a few houses nearby, grazed about by goats, guarded by many dogs, but I found this a chill and spooky spot. It seemed full of secrets, and sure enough, one of the neighbours told me that almost every night of the year people from the south clandestinely cross the river there, and creep damp and dripping through the shrubbery into Texas. 'You see that forest there?' the neighbour said, pointing to a confusion of shrubbery beside the water. 'I'll bet you there's people laying there this very minute, waiting for dark, bad men some of them, from far, far away.' I peered at the bushes through my binoculars, hoping to see glints of Russian weaponry, the smoke of marijuana rising, brown faces glaring back at me from among the leaves. All seemed deserted, though. 'Want to go and see? See if there's men there now?' asked my informant helpfully. 'No, thanks,' I said.

NEVERTHELESS, FOR ONE of my temperament, to stand on the northern bank of the Rio Grande and look across to Mexico is not generally a disagreeable experience. Drifting across the river come the unmistakable Third World smells of dust, cooking, and ill-refined petroleum, together with the intoxicating southern sounds of bells, hoots, and fevered music. What stimulations, one feels, must flourish there, what frustrations and injustices too! The very presence of that southern bank, looking often enough so much the same as the northern one, seems to speak of looser morals, freer ways, more bribable officials, less dependable mail deliveries, dirtier streets, better food, hotter sex, more desperate poverty, more horrible prisons, and an altogether better chance of adventure. In short, it offers the frisson of all frontiers everywhere, the frisson of the tantalizingly unfamiliar. And as good and bad are confused in that contemplation, so Texas too is coloured by influences welcome and unwanted from its immense and troublesome southern line.

A few miles from El Paso stands the seventeenth-century mission church of La Purísima at Socorro, built by Spaniards beside the old Royal Way from Mexico City to Santa Fe. With its carved wooden beams and its saints, angels and Madonnas, it is a cask of Hispanicism. It possesses a quality that Anglo Texas seldom honours but that Hispanic Texas, I suspect, well understands—a quality of mystic seclusion. Although the Camino Real long ago became a busy motor road, an insulating hush seems to encapsulate the little building. You can hear doves gurgling outside, and sometimes a goat bleats somewhere. You feel closer not necessarily to God, but to simplicity, which is an aspect of God, perhaps.

Time and again I felt something like that as I wandered through the frontier counties. Whenever I met Hispanics, whether they were descendants of old settlers here or immigrants from the day before yesterday, their responses somehow seemed more natural, less filtered or homogenized, than those of most Anglo Texans. They were more like Americans of an earlier age: after all, who was that boy splashing his bike across the river at Roma but Huck Finn in another incarnation? Perhaps they have not yet been caught in the straitjacket of American education, which so often teaches people to talk by rote or convention? Perhaps they are mellowed by a more ancient civilization, or a more innocent faith?

This has never been a closed frontier, and much of what is Texan is half-Mexican, really. You might say that the southern frontier, no less than the western, has made Texas Texas—many a legendary Texas hero established his reputation in these Rio Grande badlands, and the high swagger of the Texas cowboy was a Spanish swagger first. Today, though, one sometimes feels that this frontier is not merely open but actually disappearing. That mighty tide from the south, swelling out of the other half of the world, is overwhelming it. Far, far north of Presidio the flow has reached, beyond Sanderson, Alpine, and Marathon, which have been bilingual for generations, into the huge Hispanic quarters of San Antonio and Houston, up to Fort Worth and Dallas, and out of Texas altogether into the heartland of the United States.

I thought of the barge tied up at Los Ebanos. It seemed an inadequate response to this colossal momentum. If history is denied a hand-pulled ferry, it will lie low in the shrubs awhile, waiting for night.

Anonymous

The Devil in Texas

HE SCATTERED TARANTULAS over the roads,
Put thorns on the cactus and horns on the toads,
He sprinkled the sands with millions of ants
So the man who sits down must wear soles on his pants.
He lengthened the horns of the Texas steer,
And added an inch to the jack rabbit's ear;
He put mouths full of teeth in all of the lakes,
And under the rocks he put rattlesnakes.

He hung thorns and brambles on all of the trees,
He mixed up the dust with jiggers and fleas;

The anonymous poem, "The Devil in Texas," is thought to date from the early 1860s.

The rattlesnake bites you, the scorpion stings,
The mosquito delights you by buzzing his wings.
The heat in the summer's a hundred and ten,
Too hot for the Devil and too hot for men;
And all who remain in that climate soon bear
Cuts, bites, and stings, from their feet to their hair.

He quickened the buck of the bronco steed,
And poisoned the feet of the centipede;
The wild boar roams in the black chaparral;
It's a hell of place that we've got for a hell.
He planted red pepper beside very brook;
The Mexicans use them in all that they cook.
Just dine with a Mexican, then you will shout,
'I've hell on the inside as well as the out!'

Acknowledgments

"People Should Not Die in June in South Texas" by Gloria Anzaldúa from *Growing Up Latino: Memoirs and Stories*, by Harold Augenbraum and Ilan Stavans. © 1993 by Harold Augenbraum and Ilan Stavans. Reprinted by permission of Houghton Mifflin Co.

"22 November" from *Libra* by Don DeLillo. © 1988 by Don DeLillo. Reprinted by permission of Viking Penguin, a division of Penguin Books, Inc.

Introduction ©1994 by Barry Gifford. Reprinted by permission of the author.

"Un Hijo del Sol" by Genaro Gonzalez from *Growing Up Latino: Memoirs and Stories*, ed. Harold Augenbraum and Ilan Stavans. © 1993 by Harold Augenbraum and Ilan Stavans. Reprinted by permission of Arte Público Press, University of Houston.

Excerpt from *Molly Ivins Can't Say That, Can She?* by Molly Ivins. © 1991 by Molly Ivins. Reprinted by permission of Alfred A. Knopf, Inc.

Excerpt from *On the Road* by Jack Kerouac. © 1955, 1957 by Jack Kerouac; © 1983 renewed by Stella Kerouac; © 1985 by Stella Kerouac and Jan Kerouac. Reprinted by permission of Viking Penguin, a division of Penguin Books, Inc.

Excerpt from *The Last Picture Show* by Larry McMurtry. © 1966 by Larry McMurtry. Reprinted by permission of Wylie, Aitken & Stone.

"Texas" from *Locations* by Jan Morris. © 1992 by Jan Morris. Reprinted by permission of Oxford University Press.

Excerpts from *Georgia O'Keeffe: Arts & Letters* by Georgia O'Keeffe. © 1987 by Estate of Georgia O'Keeffe. Reprinted by permission of the Georgia O'Keeffe Foundation.

Excerpt from *Straight from the Heart: My Life in Politics and Other Places* by Ann Richards. © 1989 by Ann Richards. Reprinted by permission of Simon and Schuster.

Excerpt from *Travels With Charley* by John Steinbeck. © 1961, 1962 by The Curtis Publishing Co.; © 1962 renewed by John Steinbeck; © 1990 by Elain Steinbeck, Thom Steinbeck, and John Steinbeck IV. Reprinted by permission of Viking Penguin, a division of Penguin Books, Inc.

Excerpts from *Texans: Oral Histories from the Lone Star State* by Ron Strickland. © 1991 by Ron Strickland. Reprinted by permission of Paragon House.